THE PERFECT NANNY

She'll Stop at Nothing to Take Everything

D. L. Fisher

Copyright © 2023 by D. L. Fisher.

All rights reserved. No part of this book may be used or reproduced in any form whatsoever without written permission except in the case of brief quotations in critical articles or reviews.

This book is a work of fiction. Names, characters, businesses, organizations, places, events and incidents either are the product of the author's imagination or are used fictitiously. Any resemblance to actual persons, living or dead, events, or locales is entirely coincidental.

Printed in the United States of America.

First Edition: October 2023

Contents

CHAPTER 1 1
CHAPTER 2 6
CHAPTER 3 14
CHAPTER 4 18
CHAPTER 5 22
CHAPTER 6 27
CHAPTER 7 34
CHAPTER 8 37
CHAPTER 9 42
CHAPTER 10 48
CHAPTER 11 52
CHAPTER 12 57
CHAPTER 13 60
CHAPTER 14 65
CHAPTER 15 69
CHAPTER 16 73
CHAPTER 17 77
CHAPTER 18 82
CHAPTER 19 86
CHAPTER 20 90
CHAPTER 20 94
CHAPTER 22 98
CHAPTER 23 102
CHAPTER 24 106
CHAPTER 25 111
CHAPTER 26 116
CHAPTER 27 119

CHAPTER 28	123
CHAPTER 29	127
CHAPTER 30	133
CHAPTER 31	136
CHAPTER 32	139
CHAPTER 33	143
CHAPTER 34	147
CHAPTER 35	151
CHAPTER 36	155
CHAPTER 37	159
CHAPTER 38	162
CHAPTER 39	167
CHAPTER 40	171
CHAPTER 41	176
CHAPTER 42	180
CHAPTER 43	184
CHAPTER 44	189
CHAPTER 45	194
CHAPTER 46	198
CHAPTER 47	203
CHAPTER 48	207
CHAPTER 49	210
CHAPTER 50	214
CHAPTER 51	218
CHAPTER 52	222
CHAPTER 53	226
CHAPTER 54	230
CHAPTER 55	233
CHAPTER 56	238

CHAPTER 57 244

ACKNOWLEDGEMENTS 249

MY HUSBAND'S SON PROLOGUE 250

CHAPTER 1 252

CHAPTER 1

"Andrew? Say something! Are you okay?"

My husband and I are seated across from one another at our kitchen table over breakfast. It's a Restoration Hardware table, handcrafted solid pine. A beautiful table, really.

If not for the small fact that he's choking at it.

Andrew's face is red, almost a plum purple, and he's frantically yanking the collar of his shirt. I'm about to place our newborn in her bassinet so I can attempt the Heimlich when a chunk of half-eaten tofu flies from his mouth.

All this because of what I just said. *Sheesh,* you'd think I told the man his dog died.

"But you said…" Andrew's words come out labored, breathy. I watch as the vein on his temple throbs. He's sweating, even though the air conditioner is on full blast. It's *freezing.* To be fair, he almost asphyxiated himself. Still, I pull my cashmere cardigan snugly across my chest, wrapping baby Delilah in my warm embrace.

"I know what I said. It's just, I've been thinking a lot, and I don't see how we can maintain all this—" I fan my arms around the newly renovated kitchen in our coveted penthouse apartment before continuing— "without my salary." I pause to let that sink in. "I'm sorry, but I've already made up my mind, Andrew. I'm going back to work when my leave is up."

My husband glares at me as if I've just slapped him across the face. He runs a hand through his dark, curly hair, long enough for a man bun. Can you have a midlife crisis at thirty-five? Because he also wants to be called Andreas now—something about it sounding more avant-garde. The guy has really run with the whole starving artist thing.

"Look," I say, attempting to soften the blow. "Do you have any idea how quickly I will become irrelevant? It's bad enough that I'm taking two months of family leave. That's a long time in this business. There are dozens of traders gunning for my job." I hold up one finger at a time as I rattle off a list of names. "Parker Goodman, Jeremy Stevens, Chad Morgan..."

Andrew raises a hand to stop me. "Chad Morgan? Seriously, Lucinda? The Morgans are like our really good friends."

I blink at my husband in disbelief—how is he so incredibly naive? "That doesn't mean he doesn't want my clients."

"I get it, okay." He doesn't. "But your clients love you, Lucinda. You don't have to go back to work so soon—" Andrew motions toward the built-in desk in our kitchen piled with teddy bears, rattles, and enough onesies to clothe a small village. It's been a month, but without fail, our doorman comes knocking at two p.m. daily with boxes upon boxes of random stuff for Delilah. I had no idea we knew so many people. I have no idea what to do with all this crap. Overnight, our once spacious apartment has transformed into a makeshift Amazon warehouse.

Andrew abruptly stands from his chair, nearly knocking it over. "So what—who will look after her?" Right. And there's the *real* reason my husband doesn't want me to return to work. That would leave him in charge of tending to Delilah's every need. Andreas has zero intentions of being a stay-at-home dad. Andrew, maybe, but he seems to have exited the building.

When I don't answer immediately, my husband anxiously asks, "Will we put Delilah in daycare, then?"

I rub my nose against Delilah's fuzzy head, breathing in her comforting new baby and lavender scents as she lets out a sleepy coo. "I'm not comfortable with the whole daycare thing. I mean, do you have any idea how many parents send their kids to school sick?"

Andrew raises an eyebrow. "How many, Lucinda?"

"Well, since you asked, Andrew—seven out of ten. Seventy percent of parents send their kids to school sick. Seventy freaking percent! I'm sorry, but daycare is not an option."

Andrew looks at me like I'm seventy-percent alien. "How do you even know that?"

I shrug. "Mmmm—must have read it somewhere."

"Fine, then what do you suggest? Surely you can't expect me to stop working and stay home with her. Give up my dreams while you live yours? That hardly seems fair."

I'm not sure working on Wall Street is anyone's dream per se, more like a means to an end. But I'm not going to win this argument. Andrew will twist my words like he twisted my arm into funding his income-less career sculpting recycled trash.

And mark my words, if the guy tells me again right now how he's just one sale from making it big, I'll scream and kick him in his coconut-oiled shin. *That would require an actual sale, Andrew!* It's been a whole year, and he hasn't seen any of them. Not a one.

I'm trying to be supportive, but throw me a doggone bone.

"A nanny," I say.

"A nanny?"

I narrow my eyes on him—sometimes I think my husband and I speak two entirely different languages.

Andrew throws his hands up in exasperation. "I bet next you'll tell me you want to move to Staten Island and get a minivan. Oh God, you're going to expect me to do the Suburban nod, aren't you? No way! It's not happening, Lucinda."

"The Suburban nod is not a thing, Andrew. You literally just made that up. It's a Jeep wave. And besides, Suburbans are not minivans. They're SUVs."

Andrew rolls his eyes. "I don't care what they are. I'm not driving a Suburban, and I'm not moving to the suburbs. Period. Do you hear me? Not moving to the suburbs!"

I'm pretty sure the whole dang apartment building heard him.

"It's technically a borough, not a suburb," I mumble under my breath.

"What was that?"

"Nothing. Relax, Andrew. No one is moving to Staten Island or getting a minivan. We're just talking about a nanny. Please, sit back down. Hear me out." I signal to a chair across the table, and Andrew reluctantly lowers himself onto it. He folds his arms across his chest.

"If we hire a nanny, we'll know Delilah is safe at home—our home *here* in the *city* where we take *public transportation*." I enunciate the words carefully, lest there be confusion. "Think about it. Delilah will be well cared for, not one of twenty babies crowded into an eight-by-eight room. She can get out during the day—the park, the library, and music classes. She can nap in her own crib. I read somewhere that it's important to establish good sleep hygiene. I can go back to work, and you can keep sculpting. Win-win all around, don't you think?"

Andrew runs a hand across his chin, where a goatee is beginning to sprout. Did I say he was running with the whole starving artist thing? More like sprinting.

"I don't know how I feel about a stranger in our apartment."

"She'll only be a stranger at first, but then I bet she'll become like family."

Andrew rises again and starts pacing the kitchen. I glance at my watch—7:45 a.m.—this is taking way longer than expected. Doesn't he have a pile of scrap metal to meld or a blowtorch to fiddle with? I stifle a yawn.

Finally, he relents. "All right, Lucinda. I'm on board. But how do we even find a good nanny? I mean, this is our baby. We can't leave her with just anyone." Funny, now that he knows he doesn't have to stay home with her, Delilah is, once again, *our* baby.

"Don't worry about a thing, Andrew. I'll take care of everything."

My husband folds his napkin and tosses it onto his plate. Our real-life conversation has spoiled his appetite. "I'm off to the studio," he announces, walking over to our side of the table, where he quickly kisses my head and Delilah's warm cheek. "Let me know if you ladies need anything."

This time, I'm the one who rolls my eyes. Without my job, there would be no studio for Andreas to go to. His first-floor rental in the heart of Greenwich Village costs an arm and a leg. If I don't return to work, one of us will have to sell a kidney to cover the rent.

Andrew grabs his keys from the kitchen island. I listen as the front door closes and the lock clicks into place. Then I take my first deep breath of the day. I'm grateful that our conversation is over. It was painful. Needles in my eyes, painful.

Now I can focus all my energy on finding the perfect nanny. Though we've only just broached the subject, I've already thought long and hard about how we will find the ideal caretaker for our daughter. Of course, I'm not about to leave my baby with just anyone—not with all the wackadoodles out there. Unbeknownst to Andrew, I've been researching and vetting since I peed on the stick and saw the double-blue lines.

I have compiled a list of five highly qualified contenders for the job. I've spoken with them and their references over the phone, but today is the day I will finally interview each of them in person. Hopefully, in a few short hours, I will have hired the perfect nanny.

CHAPTER 2

I'm huffing and puffing like an athlete in training by the time I make it to the lobby of our doorman building. And I took the *elevator*! Holy crap, it takes a lot of crap to leave an apartment with a baby. It's pure insanity.

Delilah's not even looking at her toys yet, but somehow I have an overflowing diaper bag biting into my shoulder, numbing the fingers on my right hand. Imagine when she requires entertainment. Yeah, I'm completely screwed.

The brutal weather outside certainly isn't helping the situation. As I pass through the revolving doors onto Fifth Avenue, the stagnant air is like a noose around my neck. It's the hottest day of the year. Record-breaking, actually. And it's so ridiculously humid my sunglasses fog over the second we leave the building, blurring the bodies rushing past us on the street.

Delilah is comfortably laid out in her stroller, oozing cuteness in her pink onesie with a matching bow headband on her nearly bald head. A lightweight blanket—white with pink stars—covers her tiny body. The pediatrician warned against sunscreen until six months, so I have her porcelain skin covered despite the oppressive heat. Thankfully, she doesn't seem to mind.

I'd prefer to keep my daughter home in our air-conditioned apartment, but I promised Jenna I would meet her for coffee. I've canceled on my best friend one too many times, and she informed me this morning that she will not accept "even one more lame excuse."

Work aside, Jenna is my only connection to the real, non-diaper-filled world. Ergo, I look like a homeless person hauling all her belongings on the day the ozone layer decided it blocked its final ray.

By some divine intervention, I make it to the coffee shop before melting into the sidewalk.

"Lucy!" Jenna's voice rings through the cafe, a quaint mom-and-pop shop just down the block from my apartment. The place goes silent as everyone turns to look at her.

Typical.

Jenna is certainly something to look at with her hourglass figure and glossy, auburn hair grazing the small of her back. Her eyes are so green they don't look like they could be real. And don't even get me started on her bone structure. She could have been a supermodel instead of an influencer if she were a few inches taller.

I tug self-consciously on the hem of my stained white tee. Delilah spit up on me for the umpteenth time this morning. My daughter must have acid reflux. Or is this what babies do? I wish I had read the book sitting untouched on my nightstand—*What to Expect When You're Expecting*—back when I had the attention span to read a book. Apparently, there's a fourth trimester. A fourth freaking trimester! As if three aren't enough. I discovered this while searching the internet for answers to the question: *What the hell is wrong with my newborn child?*

I push my stroller through the crowd of caffeinating customers toward the back of the shop, where Jenna is waiting with her arms outstretched. I'm so happy to see her; I nearly burst into tears. You don't realize what a lack of adult interaction does to you until you're lacking that adult interaction. I have Andrew, but he's more man-child lately than a bona fide grownup. Isn't having a child supposed to mature you? If anything, it's turned him into Benjamin Button.

I spot a Styrofoam cup sitting on a table with my name on it. The aroma of hazelnut tickles my nostrils. When you're as close as Jenna and I, you know what the other person wants without them asking. You also know when the other one is up to something.

"Decaf?" I eye Jenna suspiciously as my fingers wrap around the steaming cup. "The pediatrician says caffeine is bad for the baby."

"Yeah, well, Dr. Ruth says undereye bags are bad for your sex life." She winks.

"Isn't Dr. Ruth like ninety-four?"

Jenna pulls out her phone to Google it. She furrows her brow. "Seriously, Lucy, how the hell did you know that?"

"I know everything, Jenna."

We've had this exchange or one like it more times than I can count. Jenna and I met on the first day of college when I nervously walked into my dorm room to find her sprawled out on one of the twin-sized beds. "I hope you don't mind, but I chose this one," she said, staring at me with her saucer-like green eyes. I scanned the room, orienting myself. Then I shrugged my shoulders. "Sleeping southward-facing is associated with better health outcomes, so I'm happy to take this one." I gingerly placed my suitcase on the bed.

Jenna burst out laughing. I smiled back at her, but as she came to learn very quickly, it wasn't a joke. To this day, my observations never cease to amaze her. At least someone appreciates them.

Jenna bends down and scoops my daughter from her stroller, cradling her in her arms. The way she's looking at her so lovingly— I'm confident I made the right decision making her the godmother.

Andrew would have preferred "anyone but Jenna," but that's because he can't imagine someone with her lifestyle raising our child, should something tragic happen to the both of us. I had hoped that making Jenna Delilah's godmother would help bring them closer. Instead, it's provided fodder for countless disagreements between Andrew and me on what's best for our child.

But just look at them—it's like I'm on the set of a Huggies commercial.

I don't want to ruin their tender moment, but I desperately need to talk to Jenna about something important. So I flash her the *I have something to tell you* look perfected over our decade of friendship.

Jenna takes the cue and gently places Delilah back in her stroller. "What's going on?" she asks, her green eyes widening as concern spreads across her face.

"So, I told Andrew today."

Her lips form a silent O. "Who'd you get—Andrew or Andreas?"

I shoot my best friend a pointed stare. "Who do you think I got?"

"Oh boy. So how did that conversation go?"

Jenna knows Andrew almost as well as me—she knows it didn't go over well. If there's one thing my husband is, it's predictable. Even his foray into repurposing trash wasn't a complete surprise. He needed something to do when he went off the deep end and took his job with him.

"It went as expected." I shrug my shoulders. "He thinks we live in the cave ages. Man provides while the woman stays home with the child."

"That's not the worst thing, Lucy, for your husband to want to take care of you."

"Come on, Jenna; you know very well that Andrew can't support us. Not since he woke up one morning and decided he's the next Andy Warhol."

Jenna ignores the jab at my husband. She's heard it dozens of times. While I hear titillating stories about my best friend's wild, single sexcapades, she hears harrowing tales of Andrew not replacing the toilet roll. Lately, we're like a G-rated Disney movie.

But as they say, I wouldn't trade it for the world. Not Delilah, anyhow.

And that's what this rendezvous is ultimately all about. I slip a hand into my daughter's diaper bag and pull out a manila envelope.

Jenna stiffens and purses her lips, looking concerned. "What's going on, Lucy?"

What does she *think* is going on? Is she expecting me to pull out divorce papers? Andrew may drive me crazy at times, but I'm not about to leave my husband. I mean, if I haven't left him yet…

"Relax," I say. "It's nothing serious. Just my narrowed-down list of prospective nannies. I'd love for you to look at the final five contenders." Jenna's face relaxes.

"Shall we?" I motion to a well-worn tartan loveseat that looks like someone plucked it right off the sidewalk on garbage pickup day. None of the furniture here matches, and the lighting is inexplicably scant considering the floor-to-ceiling windows, but the handcrafted coffee is out of this world. I sip my latte and feel the jolt of hot energy shoot through my veins. There's not a chance in hell this is decaf.

And it's going right through me. Suddenly, I have to pee like a racehorse. "Give me a second," I say as I squeeze my legs together.

Jenna looks at me, amusement playing on her lips. "Bathroom?"

There's no time to answer or to grab my bag. I'm already speed walking to the restroom on the opposite end of the coffee shop. Thank goodness there's no line, because I barely make it there on time.

Jenna is on the phone when I get back. She's always on the phone—such is the life of an influencer. But when she sees me, she sets it on her lap and pats the seat on the armchair next to her, eschewing the loveseat. We squeeze so tightly together that our knees press against each other. She places a manicured hand on my thigh. "Are you sure you want to do this? You have your savings. You could easily take a year or two. Go back to work when Delilah's in preschool."

That's easy for her to say, considering she's the one who has hundreds of thousands of Instagram followers and endorsements. With the wise investments I've helped her make through the years and her entrepreneurial endeavors, my best friend could never work another day for the rest of her life and still live more than comfortably. I, however, have a child and a fledgling art career to support.

I shake my head. "I have my reasons, Jenna. I need to do this."

It's a lot of pressure to support a family and raise a child in Manhattan. But there's also something else. Something I can't tell her. Something I can't tell anyone.

"Well, did you tell Andrew that she's moving in with you?"

"Not yet. But I'm planning on it."

"I don't think you should spring this on him, Lucy. Your husband does not do well with surprises."

As I said, she knows him well. And she's right—I should have told Andrew this morning. But I couldn't pluck up the courage to do it. "I'll talk to him tonight," I tell her as much as I tell myself. Because if I dreaded the conversation earlier, thoughts of the next one threaten to send me into a full-blown panic attack.

But I'll have to worry about that later. Delilah's nanny is somewhere in this file. I open the envelope and pull out the five resumes, one of which has an accompanying headshot.

"Now, that's something you don't see every day. Is she applying for a nanny position or starting an OnlyFans page?"

"Jenna!" I slap her hand. "That's not very nice."

"Just saying—I would not want *that* strutting around my apartment in front of my husband. Seems like tempting Adam all over again, don't you think?" As if Jenna would have anything to worry about. She's just about as perfect as they come. The one time we argued, the best dig I could come up with was that green eyes are technically a genetic mutation.

Me, on the other hand? She has a point. It's not as if Andrew and I have been hot and heavy lately. The last time we were intimate was—*oh my*—I can't even remember. It was before Delilah was born, obviously. The obstetrician said I should wait for clearance at my six-week postpartum checkup before having sex. It hasn't been six weeks. Our baby is only a month old!

And the affair. That fucking affair.

I push away the thought. It's not about Andrew and me. It's about Delilah.

Bree Miller (headshot girl) has impressed me the most of all the prospective applicants I've spoken to. And her references are impeccable. I've chatted with her parents, roommates, and employer—everyone adores her. She seems like a real gem.

Do I wish she wasn't young and attractive? Of course, I do—it would be abnormal if I didn't. But shouldn't Delilah have the best? And who knows, I may not even wind up choosing her anyway. I have four other applicants to interview as well.

I must be silent for too long because Jenna adds, "Not that I think Andrew would cheat on you with your nanny."

Would he? "No, no, of course not. I get what you're saying, though. But all the other applicants seem so—I don't know—old? Delilah won't be an infant for long. I don't want some housemaid chasing after her in a walker." That one draws a laugh. "Besides, Andrew spends most of his time in his studio. So he'll barely have any contact with our nanny at all."

"But isn't she going to live with you? How could Andrew not see someone who lives in the same apartment as him? He's not blind, Lucinda."

I press a finger to my lips, silencing her.

"Though sometimes I worry you are..." Jenna mumbles under her breath.

I ignore her comment and continue. "I guess we'll see how the interviews go. Speaking of which, I need a favor. How'd you like to spend a few hours with your goddaughter so I can meet these Mary Poppins in person? I hear babies are real men magnets." Not that Jenna needs a magnet to draw a man, but maybe Delilah would attract a nice one instead of all the worthless losers my gorgeous friend dates.

Jenna narrows her eyes at me and giggles. "That's for guys, Lucy. Babies are chick magnets. I think they may actually be male repellents."

"Well, whatever. I knew babies were some kind of magnet."

"I'd love to spend a few hours with my goddaughter, but don't you think you should bring the *baby* to a nanny interview?"

This time, I'm the one who laughs. "That would be the logical thing to do, yes, but I need to make sure I'm not dealing with any psychopaths before I let anyone put their hands on Delilah.

Anyway, there's pumped milk in her diaper bag and a pacifier if she's inconsolable."

We both look down at my baby. Lying there, she hardly seems the inconsolable type. But then, Jenna has never met Delilah in the middle of the night. Had she, my babysitting request would likely have been met with a hard no or at least some strong resistance.

"Where are you going to meet them, anyway? I assume you're not hosting them in your apartment if you're worried about psychopaths."

"Don't mock me, Jenna. You know there are a lot of crazies out there." I widen my eyes. "And for your information, I'm meeting them at the bar across the street."

"So, no baby and a bar? That's totally not crazy at all." Jenna's eyebrows knit together. "What are you up to, Lucinda Douglass?"

"Wouldn't you like to know?" I wink conspiratorially as I rise from our armchair. Then I bend over the stroller to give Delilah a soft kiss.

"Mama will be back soon," I whisper.

I wave goodbye to Jenna and head to the bar to meet our new nanny.

CHAPTER 3

Applicant number one is a sixty-year-old grandmother who recently relocated to New York from London. She wears her salt-and-pepper hair twisted into a tight bun, with literally not a single strand out of place on her head. The lady must own stock in hairspray. I read an article this morning that L'Oréal's market shares have jumped more than forty percent over the past year. I suspect the woman sitting before me may be solely responsible for that.

And then there are her shoes. She's wearing thick black clunkers that I suspect are orthopedics. She screams boarding school headmaster between the hair, shoes, and twinset with pearls, but I already have her here, so...

"Tell me about yourself, Ms.—" I glance down at the resume in my hands. "—Randall."

She smiles stiffly. "Well, I've many years of experience, as you can see from my resume. I've cared for four different families; stayed with each of them until their children were in high school. I just adore children, especially babies. They're so—" She pauses, bringing a hand to her chest. "—malleable. I believe it is my calling to help mold them into decent human beings."

'Decent human beings' doesn't sound bad. "How would you describe your discipline philosophy?"

Ms. Randall knots her hands in her lap and leans forward. She stares me dead in the eyes with a look of accusation that makes me squirm in my seat. *Why does it suddenly feel like I'm the one being interviewed?* "I suppose that depends on the child," she says. "I assure you, Mrs. Douglass, your daughter will be in competent hands with me. Children behave when they're under my tutelage, or they face appropriate consequences."

Now that sounds ominous. I shiver. "Like? Could you give an example of an appropriate consequence?"

"Like if Thomas, say, were under my care and used a naughty word, I would wash his mouth out with soap. It's a wonderful deterrent against what you Americans call 'potty talk.' As for Thomas, I promise he would never use that word again."

I get the sense Thomas isn't hypothetical. And then, I think of my precious Delilah ingesting Dove. Needless to say, that interview lasts all of ten minutes. I'm not about to pay someone to poison my daughter.

I'm incredibly anxious as I await my next applicant. I hope this interview goes better than the last. It can't go any worse, right? I exhale a sigh of relief when the front door to the bar swings open. Applicant number two is at least twenty years younger than Ms. Randall, with a dark, loose bob that skims her shoulders. She's similarly well put together—in slacks and a button-down shirt—but unlike Ms. Randall, she doesn't look like she was plucked from a knitting catalog.

"Hello," I say, extending a hand. "I'm Lucinda Douglass. It's so nice to meet you in person."

"Renee Cohen." She slips her hand into mine, and I'm relieved to find she has a firm handshake. Psychological tests show that those with a firm handshake are genuinely interested and less neurotic than those without. Shaking Ms. Randall's hand was like holding a limp noodle.

There's something else I notice almost immediately. When Renee Cohen smiles back at me, deep creases line her dark brown eyes. And then, there's also a noticeably large gap between her front teeth. *Great*, Jenna and her ridiculous talk about hiring an attractive nanny are stuck in my head now.

Because what if she's right? Would I be opening Pandora's box by inviting a younger woman into our home? Is now the right time in our lives to be tempting fate?

Is there *ever* a good time to tempt fate?

"Please, make yourself comfortable." I signal to the bar stool next to mine. Once she's settled, I dig into my lengthy list of questions. You can't be too careful these days, can you? I printed the list online—fifteen questions to ask your prospective nanny. They run the gamut from 'What made you want to become a nanny?' to 'What are your qualifications?'

"I have a college degree in childhood education from UConn and a master's in child psychology from St. John's. I'm first aid and CPR certified," she tells me.

"Wow," I say, jotting down a few notes on her resume. "That's very impressive."

The waitress comes over to take our drink orders. I check the time on my watch—10:30 a.m. I've been sitting here for almost an hour. But if things keep going like this, Renee Cohen will be my last interview of the day. My last interview ever. Sorry, not sorry, three, four, and five.

"Iced tea for me, please," I tell her.

"And for you?"

"I'll take a vodka martini on the rocks with blue cheese olives." Renee hands back the drink menu. At first, I think she's joking, but I realize she's dead serious when she doesn't call the waitress back as she leaves to place our orders. My jaw is on the floor. This is just about the last of all the things I was expecting. Drinking vodka at a job interview for a nanny position? Drinking vodka at a job interview for a nanny position at 10:30 in the freaking morning?

No ma'am. I'm not about to throw my daughter into the arms of an alcoholic.

Thank you, next.

Unfortunately, three and four don't even show up for their interviews.

Five is my last shot before it's back to the drawing board. I wanted to come home today with something concrete to show Andrew how serious I am about all this. To show him that I've got the situation under control. Besides, I'm running out of time before I return to the office.

I sip on my iced tea while waiting for Bree Miller to arrive. Then I shoot a text to Jenna to check on Delilah.

All good?

I'm nervous in a way I can't quite explain. It's my first time leaving Delilah with anyone other than my husband. It's been less than two hours, and I'm already crawling out of my skin. I'm not sure how I'll manage to leave her for entire days at a time.

It will somewhat assuage my guilt if I know she's in good hands. But the way things are looking, I'm seriously starting to doubt those hands exist.

And worse, I'm starting to question all this.

Am I making a terrible mistake?

I chew on a cuticle as I stare at the three dots pulsing on the screen. Why is it taking Jenna so damn long to write back?

After a few minutes of agony, a text comes through.

Relax, Lucy. She's sleeping like a baby.

I exhale a sigh of partial relief. I've been at this for nearly two hours now. It's not even lunchtime, and I'm ready for this day to end. Bree Miller is my last hope. That is, if she shows up at all. Based on the appearances so far, there's only a fifty percent chance that I don't get stood up again. I stare at the door for what feels like an eternity, willing it to open.

And then it does.

And it's her.

CHAPTER 4

The tension instantly releases from my shoulders. My prospective nanny is not quite the sexpot Jenna had me worried about. She's dressed casually and modestly in athletic pants and an oversized T-shirt. Her blonde hair hangs loosely around her shoulders, neat but not overdone. Other than a touch of mascara, her face is makeup-free. She looks like a fresh-faced, down-to-earth, twenty-something-year-old.

Just like I did before life caught me in a chokehold.

"Mrs. Douglass?" I start at the sound of my name. Bree Miller is standing in front of me, wringing her hands together.

"Hi, yes," I say. "I'm so sorry—I must have zoned out. I have total baby brain. Please, call me Lucinda. Mrs. Douglass is my mother-in-law."

Bree giggles nervously. "I'm Bree—we spoke on the phone. I wasn't sure I had the right person. You do not look old enough to have a baby."

Wow, I might love this girl already.

I look her over. So far, Bree Miller is the only candidate I can picture on the floor with Delilah—exploring, painting, playing in the dirt, and doing all those other things kids with a healthy childhood do. And there's also the fact that I've got no one left to interview. So I *really* want this arrangement to work out.

The waitress returns to our table to take Bree's order. "Can I get you something to drink, Miss?" Bree's eyes dart across the menu.

On the outside, I'm composed, but my insides are screaming: *For the love of God, please don't order a vodka martini on the rocks with blue cheese olives!*

"Water with lemon would be great." I unclench my fists.

Before I can ask the first of my lengthy list of questions, Bree reaches into her bag. "I know it's early, but would you like a piece of chocolate?" She pulls out a Baci wrapped in fancy silver foil like a small gift.

"Wow," I say as I gratefully take the chocolate. I haven't eaten a thing today in all the hoopla with Andrew and these interviews. And, "These are my favorite chocolates in the entire world. I haven't had one in years. I had no idea they still made them."

"That's so funny," she laughs. "Mine too. You know what they say—chocolate is good for the soul."

"I say that all the time." A grin spreads across my face as I pop the heavenly ball into my mouth.

The waitress returns shortly with Bree's water and a refill for me. I take a long sip and begin the interview, though it feels more like a formality. Because chocolate and compliments aside, something about this girl makes me trust her.

Of course, Jenna always needles me about how I trust too quickly. But I think that's more of a 'her' problem than a 'me' problem since she doesn't seem to trust anyone. Except for me, of course. But even that took a while.

"Tell me about yourself, Bree. What makes you want to be a nanny?"

"Oh, I just love children. I have six younger siblings, and I've helped raise them. One of my sisters is special needs, and we are especially close. I still go to visit my family in upstate New York whenever I have the chance. But don't worry, you and your family will come first."

I glance down at her resume. "I see you've been working at a preschool since you graduated from NYU, which, coincidentally is my alma mater as well. Why are you looking to make the switch? I have to be honest; there's not much upward mobility here."

Bree takes a deep breath and rests her hands on her knees. "I don't want you to think poorly of me—" She pauses as I wait for some bombshell to end this interview like the two before. "I feel too stretched in the preschool environment. I'd much prefer to focus on one child I can watch grow. A child I can grow with. That's what drew me to childhood education in the first place. I'm not in it for the money." My body relaxes.

Bree's resume was impressive, but *this*... My insides are melting.

I cross my fingers at my side. "What is your philosophy on behavioral discipline?"

No soap. No soap. No soap.

Bree tucks a loose strand of blonde hair behind her ear. "I'm a huge believer in positive reinforcement. I'm not a fan of punishments." She focuses her blue eyes on mine. "Of course, there are consequences in life for negative behaviors. But I much prefer timeouts and talking to a child at their level so they understand why whatever they did wrong was wrong. So they can learn from their mistakes. You know?"

I smile widely. "Yes, I know, and I couldn't agree more." No Dove for Delilah.

Bree seems perfect, almost too good to be true, but that headshot is niggling at me.

"Could I ask you a somewhat personal question?"

"Of course, you can. Fire away."

"Why the headshot? Are you hoping to make it on Broadway or as an influencer or something? My best friend Jenna is an influencer, and she won't even go downstairs to get the mail without a headshot hidden somewhere on her."

Circles pop on the apples of Bree's cheeks. "You think it's cringy I sent a headshot, don't you?"

"No, no, no," I reassure her. "It's just—Delilah's only a month, and we may have more kids one day." *Assuming, of course, we make it to one day.* "I'm a big planner, and I need to know if this would just be tiding you over until something better comes along."

This time, Bree smiles widely. I can't help but notice how perfectly straight and white her teeth are. "I got the headshot idea from the Real Nannies of the Upper East Side Facebook page. Something about helping you stand out from the crowd—I know, I know, it was a silly idea. But honestly, I'm not going anywhere. There is nothing I would rather do than spend my days exploring the city, painting, and digging in the dirt with your daughter."

It's as if she's read my mind.

I glance down at my list of questions. When you know, you know, and I know Bree Miller is meant to be Delilah's nanny.

She's also the last candidate I have to interview. And there's the fact that my nipples are starting to leak. I need to get back to my daughter.

So really, the only question I have left is, "When can you start?"

CHAPTER 5

"You have to be kidding me! You hired the headshot?" Jenna stands in her kitchen with a hand on her hip. I'm perched on a barstool, nursing an icy glass of water. I've had so much to drink over the past few hours that I will be peeing all day and night. But gosh darn it, I've never been so hydrated in my entire life.

I've already breastfed Delilah and placed her peacefully back in her Bugaboo. Once again, she's out like a light.

"I did. But..."

"But what?"

"The other applicants were just awful, Jenna. No, beyond awful. One said she'd wash Delilah's mouth with soap; another drinks vodka martinis at ten in the morning. Ten in the freaking morning!" Jenna pushes her bubbly glass of Prosecco to the side. "Two of them didn't even show up. They texted they were on the way and then ghosted me. Seriously, who does that?"

"So let me get this straight—you're hiring the headshot because she *showed up*? You've known this girl for all of a minute. And what the hell kind of name is Brie? Seriously, is the girl named after a block of cheese? I'm telling you, it's a red flag if I've ever seen one."

I'm not sure how your parent-given birth name could be considered a red flag, but...

I stifle a giggle. "That's B-R-I-E, Jenna. She spells it B-R-E-E. See the difference?"

Jenna taps her freshly manicured red nails on the countertop. "Well, what's her last name?"

"Miller."

"Oh my goodness, Lucy." She brings her hand to her chest. "You're hiring a cheesy beer? That's even worse."

"For the love of God, Jenna, the girl was not named after a cheese, and I'm pretty sure she can't take credit for her last name either! And by the way, there are twenty-eight million Millers in the world. And I don't mean the *beers*!"

Jenna rolls her eyes. "Whatever. I'm just saying. I would have thought you'd pick someone a little more experienced in the childcare sector as opposed to a soft-core porn star wannabe."

I shoot my friend a pointed stare. "Wow, that's a whole lot to extrapolate from a single picture, Jenna."

Her voice softens. "It's just, you're letting this stranger move in with you, Lucy. Are you sure you're not making a mistake? You know I only want what's best for you."

"I guess you can't know for certain you're making a mistake until you make a mistake, right? Anyway, I have a really good feeling about her."

"You and your good feelings..." Jenna shakes her head at me, and her curled hair bounces around her in waves. It's as if there's a fan blowing on her as she shoots a Pantene commercial. Her eyebrows knit together, creating a crease between her eyes. It's gone just as soon as her face relaxes. I used to get that angry line between my eyes only when emoting, but it doesn't seem to want to go away now.

Jenna's got me beat in the genetics department, but she also clocks a solid eight or nine hours a night instead of eight or nine minutes in a row.

It's all fine and dandy now—well, not really—but it definitely won't be when I'm tasked with risk assessments, calculations, and other people's money. And if all goes according to plan, in one short month, I'll have to drag my butt out of bed and be fully functional at work. Will Delilah even be sleeping through the night by then? Will I have to sleep-train my little peanut? Let her cry it out? I'd sooner poke myself in the eye with a tweezer. And we all know Andreas isn't about to do it either.

Is this a mistake?

I'm lost in thought as an interminably long silence stretches between us. "Fine," Jenna says finally. "But don't say I didn't warn you. Bree Miller has trouble written all over her airbrushed face."

—

Jenna's warning sticks with me as I stop in the corner shop on the way back to my apartment, though I'm trying hard not to think about it. I've already told my boss and clients I'll be back on the trading floor on October 1. I offered Bree the nanny position, and she happily accepted—I can't exactly go and take it back. Can I? No, no, of course, I can't. Bree is probably putting in her notice at work and breaking the news to her roommate that she'll be moving out next month as we speak. I'm not about to leave this poor girl jobless and homeless to boot simply because my best friend takes issue with her name sounding like cheese—correction: a cheesy beer.

Speaking of cheese, I grab some fresh chunks of mozzarella, eggplant, bright red cherry tomatoes, and an assortment of herbs to make Andrew's favorite sauce. Last but not least, I throw a big ol' stick of butter into my basket. I plan to butter my husband up before dropping my second bombshell of the day—the one I should have told him this morning. Delilah starts to stir in her stroller. She has slept through the better part of the morning and afternoon. That does not bode well for our evening at all.

Then, neither does the surprise that'll come knocking around eight o'clock. Bree insisted on coming by to meet Delilah and Andrew tonight. I mean, Delilah will most likely be sleeping, but Andrew... well, let's just hope my gourmet dinner for two puts him in a good mood.

Too soon? I know we only just discussed the possibility of hiring a nanny this morning, but hopefully, a quick rip of the Band-Aid will be less painful than a slow peel.

It's already four p.m. by the time I return to our apartment. I slide Delilah into her swing, which gently rocks her back and forth while playing a soothing Mozart piece. It's relaxing. *Really* relaxing.

So relaxing, I must fight the temptation to sink into the couch and lift my feet because I know I'll be out cold once my butt hits the cushion.

I can't afford to fall asleep right now. I've got some serious wining and dining to do.

I leave Delilah peacefully rocking in the living room so I can get to preparing my butter-you-up meal. Thankfully, the eggplant is already breaded and fried (I'm not Martha Stewart!). Though, I do make my own sauce. I chop the tomatoes, onions, and garlic and bring them to a slow boil on the stove. I throw in some salt, pepper, oregano, basil, a bay leaf, as well as half the stick of butter and leave the magical mixture to do its thing.

Then, I pour myself a generous glass of red wine. Of course, I shouldn't drink while breastfeeding, but what can I say other than it's been a day? And if this morning is any indication of what's to come, it should be a heck of a night. Knowing my husband as I do, we're talking fireworks.

I take a long sip, allowing the alcohol to warm my body and soothe my nerves.

Once the ingredients have reduced to a simmering paste, I begin layering the slices of eggplant with the sauce and mozzarella cheese. And, of course, the remaining butter. I grate some fresh Parmesan on top, and et voilà! I slide my masterpiece into the oven. While the eggplant cooks, I whip up a salad and start fettuccine on the stove. Then I set the table with our wedding china and light two taper candles.

The scene is absolute perfection—the perfect dinner to warm my once-perfect husband to the perfect nanny.

I'm about to sit down and enjoy my glass of wine when I'm startled by a knock at the door.

Who could it be?

It's a little late for packages.

A second knock.

Hmmm... I didn't receive any notification from the front desk about a visitor.

Could someone have the wrong apartment? Only one other unit shares the top floor with us. Our neighbor is in her eighties, and her grown children rarely come to visit. But even so, they at least know which apartment is hers. I mean, they stand to inherit it.

"Coming," I call out, wiping my hands on my already-stained shirt. I should probably slip into something a little more seductive before Andrew gets home. Maybe run a comb through my hair?

I squint an eye against the peephole.

What is *she* doing here?

CHAPTER 6

"Hey, Lucinda." Bree is standing in my doorway, grinning from ear to ear, with two large suitcases clutched at her sides and a teddy bear tucked under her arm. To say I'm confused is an understatement. I mean, when I told her she could come by tonight, I meant it like, *hey why don't you come by to meet Delilah and watch how I put her to bed?* It doesn't take two oversized suitcases to put a baby to bed.

"How did you get past the doorman?" I ask, completely caught off guard.

"I told him I was your sister."

"*Sister?*"

"Yeah, he said he could totally see the family resemblance. Nice guy."

Hmmm. Should I be flattered that our doorman Ashton thinks I resemble an attractive twenty-year-old? Or suggest he invest in a pair of glasses? Who's to say he won't one day let in an armed man claiming to be my mother?

Bree and I look nothing alike—she's over a decade younger than me and doesn't have crow's feet or stretch marks. I pulled a white hair from my scalp the other day. The only thing white on Bree's head is her sun-kissed highlights.

And then there's the luggage. "What's with the suitcases, Bree?"

"My roommate was pretty pissed when I told her I'd be moving out next month, so I figured now was as good a time as any. Don't ya think?"

I rack my brain for a response, but there are no words.

I glance down at my watch, then stare at Bree standing awkwardly in the doorway. It's only five-thirty. There's something to be said for punctuality, but two and a half hours early? A whole *month* early? Andrew isn't even home yet. I haven't had a chance to tell him Bree is moving in with us. Or that I hired someone, for that matter.

"I'm sorry," Bree says, her face falling. "I shouldn't have shown up so early and expected you to be okay with me staying. I was just so excited to meet Delilah and wanted to get a chance to snuggle her before she went down for the night. And truthfully, I didn't have anywhere else to go. I didn't mean to interrupt—" She glances over my shoulder at the romantic table set for two and then looks down at her feet. "I'll figure something out and come back later," she says in a low voice as she turns to walk away. She looks so tiny with her giant suitcases, childlike. I think of my child, and I feel terrible.

Just awful.

"Bree, wait."

She whirls around quickly with a look of hope in her pale blue eyes.

"You don't have to go. It's fine, really. Please, come in." I open the door fully and scooch to the side to make room for her—the first of many dances, I'm sure, as we all get used to our new living arrangement. The one I just need to tell Andrew about.

Oh, God. Andrew.

Guess who else is early…

I hear my husband's footsteps padding down the hallway as a loud beeping noise fills the apartment.

And smoke. So much smoke.

"My eggplant!"

I start running toward the kitchen, stopping short momentarily to rattle off instructions to Bree. I point toward the living room, talking a mile a minute— "Delilah is in there asleep in her swing. If she wakes up, you can bring her to your room. It's down the long hallway, second door on the right. I'm sorry, I haven't had a chance to set out towels or anything…"

"Please, Lucinda. I know I've caught you off guard. I'll figure it out. Go, take care of your dinner."

I smile weakly, then sprint into the kitchen and grab a dish towel. I rip open the oven only to be blasted in the face with plumes of thick, black smoke. I'm about to reach for the fire extinguisher, but there aren't any flames. It looks like my eggplant parmesan put the fire out (and started it?). Either way, it's burnt well beyond recognition. Ironically, my magical stick of butter probably sped up the process.

Could things get any worse right now?

"What in the hell is going on, Lucinda?"

Why yes. Yes, they can.

Andrew is standing in the kitchen with his hands on his hips squinting at me, his eyes tearing as if I sprayed him with Mace. His gaze flits to the tray in the oven, displaying what now resembles an incinerated boot. "You cooked," he says, shaking his head. Then he coughs loudly into the crook of his arm.

"I tried," I respond tightly, attempting to hide my embarrassment at the colossal failure meant to be our dinner. Okay, so now you know—I'm not the gourmet chef I may have made myself out to be. As if on cue, bubbling water boils over the pot, sizzling loudly on the stovetop. Because I completely forgot about the fettuccine. So much for al dente.

"There's a salad." I hold up a piece of lettuce. It hangs limply in my hand, another victim of the over-boiled water and heavy smog. What a fricking disaster.

Andrew cracks a window in the kitchen, allowing some of the smoke to escape. He steps onto a chair and pulls down the smoke detector from the ceiling, removing the four double A batteries so the beeping finally stops.

Without it, I can hear my heart beating in my chest. It's loud and fast and incredibly irritating. Not nearly as irritating as my news will be to Andrew, though. I'm seriously reconsidering the benefits of a slow peel.

"Where's Delilah?" he asks. "I can take her outside while you're figuring out dinner. Maybe we can order pizza or something? She probably shouldn't be breathing in all this smoke." Andrew swats at a wall of smoke with a hand.

"She's in the living room." He turns to leave. "But wait, before you go, I have to tell you something—"

Too late.

Andrew practically runs smack dab into Bree, standing in the kitchen archway with Delilah pressed against her chest. I can't even take a deep breath to calm my nerves because of all the damn smoke.

"Sorry to interrupt," she says. "It's just—I think Delilah is hungry." *Hungry?* I eye Bree curiously. I'm not sure where she got that idea from since Delilah is fast asleep in her arms, but okay. If she says so, it must be true. Our brand-new nanny knows my baby and her feeding schedule better than I do.

Oh, God. What's wrong with me?

I quickly compose myself. "Bree, this is my husband, Andrew," I say by way of introduction. "Andrew, this is Bree, our—"

"Live-in nanny," she interjects.

Well, that's one way to break the news, I suppose. Band-Aid, meet rip.

"I'm sorry, our *what?*" All the color drains from my husband's face. "Lucinda, could I have a word with you in private? NOW."

Jenna was right. I should have broken the news to Andrew this morning that I had advertised for a *live-in* nanny. To be honest, I was too afraid he would say no, and I wouldn't be able to convince him otherwise. I can't afford to show up to work late in the event my nanny gets stuck in traffic or something. I figured a nanny can't be late when all she has to do is walk out of her bedroom door to report for work.

I planned on telling Andrew all this *before* Bree moved in—I did—I just didn't want to overload him with too much all at once. Well, that backfired bigtime. But how was I to know Bree would show up with luggage when she wasn't supposed to move in for another month?

"I can take Delilah into my room so the two of you can talk," Bree offers. "Do you have a bottle I can give her?"

"*Her room?* Where is *her* room, Lucinda?" Andrew's voice has risen at least five octaves. I think he may be going into shock. That, or doing the math of where our new nanny's bedroom is located. I feel like a real asshole now. I also should have consulted Andrew before offering his drawing room as a nanny suite. But our apartment, though spacious, is only a three bedroom. Apart from sleeping between Andrew and me, where else was there for Bree to go?

"What the hell is going on, Lucinda?" Andrew asks through gritted teeth. The muscles in his jaw twitch. He looks like a powder keg ready to blow. I expected him to be upset, but not *this* upset. Because aren't new-age artists supposed to be calm? New-age-y?

"Just give me a minute—I can explain." I turn to Bree. "There are bottles in the fridge. Warm one up for two minutes, and you're good to go. Please, burp her well, or she'll be up all night with gas." Who am I kidding? Delilah will be up all night with or without gas.

And I have the feeling Andrew and I will also be up all night, arguing over our new nanny.

Bree grabs a bottle from our fridge and warms it up as Andrew and I stand awkwardly looking anywhere else but at each other. At least, I know I am. Bree coughs loudly into her arm while waiting for the bottle warmer to beep. Finally, after what feels like two hours (as opposed to two minutes), the timer goes off.

"I can put Delilah to bed," Bree offers. "So the two of you can *talk*."

"That would be wonderful, Bree. I really appreciate it."

"Anything I can do to help." Bree takes the bottle and Delilah into the other room, leaving me alone with my husband's wrath. Good times.

And he wastes no time unleashing it. "A live-in nanny, Lucinda? Don't you think that's something we should have maybe discussed? You only just mentioned the possibility of even hiring a nanny this morning. I'm pretty sure you didn't say anything about her living with us."

I hang my head. "You're right, Andrew. I was waiting for the right moment to bring it up."

"And you thought the right moment was when she'd already moved in? I don't get you sometimes."

Well, when he puts it that way.

I chew on a fingernail. "What can I say? She was early."

"So let me get this straight—it's *her* fault *you* didn't tell me you hired a live-in nanny because she was punctual?"

"Not punctual, Andrew. Like three hours early. See the difference? And, for the record, she wasn't supposed to move in until next month. Not until I had time to talk to you about it."

Andrew shakes his head at me. "The point is, you already told her she *could* move in without talking to me. This is supposed to be a partnership, not a dictatorship, Lucinda. You don't get to make all the decisions."

He's completely right. And I do feel bad.

"You're right, okay." I close the space between us and place a hand on my husband's chest. The anger slowly melts from his face as I slide my fingers down to his stomach. My actions have me feeling guilty; the wine, amorous.

I haven't touched Andrew like this in a while. I'm usually too caught up in his wise assery these days to want to go anywhere near him. I don't think I've so much as looked at him since Delilah was born.

If I'm being honest, he looks good.

Seriously, when did the guy get abs?

Sometimes I forget all the things that made me fall in love with him in the first place.

"Look, Andrew" I say. "We haven't been able to have sex since Delilah was born, and we can technically do it RIGHT NOW." I wink, moving my hand as low as it will go without downright fornicating in the kitchen. "See how good it is having a nanny around? See what we're able to do? I promise this will be a good arrangement for all of us; you'll see."

It will take some serious making nice to smooth this one over. And if there's one thing I know about my husband, it's how to make him forget he's mad at me.

"I thought you had to wait for your six-week checkup?" Andrew chews on his lower lip as he says this.

"I think I can make an exception this one time." I wink conspiratorially.

What's two more weeks?

Andrew lifts me off my feet and twirls me around in the air. I let out a small gasp.

Maybe I do still love the guy a little.

I'm trying to enjoy the moment. Yes, this new arrangement will take some getting used to for all of us. We just need to communicate and set some boundaries.

I tell myself this as I catch Bree in the corner of my eye, watching us.

That's not weird. *Is* it?

CHAPTER 7

My husband and I had sex, folks. Plot twist, considering...

Afterward, Andrew immediately drifted off to sleep. I've been listening to him softly snoring as I rest my head on his chest. His pecs are notably hard and defined for a man in his mid-thirties. I wonder if he's been taking a daily break from his sculpting to work out. His stamina was better than I remember, or maybe it's just that I've lost mine.

Less pleasant thoughts flit through my head, but I push them away. Things are different now—we have a child together. The past is in the past.

My stomach lets out a low grumble. I'm utterly ravenous. In all the excitement of nearly burning down our apartment—of fighting and making up—Andrew and I both forgot about dinner. Probably a good thing, too, considering how I murdered it.

I gently peel myself from Andrew's embrace and slip out of bed. I wrap myself in the silk robe draped across the velvet bench at the base of our bed. Then I feel around with my toes in the dark, searching for the slippers I abandoned in the heat of the moment. Once my feet are snugly tucked inside, I tiptoe out of our bedroom.

I check the time on my watch—it's already twelve a.m. I guess we had quite a bit of making up to do.

I haven't heard a peep on the monitor since Bree put Delilah to bed a few hours ago. The apartment is surprisingly quiet for this time of night. Delilah is due for a feeding, a fact she will let us know with a wailing cry. And one thing you should know about Delilah is that she doesn't just cry—she screams bloody murder. On one of our first nights home from the hospital, the police showed up at our door to investigate what may have been a serious domestic event. Our elderly neighbor was awoken by the screaming (and for context, she is partially deaf). "Bloody murder," she told them. The police asked to search the apartment to ensure we were all accounted for and no one was seriously injured or *bloody murdered*. They realized it had all been some silly misunderstanding once they saw Delilah, red-faced and teary-eyed, with her little baby fingers balled into tight fists.

Well, that's what they called it— "a silly misunderstanding." Try me again two months from now, and they may find that nosy Mrs. Henderson was on to something. It won't feel like a silly misunderstanding when they come to find I've murdered my husband in a fit of sleep-deprived rage.

I creak open the door to Delilah's room. Her white noise machine gently whirs, and I hear the faint sounds of her breathing. I suddenly stop short before making it to the crib. My heartbeat quickens in my chest. The hairs on my arms shoot up, and a prickly sensation slides down my spine. I whip my head around the room, expecting to find Andrew or Bree in the darkness. It doesn't feel like we're alone. But there's no one there.

It's strange—I've had this feeling before. Just yesterday, as we made the short trek from our apartment to the coffee shop, I felt like someone was following me. I looked over my shoulder, searching for a familiar face or someone out of place. But no one was even looking at me.

This sleep deprivation thing has me going mad. Absolutely mad.

I shake my head and lift Delilah from the crib, gently changing and nursing her. Her body is curled in the fetal position and warm from sleep. Delilah and I have developed a nighttime routine during this first month of her life—first, I change her diaper and onesie, and then I nurse her. At some point mid-feed, Delilah unlatches from my breast and proceeds to have an explosion that shakes the room, forcing me to abandon the feeding and start all over again. Feeding my daughter in the middle of the night is an hours-long affair.

But by the good grace of God, that doesn't happen tonight. After she's well burped, I place my baby back in her crib and chance one more look around the nursery, unable to shake the icky feeling crawling under my skin.

Satisfied at least for now that we're alone, I gently close Delilah's door behind me and hurry back to our bedroom. But something isn't sitting right.

I'm not so hungry anymore.

CHAPTER 8

You can tell just by looking at my husband that he got lucky last night. He's humming to himself as he flips pancakes on our griddle. I've never heard Andrew hum before. It sounds like someone released a songbird in our kitchen. Was I *that* good? Or does his sudden affinity for humming have something to do with the hot twenty-year-old minding our baby? I guess it didn't take him very long to adapt to our new arrangement.

Why am I even thinking like this? It must be the hormones—dang fourth trimester.

I sneak up behind Andrew and wrap my arms around his muscular waist. I nuzzle my face into his neck. "Good morning, handsome," I whisper into his ear, pausing long enough to let my tongue linger on his earlobe. "Breakfast smells amazing."

After convincing myself I was being paranoid last night and logging a few hours of much-needed shut-eye, my appetite has returned with a vengeance.

"And good morning to you, beautiful. I made yours just as you like with fresh blueberries." Andrew places his spatula on the countertop and turns to face me. God, he looks maddeningly sexy in an apron. After last night, I'm not quite as bothered by the goofy man bun. It's probably just a phase. He's obscenely good-looking when he sports a more traditional cut. Maybe *too* good-looking? Do I want people staring at us wondering, *what is* he *doing with* her? On second thought, I hope he grows his hair down to his ass. But then he might look like Jason Momoa. I should just go ahead and change my name to Lucinda 'Completely Screwed' Douglass.

Andrew breaks through my thoughts. "I'm taking orders. Can I interest you in a repeat of last night?" He winks at me, and my entire body tingles.

So it *was* last night that has him humming like a songbird in heat. Go me!

"What about the pancakes?" We both glance over his shoulder. Despite the distraction, his pancakes are perfect—fluffy and golden brown—unlike my unsuccessful attempt at eggplant parmesan. As a reminder, in case that embarrassing disaster somehow slipped my mind, our kitchen still reeks of the smoke that sticks to paint in the walls long after a fire.

Andrew keeps my gaze as he slips his hand behind him and turns off the griddle. Then he pulls me in for a kiss. Within seconds, we're making out like teenagers, with his hands fisted tightly in my hair. I honestly don't know what has gotten into my husband.

"Morning, lovebirds."

Andrew and I startle as if caught in the act. Which, if Bree had shown up a few minutes later, may very well have been the case. I mean, up until last night, we could have had sex on the countertop without anyone the wiser. Not that we have sex on the kitchen countertop, but still. We *could* have.

I'd forgotten Bree was even here. And now, I'm so flustered that I can't even bring myself to make eye contact. As I stare at the floor, I notice Bree hasn't bothered putting on pants this morning. It certainly didn't take her very long either to make herself at home.

Andrew clears his throat. "Uh, good morning. Are you hungry, Bree? I made pancakes."

"Famished, actually. I was up all night with Delilah. I'm not sure what you're eating, Lucinda, but she's awfully gassy. You may want to switch to a sensitive stomach formula or lay off the caffeine and chocolate." She winks at me. "Don't worry, she's *finally* asleep now."

My cheeks flame red. Did Bree just accuse me of *poisoning* my daughter with breast milk via the one-inch ball of chocolate *she* gave me?

Andrew chuckles as he places a heaping plateful of *my* blueberry pancakes in front of Bree. That's okay, I guess—once again, I've lost my appetite.

"She got you pegged pretty quick, Luc, didn't she?"

And there it is—the wise assery I was talking about. Andrew never used to poke fun at my expense. Or maybe it just didn't get to me before the affair. *This* is the reason I don't know if I should slip into a swimsuit or a snowsuit when I'm around my husband. We are so hot and cold, I fear I may simultaneously die of heatstroke and hypothermia all in one fell swoop.

I force a tight smile. Something else is also bothering me, aside from the obvious. Bree couldn't possibly have been up all night with Delilah. When I checked on my daughter around midnight, she was out cold in her crib. I sleep-fed her, milk spilling out the sides of her mouth, dribbling down her chubby pink cheeks. Not to mention the fact that I sleep with Delilah's baby monitor so close to my face, it could double as a pillow. Surely I would have heard her if she were quote-unquote up all night.

Why would Bree say something like that?

Bree smiles appreciatively at the plate in front of her, opening her mouth wide for a generous bite of pancakes. When she's finished chewing like she's filming a commercial for IHOP, she gushes, "You didn't tell me you were married to a gourmet chef, Lucinda." *A gourmet chef?* Sheesh. It's not like Andrew made bananas foster Belgian waffles or eggs benedict from scratch. He literally used Pearl Milling Company's just-add-water pancake mix. I can see the box peeking out from behind the coffee machine.

Am I being paranoid? Because it sure seems like Bree is flirting with my husband. No, not *seems*. She is *definitely* flirting with my husband. And where are her gosh darn pants?

Someone, please, remind me why I wanted to hire a live-in nanny... Anyone? Anyone?

Andrew once again clears his throat. If I didn't know better, I'd think he was coming down with something. But my husband does this whenever he's nervous or uncomfortable. I'm guessing now it's a combination of both.

"So, what's on the agenda for today, ladies?" Andrew leans back against the counter, fidgeting with his apron. Another tell that he'd rather be anywhere but here.

"Oh, you know, this and that," I say, composing myself. "Maybe we can get some fresh air and take Delilah on a walk to Central Park."

"That sounds lovely," Bree says through a mouthful of pancakes. "Only—"

"Only what?" I ask, struggling to imagine what she's about to say. *Fresh air can cause febrile seizures?*

"Well, in my haste to pack so I could start for you as soon as possible, I kind of forgot my sneakers." She lowers her eyes. "I don't have any walking shoes."

"Oh, don't even worry about that. Lucinda has a whole closet full of walking shoes. Don't you, Lucinda? What size are you, Bree?" Andrew takes a long swig from his glass of orange juice. He looks awfully pleased with himself. It's so thoughtful of my husband to offer out my shoes.

"Seven," she replies. "I'm sure Lucinda's feet are smaller. She's so tiny." That is not true, but my irritation somewhat subsides.

"I'm a size seven as well."

"Well, hot dawg. What are the chances?" Andrew pumps a victorious fist in the air.

I regard my husband curiously. In the time I've known Andrew, I've never seen him get so excited over a pair of shoes. He didn't even know my shoe size though we've lived together for over a decade.

"Seven is the most commonly purchased size in women's shoes, Andrew, so the chances are pretty high."

"Right." Andrew rolls his eyes. Our postcoital bliss has worn off, and things are apparently going south fast. I'm starting to think my husband no longer appreciates my mental Rolodex of valuable information. Or perhaps it's the fact that I corrected him in front of the virtual stranger devouring pancakes in an undershirt in our kitchen. I guess I'll have to work on that.

"Well, enjoy your walk," Andrew says tightly, all hints of his earlier jubilation gone. "I'm off to the studio."

"I'd love to see your work one day," Bree says, beaming.

Andrew smiles widely at her. "Well, I'll just have you down to the studio one day. I'll have my people call your people." They both laugh at his joke. Funny, because he never asks me down to the studio.

Andrew tosses his apron on the island and grabs his keys. Then he walks out, letting the front door slam behind him.

This time, there's no kiss goodbye.

CHAPTER 9

My husband's departure was decidedly chilly, but the weather outside is fantastic today. A cold front blew through last night, and the temperature dropped fifteen degrees. There's a gentle breeze and a few puffy clouds; otherwise, it's clear blue skies all around.

While pushing Delilah's stroller along the sidewalk, I take a sip from my Hydro Flask, filled to the brim with iced Mother's Milk tea. Andrew brews me a fresh batch every morning. The lactation consultant in the maternity ward called the stuff 'literal magic' for promoting milk production. Lest I forget how important a mother's milk is to a growing child, the hospital sent me home with a T-shirt and mug reminders that *Breast is Best*. Genius marketing strategy. I've been drinking this stuff twenty-four-seven.

It costs more than a dollar a teabag, so I wasn't complaining when Jenna sent me a screenshot of an Instagram giveaway where I wound up winning a lifetime supply. That in itself almost makes me want to have more babies. Plus, there's something abnormally satisfying about pumping out cartons of milk. If there were an award for milk production, I'd be a shoo-in. I guess I'll never know if it's me or the tea because I've no reason to stop drinking it—not while breastfeeding, anyway. Maybe not ever with my lifetime supply.

"Here, let me help," Bree offers, taking over the stroller duties so I can properly drink my tea. It is a welcome change to have the use of both hands. At the same time, no less (#mindblown)! Still, having someone other than myself or my husband pushing Delilah in her stroller is strange. Something else I'll have to get used to.

It's not been twenty-four hours yet. These things take time. I can't even remember why I was annoyed with Bree this morning. Does it really matter that she likes to sleep in an undershirt and thinks Andrew is a good cook? Delilah slept better last night than she has since she came home from the hospital. Our nanny could streak through our apartment at this point, and I'd probably still let her stay.

But for now at least, Bree is fully clothed, striding confidently beside me in the Golden Goose sneakers I treated myself to when my feet swelled, and heels became a non-option. They're white leather with hot pink trim and glitter stars. If I were in her position, I would have grabbed a pair of actual walking shoes, like my perfectly sensible Nikes, but I can't fault her for liking sparkly things. *It's just a pair of shoes*, I tell myself—just a seven-hundred-dollar pair of shoes.

And my husband did tell her to have her pick.

We stop at a crosswalk, and I look down at my bright-eyed and bushy-tailed daughter. She stares at me with her big blue eyes, and then, out of nowhere, she flashes her toothless pink gums.

Oh. My. God.

I swear, Delilah just smiled at me.

"Did you see that, Bree?" I nudge her gently with my elbow, unable to pull my eyes from my daughter's face. "Delilah just smiled."

Seriously, you'd think winter was ushering in spring the way my heart is melting.

"I'm sorry to be the bearer of bad news, Lucinda, but babies don't actually smile at four weeks. It's probably just gas."

Geez. What's with this girl and gas?

I'm about to say something, but I stop as an uneasy feeling suddenly settles over me, and not from the disappointing news that my daughter's loving grin was a product of newborn flatulence. My heartbeat quickens in my chest as I whip my head from side to side before throwing it back over my shoulder. I can't shake the feeling someone is out there watching me.

But I don't see anyone other than Bree giving me a side eye. *What in the world is happening to me?*

I'm taking one last look around when I catch sight of a sign for Ivybrook Preschool. What a coincidence—the preschool Bree worked at up until yesterday is just around the corner from my apartment.

Bree is oblivious, scrolling through Instagram as we wait for the light to change. "Hey, Bree," I say. "Look." She follows my finger with her eyes to the Ivybrook sign and the gaggle of noisy toddlers assembled in a zigzag line with a few teachers outside. "Was that your class?"

"Huh?" She looks confused.

"Is this not the Ivybrook preschool you worked at?"

"Oh," she says, with a slight giggle. "Yes, but no, that's not my class." She goes back to her phone without giving the place a second glance.

My first job was in college at a nightclub in the West Village called Angles. I cleaned bathrooms and waited tables until I worked my way up to mixologist. More than a decade later, I'd be leapfrogging over people waiting behind the velvet rope to get back inside. Granted, that could be because I don't get out much these days. But still, it's been all of eight hours since Bree handed in her resignation, and she's utterly apathetic. That seems strange, doesn't it?

Come to think of it, when I offered her the job, Bree didn't even ask if she could grant Ivybrook the standard two weeks' notice. She literally went to work yesterday morning and quit that same afternoon.

I'm curious, and about to ask if she knows the teachers from this other class and wants to stop over to say hello (though I get the sense she doesn't) when the walk sign flashes green. Oh well. Now that she lives so close, she'll have all the time in the world to visit. And if they are upset with her because the wound is so fresh, time heals *most* things.

We cross Fifth Avenue to head into Central Park. Because of the fantastic weather, the park is bustling today with all walks of life—runners, bikers, sunbathers, and little kids hanging like monkeys on the playground equipment. Bree and I settle down on a bench near the playground. I inhale the fresh summer air. The city recently planted an assortment of flora in this area of the park in Phase I of an effort to beautify all of Central Park.

I'll likely be sitting in this very spot watching Delilah play in a few short years. But for now, she's still a newborn who doesn't sleep through the night. And so, my eyelids are heavy like bricks. I close them and let the sunlight warm my face. I wish I could stay like this forever. I deserve a few minutes of uninterrupted peace, don't I? How about one minute? Thirty seconds?

Nope. Apparently not. My phone rings loudly in my pocket, shattering the short-lived solitude.

Chad Morgan's name flashes across the screen. I hold the phone in my hand, internally debating whether or not I should answer. I so *don't* want to deal with work right now.

I feel Bree's stare as she watches me decide what to do. "Do you want to take that?" she asks. "I can sit here with Delilah."

I hesitate for a moment. I'm going to have to cut the cord at some point. And I know I'll have to deal with Chad and work before I go back. Besides, he's already interrupted whatever relaxation I was settling into.

"Thanks," I say. "I won't be long." I hit the accept button as I walk to a slightly quieter area away from the playground. I tuck myself behind a Great American Elm tree.

"Finally," Chad breathes into the phone before I've even had the chance to say hello. "Why haven't you returned any of my calls?" There's a not-so-subtle hint of annoyance in his voice.

"I'm sorry, Chad, I've just been swamped. I do have a newborn baby, you know?"

"Yes, I'm well aware of that." His voice softens. "Listen, we should get together and talk before you return. A lot is going on and—"

A loud, high-pitched shriek travels from the playground.

"Lucinda, are you there?" Chad's voice becomes distant as I drop my hand and start running. My heart races in my chest as I turn the corner and spot the source of the commotion. A man dressed in head-to-toe black has his fingers wrapped around the handle of Delilah's stroller. Bree seems to be pulling in the opposite direction, fighting him off.

"Stop!" I scream as I run full speed toward them.

The man looks up as I lunge, momentarily freezing as his dark brown eyes connect with mine. Without warning, he releases the stroller and sprints off, disappearing into the park.

I suck in a breath. The stroller wobbles back and forth as if it might topple over with my daughter inside before righting itself.

Bree stumbles back, falling onto the bench.

"Delilah," I cry as I reach into the stroller, lifting my baby and smothering her with kisses. I kiss her head, eyes, and cheeks and then check her body from head to toe. Then I kiss and check her all over again. Thank God, Delilah is completely unscathed, blissfully unaware of the fate she just narrowly escaped. I can't bear to think of what that fate might have been.

How could something like this have happened? Were we being followed? Why would someone try to abduct my child? My head is spinning with every unpleasant possibility it can conjure.

Once again, I'd almost forgotten about Bree.

"Bree," I say, gently touching her shoulder. "Are you okay?"

She jerks her head up to look at me, and I gasp. "Jesus Christ, your face!" Bree's right eye is the color of a 7-Eleven slushie—one of those concoctions Jenna and I made nightly in college—black cherry mixed with blue raspberry. It's also the size of a golf ball and swollen shut.

She exhales loudly. "I don't know. It all happened so fast. That bastard elbowed me in the face. There was no way in hell I was letting go of that stroller."

I shiver at the thought of what might have happened if she had.

"You saved her," I manage through tears. "You saved my baby. I owe you her life, Bree.

Seriously, she can have every last pair of shoes in my closet. Because if that's not the perfect nanny, I don't know what is.

Once I've stopped profusely thanking Bree, I scream at the top of my lungs, "Someone, please, call 9-1-1."

CHAPTER 10

I feel stuck in a nightmare from which I can't wake up.

It's been thirty minutes since the masked assailant disappeared into the sea of unmasked normal human beings in Central Park. I can't believe someone tried to kidnap my baby in broad daylight in a crowded park. Moreover, how a masked man dressed in all black strolled through Central Park on a hot summer afternoon without anyone stopping him. What happened to #SeeSomethingSaySomething?

I mean, I guess things happen. It's a wild world we're living in. There was that man draped in a blanket who tried to kidnap a young girl walking with her grandmother on a New York City street corner. It was only a few years back.

But the blanket—I don't know—it seems more *spontaneous*. This guy's outfit, with a ski mask and gloves, feels awfully premeditated, not just some spur-of-the-moment crime of opportunity. It's as if he came to this area of Central Park for one thing and one thing only—Delilah. And then there's this feeling I haven't been able to shake.

Maybe we *should* move to the suburbs. We don't have to get a Suburban. I'll take an Escalade. Maybe a Range Rover?

I call Andrew while waiting for the police to arrive to take our statements. Predictably, his phone goes straight to voicemail. Artists don't appreciate being bothered when they're knee-deep in their craft, which for Andrew is spare tires and recycled cans of cola.

Getting in touch with him when he's at work in his studio is impossible.

It wasn't always like this. Until a year ago, Andrew was gainfully employed at a nine-to-five—okay, nine-to-sometimes-eleven—job. He was an up-and-coming lawyer at a prestigious firm, on track to eventually make partner. His clients and colleagues loved him, especially all the young paralegals. They loved him a little *too* much.

Andrew's hair was closely cropped to his scalp back then (hubba, hubba), and he wore a suit and tie instead of oversized paint-splattered jeans. Which, by the way, he now wears every single gosh darn day. I went through his drawers last week. Should I be relieved or disturbed that he has half a dozen of the same paint-splattered jeans? What would Jerry Seinfeld say?

In any event, my husband was going places.

Now: *It's Andreas. You've reached my voicemail. I'm currently busy creating a masterpiece. Hold on a second while I grab a brush (shuffling). All right, what do you need to tell me? And go...*

The guy has completely lost his goo.

Call me back as soon as you can, Andrew. There was an incident at the park. We're all okay, but I need you to call me. Uh, thanks. Bye.

Bree and I look at each other as the playground fills with the sounds of sirens. Well, half of her looks at me since one of her eyes won't open. Within minutes, we're surrounded by police and paramedics.

"Ma'am," a uniformed officer addresses Bree. "Is your baby injured?" Oh my God, he thinks Bree is Delilah's mother. What does that make me—the *nanny*? And she doesn't even correct him. She says, "No, thank God, she's unharmed."

Am I overreacting? I mean, she did save Delilah's life. She probably didn't even realize what he asked her. Judging by how her bruise is spreading across her face, I wouldn't be surprised to learn she has a concussion.

Still, I clear my throat. "Actually, Delilah is my daughter." The portion of Bree's face that isn't black and blue turns bright pink, almost magenta. Her body stiffens. So maybe she did realize.

"Can you tell me what happened? Ms.—"

"Douglass. Lucinda Douglass."

Now my face reddens. Because while I know what happened once I confronted the would-be kidnapper, I wasn't there as the events unfolded. I was hidden around a corner on the phone with Chad. He didn't even get the chance to tell me what he needed to tell me, and it sounded important.

I must be silent for too long because Bree pipes in. "I can tell you what happened. I was there for the *whole* thing."

The officer nods as he flips open a notepad to take down the report. "I was just sitting on this bench when this man came running up and grabbed our stroller out of nowhere."

"Did you recognize this man?"

"Unfortunately, no. He had a black ski mask covering his face. And he was wearing black leather gloves. He looked like he was about to rob a bank."

Or attempt to kidnap my daughter.

The officer's jaw tightens. I know what he's thinking: Gloves equal no prints. Mask equals no description. No prints and no description. They can't even attempt a composite sketch, as we have no freaking clue what the guy looks like. The only things we've got to go on are his brown eyes and apparent affinity for black.

Holy shit, they're never going to apprehend him. Which means he's just somewhere out there. He's going to come after us again and—

"And where were you, Ms.—"

"Douglass," I remind him. Gosh, is it that hard to remember? He wrote it down, for goodness' sake.

"I..." The officer's eyes widen as he taps his pen against his notepad, waiting for my response. "I had to take a work call," I admit as my cheeks flame.

"Oh, I see." He jots something down on his notepad. I try to peek at his notes, but he swiftly shuts the pad.

Then he reaches into his pocket and pulls out a card. "Well, whoever it was, it looks like he's gone for now. If either of you ladies remembers anything else, you can call the station."

I nod, but I don't feel better that he's gone. I won't feel better until the man who tried to take my daughter is caught and locked away.

CHAPTER 11

The paramedics spend an inordinate time fussing over Bree. I get it, I do, but I want to go home. Out of nowhere, thunder clouds have ominously rolled in, and the last thing we need is to get stuck in a major downpour, stroller and all. I'd say we've been through enough today.

And despite their persistent recommendations, Bree has made it abundantly clear that she does not wish to go to the hospital for further evaluation. She wants to go home too. For the love of God, let the girl go home!

Unsurprisingly, I haven't heard a peep from Andrew. I left him another message, a little more pointed this time—something along the lines of, *someone tried to kidnap your daughter; pick up the goddamn phone.* After I hung up, I may or may not have strung together a series of expletives.

Seriously, folks—how can you go without checking your phone for an *entire* day? It's not normal. Our world almost ended while Andrew was busying himself making 'happy little trees' or whatever he's working on.

I'm about to leave my husband another message, one in which I don't hang up before the cuss words flow, when I hear a familiar voice.

"Lucy? Is that you? Oh my God, it *is* you! What in the world is going on?"

"Jenna?" I blink my eyes rapidly to make sure she's not some mirage in the park. I wonder for a split second what she's doing here, but then realize I don't care. All that matters is that she's here. I'm so incredibly happy to see her that I actually burst into tears. Jenna pulls me in for a tight hug, soothingly rubbing the back of my head.

She looks absolutely gorgeous, angelic even. Her auburn hair hangs in loose waves that graze all the right places of her gauzy white dress. And her eyes look bigger and brighter than ever—dusted with bronze shadow and amethyst liner. Crap, I bet she's here to shoot footage for her Instagram account or some ad sponsorship. The fact that I'm ruining her perfect outfit and flawless makeup with the snot bubbles I'm blowing into her hair and all over her body makes me sob even harder.

And here I thought almost having your child kidnapped and a subsequent police investigation in the middle of Central Park during peak tourist time on the perfect summer day constituted making a scene…

When I've stopped ugly crying, Jenna pulls back to look me over. She's glowing. My slobbering seems to have given her chest a lovely sheen.

"What happened, Luc? Are you okay?" She takes my hands in hers.

I draw a deep breath. "Actually, no. I'm not okay. Someone tried to kidnap Delilah."

"Wait, *what?* What do you mean someone tried to kidnap Delilah?" It does sound almost unbelievable hearing her say it. But it happened. I saw it happen.

"There was a masked man, dressed in all black—" My sentence trails off. I don't have the air or energy to tell her the story. I will start crying again if I try, and I'm already red and blotchy enough, not to mention the ice pick headache poking at my left eye.

"I can tell you what happened." We both turn to look at Bree as she rises from the park bench. *Dear God.* And I thought I was a hot mess. The girl looks bad. *Really* bad. Like being on the losing end of a throwdown with Ewan McGregor bad.

"Who are you?" Jenna slips her sunglasses down the bridge of her nose and looks Bree over skeptically. I sure hope she likes her. Jenna is a hard shell to crack. It's bad enough that she and Andrew don't care for one another. I can't very well have her clashing with my nanny on top of that.

"I'm Delilah's new nanny, Bree."

"Oh right," she says, giving me a side-eye. "The cheese. You look different in person than in your headshot."

"Jenna!" I slap her arm.

Bree seems unphased, thankfully. To be fair, I did tell Bree at our interview that Jenna essentially stuffs her bra with headshots. So as they say, the pot has now officially met the kettle.

I listen, still somewhat in shock, as Bree recounts the story of the masked man and her rescue. By the time she's finished, my best friend's jaw has all but hit the pavement.

Jenna shakes her head. "That's absolutely insane," she says. "And neither of you got a good look at him?"

"He was wearing a ski mask." I pinch the bridge of my nose, trying to remember something, *anything*. "The only thing I saw was his eyes."

"Was there anything distinctive about them?"

I shake my head, then throw my hands up in frustration. "They were brown. I don't know, Jenna. It all happened so fast. There might have been something, but I can barely see straight right now, let alone piece together a coherent memory." And I don't have to state the obvious—more than half of the world's population has brown eyes, present company included. They're about as indistinctive as indistinctive gets.

"I can't believe what this world has come to," Jenna offers, shaking her auburn head of loose curls.

"You and me both."

We fall silent with our thoughts for a moment before Bree interrupts. "Where do you live, Jenna?"

Well, that was random.

Jenna seems to think so as well. She moves a hand to her hip. "Greenwich Village. *Why?*"

"I don't know..." Bree curls a lock of blonde hair around her finger. "Just wondering what you're doing in this part of *Central Park*. Super coincidental..."

My body momentarily stiffens. Is Bree right? What *is* Jenna doing in this park? More, what is she doing in this *section* of the park? It's not like Jenna has any kids. Central Park is two and a half miles wide. Plus, she lives in Greenwich Village, practically across the street from Washington Square Park. It's a perfectly good park.

Jenna's cheeks color. "I'm meeting someone," she says. And then adds, "A friend."

"A friend? Which friend?" I strain my neck, looking around the park for a familiar face. "I know all of your friends."

Jenna's eyes drop as she plays with the strings on her dress. "Look, it's a date, okay? You don't know him. It's a guy I met on Tinder."

"Oh...so a swipe right kind of friend." Bree giggles into her arm.

Duh, of course, it's that kind of friend. Not only does Jenna have tens of thousands of Instagram followers, she's also a professional serial dater. Andrew and I have personally set her up dozens of times, and while she's always game for a meet-up, her relationships never last very long. It's only a matter of time before Jenna finds something wrong with whomever she's seeing at the moment. I worry her standards are so high she may never meet the one and miss out on experiencing the indescribable wedded bliss my husband and I share. On second thought...

I laugh along with Bree, but my insides are roiling. Why wouldn't Jenna tell me she had a date today? We tell each other everything. I'm about to grill her, but then I stop myself. Is Tinder that spur-of-the-moment hookup thing? Maybe she just swiped right a few minutes ago. Or is it left? God, I'm getting old.

It's almost impossible that Jenna and I are the same age. And as if to further draw attention to the spinster thing I've got going on, I'm compelled to bring up dating safety. "Well, I'd say I'm happy you've exercised good judgment by meeting during the day in a public place, but..." I throw my hands in the air. It didn't work out too well for us, did it?

Jenna shakes her head. "I'm fine, Luc. It's you I'm worried about."

Geez, I can't ever imagine why.

"I'll be okay," I say, without any hint of believability. "We should probably get going, though. It's been a long day, to say the least." I lean in to air kiss Jenna on the cheek so as not to mess up the makeup she expertly applied for the date she didn't tell me she had.

"Yeah, you look exhausted, Lucy," Jenna says gently. I mean, as gently as you can tell someone, they look like crap. "You should go home and get some rest."

She's right, of course. I should go home and get some rest. But I won't. I'll toss and turn and think about what almost happened to Delilah today. The truth is, I'll be lucky if I ever find sleep again.

CHAPTER 12

MANY YEARS AGO

It was the middle of the night when my father woke me with a close-fisted jab to the upper arm. "Get up. It's time," he grumbled as I tried, dazed and confused, to rub the sleep from my eyes while holding back tears from the impact.

My arm pulsed with a fresh surge of pain as I rolled onto my side. All I wanted to do was sleep, but that wasn't an option. If it were, perhaps I wouldn't have had this uneasy feeling in the pit of my gut.

I shuffled out of bed as quickly as possible and headed down the stairs of our two-story Cape Cod. Our house was adequate for four, maybe five, but for a family of eight?

And it wasn't just the fact that we were bursting at the seams. The house needed some serious cosmetic work and, I suspected, structural as well. Take the stairs, for example. Every step moaned loudly as I descended to the main level, my footsteps like cannons in the cavernous space. There were spots where you could see the wood splintering as if the floor could give way at any moment.

I found Mom sitting in the living room, tears spilling down her round face. She brushed the back of her hand beneath her eyes and forced a weak smile when she saw me. "Take care of your brothers and sisters while we're out, okay?"

I nodded obediently. I always did.

My dad extended a hand to help my mom up from the threadbare loveseat in our living room. That's when I saw the blood. A giant red pool of it. That couldn't be normal, could it? I watched the trail as my parents walked out the front door.

I tried not to worry, but the minutes stretched like hours. I let myself into my father's office and fired up his computer. It was a beat-up old thing, but it worked all the same, even if it was slow as molasses.

I knew better than to complain. When my dad was growing up, he had to use his legs to walk to the library and read an actual encyclopedia to get information. And his dad had to walk five miles through the snow to get to the only library in their county. All I had to do was press a few keys and wait for the information to appear at my fingertips.

"You're as spoiled as rotten fruit," he told me whenever I sat at his desk to do work for school. I shook it off. He'd said worse. At fifteen, I strongly suspected I was my father's least favorite child. Not that he wanted any of us, it seemed. Yet here they went, having another—my sixth sibling. Seriously, who needed so many darn kids?

My fingers trembled as I typed into the Google search bar: *causes of heavy bleeding in pregnancy.*

A sick feeling washed over me as I scanned the results. The top relevant hit was for placental abruption—a condition where the placenta spontaneously detaches from the womb; it can cause life-threatening problems for both mother and baby. I brought a hand to my mouth and backed away from my father's desk as if I might unsee what I saw.

I paced into the living room, a strong sense of dread unfurling inside me. It looked like a bloody crime scene. I took a deep breath, steeling myself for the arduous task of cleaning my mother's blood off the loveseat and carpet.

We must have had some Clorox somewhere, I thought. My father used it on my skin when I gave myself a tattoo with a permanent marker. Bleach. Yes, bleach. My father said it removed everything—hopefully, even blood.

I'd have to be quick, though. The baby was fussing upstairs. Soon all my brothers and sisters would be awake. I'd have to feed them and then get them off to school. I had to get rid of all this blood before they saw it.

I turned toward the kitchen to check the pantry where we kept our cleaning supplies but was interrupted by a series of raps at the door. I whipped around and spotted our neighbor Judy standing at our front door with a hand pressed against her forehead as she squinted through the glass.

What was *she* doing here?

I dragged my feet to our entryway and begrudgingly unlocked the door. Judy stared at me with her hazel eyes. Her pupils were almost vertical, like a cat's. It gave me the creeps. I kept my distance as much as possible. Easier said than done since she lived next door and was now standing at our door.

I momentarily stared at her, wordless, noticing how her usually flawless face had taken on a greenish tinge.

Judy placed a manicured hand on my shoulder, and I winced. "I'm so sorry to have to be the one to tell you this, sweetie, but your mother is dead."

CHAPTER 13

I awake with a gasp in our chaise lounge to the sound of a key turning in the front door. I'm not sure when I nodded off. I check my watch—7:30 p.m.—well, it's about freaking time. With the exception of last night, Andrew leaves earlier and earlier every morning and gets home later and later every evening from his studio. It's as if he's trying to avoid us.

Or perhaps there's someone else.

I shake the thought.

I've given up on asking Andrew what he does all day. I used to feign at least some level of interest, but not lately. I think about it sometimes, though. For all I know, his studio is a front for a drug den. I've considered dropping by unannounced, but there's that whole ignorance is bliss thing to consider. What if there's something to it? Something I don't want to know.

"Lucinda?" I listen as Andrew kicks off his Hey Dudes by the front door. It sounds like one makes it in the closet. I hear a slow shuffle as Andrew retrieves the other shoe and tosses it inside, before closing the door.

He doesn't seem to be moving about in a hurry. There's also the notable lack of urgency in his voice as he called out my name. Surely he must have gotten my messages by now. His calmness strikes me as strange. Incredibly strange.

I rise from the chaise and make my way toward the kitchen. The aroma of sesame chicken almost masks the smell of the previous evening. *Almost.* Bree was a doll and ordered in Chinese for us. I told her to hold on to my credit card so she has it for incidentals, like a sudden craving for moo goo gai pan. And then I gave her the night off, with strict instructions to ice her eye. It's pretty scary looking, but all things considered, it could have been much, much worse.

Bree insisted on putting Delilah to bed first. I checked on my daughter twenty minutes ago before I nodded off on the couch, and she was fast asleep in her bassinet. I think I may have hired the baby whisperer.

As expected, I find Andrew in the kitchen, where he's stopped looking for me as he examines the egg rolls stacked neatly into a pyramid on our island. I'd love to take credit for the aesthetic presentation, but it was all Bree.

"Andrew." He glances up at me briefly, then back down at the egg rolls.

"Vegetarian?" he asks as he breaks one open, turning it over and over in his hand to inspect it.

Your daughter was almost fucking kidnapped today. "I wouldn't know, Andrew. Bree ordered it."

"Well, did you tell her I'm a vegetarian, Lucinda? It's just four words—Andrew. Is. A. Vegetarian. See, easy peasy." He smirks. Possibly joking, possibly serious. Either way, I'm not too fond of his tone. After he sided with Bree at my expense this morning, the only thing I'm fond of right now are his abs. He's got really great abs.

I plaster on the fakest smile I can muster. "So sorry, honey. I was a little busy reminding Bree to ice her eye and getting over our daughter almost getting abducted while her father was MIA all day."

"Wait, what?" Well, that certainly got his attention. Andrew drops the egg roll onto the kitchen tile. Bits of cabbage and carrots go flying everywhere. It's very dramatic. Either he's genuinely surprised that someone tried to kidnap his only child, or he just realized it's pork.

I wonder how he'd react if I told him.

Oh, who really cares. I'm physically and emotionally drained. The last thing I want is to fight with my husband right now. I plop down on a chair at the kitchen table, and Andrew follows, staring at me with his big brown eyes as concern spreads across his face.

"It was the scariest, craziest thing ever. I'm still shaking, Andrew. Look—" I hold out a trembling hand. I take a long sip of tea to moisten my throat, and then I tell him the story that keeps playing on a loop in my head. By the time I've finished, Andrew is also shaking, his face as white as a sheet. It turns out he didn't check his messages. Again, odd. But in the grand scheme of things, Andrew not listening to my frantic voicemails is the least of my concerns.

He opens his mouth to say something but doesn't get the chance. There's a loud knock at the front door. It's just a knock, but it gives me full-body chills.

It's like eight o'clock right now. Who would be showing up at our door without warning at eight o'clock? And why isn't our doorman ringing us first?

I'm on the edge of my seat as a male voice introduces himself to my husband as a detective from the NYPD. For a moment, I feel the slightest glimmer of hope. Maybe he's come to tell us that they found the guy. We'll press charges, naturally, and put this nightmarish day to rest—after we figure out why he targeted my daughter in the first place.

Because let's be honest, until that question is answered, I may never leave our apartment again.

Ahem. My eyes shoot up at the sound of Andrew clearing his throat. Standing next to him is a burly man with close-cropped silver hair. He's dressed casually in street clothes, a badge affixed to the waistband of his pants. My heart hitches in my chest.

"Lucinda, this is Detective Dick O'Brien. Detective, my wife, Lucinda Douglass."

I nod in the detective's direction. My mouth feels too dry to speak. I'd say it's the MSG from the Chinese food, but I haven't had a bite to eat yet. I take another swig of tea. At this rate, my breasts will be flowing like a fountain this evening.

"I'm sorry to bother you this late at night, Mrs. Douglass. I'm the detective assigned to your case. If we could, I'd like to clear up some details about what happened at Central Park today. May I ask you a few questions?"

"Yes, please sit down." My voice cracks as I motion toward the chair across from me.

Detective O'Brien lowers himself onto the chair. He's wearing a long trench coat that skims the floor when he sits. That storm wound up rolling through, and the rain is now coming down sideways in torrents, pelting our windows as if trying to break through the glass. Droplets roll down the sleeves of his coat, dripping onto the kitchen tile in pools. It must be pretty serious for him to have trekked through the city in this weather at night, unable to wait until daybreak and sunshine.

Well, we'll soon find out just how serious it is.

Detective O'Brien pulls a notebook and pen from his jacket and then locks his hazel eyes with mine. I flash back to the brown eyes staring out from the ski mask at the park and shiver. Something niggles at me, the glimmer of a memory, but I can't grasp onto it. It's been like this all day.

"I've been looking over the police report, and there seem to be some inconsistencies I'd like to clarify. I have you as an eyewitness to the attempted abduction, but there's a note about you not being there. Were you or were you not there, Mrs. Douglass?"

Oh God, I want to die. "I was there. For some of it," I admit.

"What do you mean you were there for some of it?" Andrew pipes in, folding his arms across his chest. "You didn't tell me you weren't there for the whole thing. Where were you, Lucinda?" Andrew's tone is accusatory, like this is all my fault.

The detective raises his eyebrows. "Yes, Mrs. Douglass. Where were you when the attack took place?"

My heart is beating so loudly in my chest that I'm afraid they both can hear it. I bury my hands in my lap to stop them from shaking. I keep my gaze fixed on the detective, unable to look at my husband.

Then I take a deep breath. "I briefly walked away to take a work call and left Delilah with our nanny. I heard screaming, and that's when I found the masked man with his hands on her stroller. I sprinted toward them, and he took off running into the park."

"I see." Detective O'Brien scribbles a note. I can just imagine what it says—*the terrible mother left her baby with the brand-spanking-new nanny while she took a work call.* When did it become a crime to take a work call? Imagine the backlash if it had been a Zoom. Or—*gasp*—Skype.

"If this is a taste of what's going to happen when you're at work, Lucinda, you are so *not* going back." Andrew stomps a socked foot on the ground.

This time Detective O'Brien clears his throat. "Is there anyone you know who might wish to cause you or your child harm? An ex, neighbor, coworker? Because I've seen more child abductions than I care to discuss, and to be honest, this one seems highly premeditated."

I open my mouth to speak, but the words don't come out. Because this is what I feared all along—someone planned this attack and targeted Delilah.

But who?

And what's to stop it from happening again?

CHAPTER 14

I feel dizzy, my breath coming in small gasps. Because our situation wasn't dire enough, now I'm hyperventilating. I grab the edges of the table to keep from passing out. The room swirls around me as I try to regain my composure.

"Sorry, Detective. Just a second." Andrew jogs to the pantry, retrieving a brown paper lunch bag. I'm not even sure why we have them—I don't think Andrew or I have once brought a bagged lunch to work. He shoves it into my hand. "Breathe, Lucinda."

I hold the bag over my mouth and breathe in and out until my respiration slowly returns to normal. I should feel calmer, but I don't.

"Are you okay to continue?" Detective O'Brien asks, pen perched between his fingers.

"As okay as I'll ever be until you track down this man. To answer your question—I don't know who would want to hurt us. I have a good relationship with my coworkers, clients, friends..." *Husband.*

I look over at Andrew, who briefly left the room, returning with Delilah cradled in his arms. He seems genuinely concerned, *now*. But how does a man go an entire day without checking in on his wife and newborn daughter? Does he even care about us?

"In cases like this, Mrs. Douglass, it's often someone you know."

"I'm aware of that, Detective. Strangers account for only one percent of childhood abductions."

Detective O'Brien's eyebrows fold toward one another, creating a deep crease between his hazel eyes. He clears his throat. "Exactly, which means ninety-nine percent of cases are personal." The air in the room is thick with possibilities. I fidget in my chair as the silence between us lengthens, and my stomach clenches with a fresh wave of anxiety.

He turns to Andrew. "Speaking of which, where were you all day, Mr. Douglass?"

Andrew freezes mid-bite. Oh my, he's eating the egg roll. A small cube of pink meat lands on Delilah's head. When he's finished chewing and swallowing the pork-laden fried appetizer, he licks his lips and takes a long sip of water.

"I was in my studio all day. I didn't even leave for lunch."

"Can anyone else account for your whereabouts?"

I stare intently at my husband. Andrew's hands are still, his expression relaxed. He certainly doesn't look guilty of anything. So why is Detective O'Brien questioning him about his whereabouts?

"There's a camera directly outside the building that records everyone who comes and goes. I'm sure the landlord could provide the security footage. I arrived at 8:30 a.m. and returned home just a few minutes before you."

Andrew writes down the address and landlord's name on a yellow Post-it and hands it to Detective O'Brien, who sticks it to his notepad and turns back to face me.

"Just one more question for now, Mrs. Douglass, and then I'll get out of your hair. Do you smoke?"

I repeat his question aloud, wondering if I heard him correctly. "Do I *smoke*?"

He nods, quite serious.

"I don't smoke. But what does that have to do with anything?"

It's such a random question, so out of left field, I almost start laughing. *Almost.* Nothing about our current predicament is even remotely funny.

And then I shrink in my chair because it occurs to me that he may be referencing the overwhelming stench in our kitchen. Maybe he's trying to get a more complete picture of the mother who abandons her baby in the park for a work call and can't cook a decent meal for her family without nearly burning down the place. Although, that would be a lot to deduce, even for the most seasoned detective.

So *why* is he asking if I smoke?

Detective O'Brien reaches back into his jacket pocket and pulls out a book of matches sealed in a plastic evidence bag. "We found this in the area of the playground where your daughter was attacked. Do you recognize it?"

He pushes the baggie across the table. I pick it up with trembling fingers. *The Loungebook Pearl.* Of course, I recognize the matchbook. It's from the bar/restaurant across the street from my office. I nod. "Yes, I'm familiar with the place."

"But these don't belong to you?"

"No, Detective, as I said, I don't smoke. Never have. And I can assure you, I don't carry around a book of matches in the event the craving one day randomly strikes."

"Duly noted. Have you visited this establishment before?"

"Well, yes…" My mouth goes dry as I realize what Detective O'Brien is getting at. "You don't think it's a coincidence that you found these at the park? I'm sure lots of people go there. It's a popular place." Albeit some fifty-something blocks, the equivalent of five miles away.

Detective O'Brien narrows his eyes at me. "I don't believe in coincidences. And here's the thing. These were found on a children's playground. There are no smoking signs posted everywhere. So I ask myself: Dick, what are the matches doing there? And the only logical explanation I can come up with is that whoever tried to abduct your daughter dropped these during the struggle. I will run prints on them, but I'm not too optimistic, given the fact that the perp was wearing gloves. But other than these matches, we have nothing else to go on right now. So if you think of anything—*anyone* who may have had a reason to harm you, please call me directly."

It's evident from the tenor of this conversation that this crime will likely become a cold case. Unless that is, the guy tries to strike again.

Detective O'Brien slips a business card across the table with his cell phone number scribbled across the back. "In the meantime, stay ultra-aware of your surroundings, Mrs. Douglass. You got lucky that the guy got spooked and ran away. If this was a targeted incident, you might not be as lucky next time."

I'm not sure I'd consider someone you may have disgruntled trying to kidnap your child lucky, but I get what he's saying. Maybe next time, the guy won't get spooked.

Maybe he'll get what he came for.

CHAPTER 15

I fall asleep with Delilah on my chest, unable to put her down after my disturbing conversation with Detective O'Brien. I plan to—I don't know—maybe never shut my eyes again.

Unfortunately, that plan is extremely short-lived.

I'm not sure when I nod off, but I wake with a start to the nursery, dark and quiet. The only sounds are our sleepy breaths and the falling rain outside. My eyes flutter for a moment, heavy, but I force them back open. If I let them shut again, I will not leave this spot tonight. And clearly, I'm too wiped to stay awake.

I hadn't expected to be the mother who falls asleep while nursing her baby. Most people know by now that sleeping with your baby on your chest isn't safe. If you're not being warned *Breast is Best* ad nauseam, it's *Back to Sleep*. But it's easier to be pragmatic when you're not bone-crushingly exhausted. Besides, I also hadn't expected to be the mother who nearly has her child abducted in broad daylight. And yet, here I am. There's nothing and no one who could have prepared me for that.

I gingerly rise from the rocking chair, moving as slowly as possible so as not to wake Delilah. I place her down gently in her crib, my hand lingering on her belly so she knows I'm still there. Satisfied she's staying asleep (for now), I tiptoe from her crib, switching on the white noise machine before I go. The room whirs as I slip the door closed behind me.

I'm padding quietly down the hallway when I stop dead in my tracks. I hear movement, shuffling. Then I notice the light on in Bree's bedroom. I press the side of my Apple Watch and see it's now 2:30 a.m. What is she doing awake?

Bree's laughter creeps under the door. I inch closer, my stomach in knots.

"Stop," she whispers. "We shouldn't."

Shouldn't *what?* What the hell is going on in there?

My fingers instinctively move toward the knob. My hand trembles against the cool stainless steel. I slowly twist it, and then—

"Lucinda?"

My hand flies from the door like it's been set on fire. My heart is beating a mile a minute. It feels like it might explode from my chest. "Jesus, Andrew," I manage through gritted teeth. "What are you doing?"

"What am *I* doing? I think the better question is—what are *you* doing? Are you spying on our nanny?"

How do I tell my husband that I thought for a moment that he was in there with Bree?

I feel like a complete ass now. This woman saved my child, and here I am thinking she's sleeping with my husband.

"I wasn't spying," I lie. "I was checking to make sure Bree was okay and didn't need anything after what happened today. You didn't see how bad her eye looks."

"Well, please, don't let me stop you then." Andrew motions back toward her door, challenging me to my deception. Yes, my husband can be a giant jerk sometimes.

I pause for a moment, debating what to do. I mean, I hadn't even knocked. I can't very well barge in there, even if that's what I was about to do before Andrew stopped me. Now that I know he's not in there, I realize what an idiot I'll look like in front of them.

"Um, I think I hear her laughing," I say. "She must be on the phone or something. On second thought, I don't want to disturb her."

Though I'm dying to know what she *shouldn't* be doing, I know at this moment, Andrew kiboshed any chance of me finding out. It's not like I can just stand here eavesdropping while he watches me. Because that won't make me look crazy or anything.

As I turn to head back to our bedroom, Andrew grabs my elbow. "That's your problem, Lucinda. You can never admit when you do something wrong. You refuse to take responsibility." It strikes me we're not talking about me standing outside of Bree's door anymore.

There are a million and one things I could say, but I don't say anything. I shrug off Andrew's hand and walk away.

—

Andrew is gone when I wake up in the morning, and I would be lying if I said it didn't bring me some relief. With the way we've been getting along, I'd much prefer to play chair detective on my own.

The rain has finally abated, and the sun is streaming through our blinds. It's all very serene until Delilah's cries pierce the silence. I scramble to get out of bed and wrap myself in my robe, but the cries stop almost as quickly as they start. Bree must have gone to soothe her.

I stare at Andrew's empty side of the bed, wondering how we got here.

I've read studies on the relationship between love and hate. One found that the deeper you love a person, the deeper your hatred toward them is when you factor betrayal in. So our propensity to hate our partner depends on the depth of our love toward our partner and the cause of the relationship's dissolution. I can't help but wonder—where would we be right now without the betrayal? Would I still be head over heels, madly in love with my husband? And he, with me?

I open my nightstand drawer, grabbing the Manila envelope buried beneath a random collection of magazines and miscellanea. I pull the photos from inside.

A year ago, this envelope appeared in our mailbox with my name scribbled on the front in cursive handwriting. There was no stamp and no return address. It materialized one day, seemingly out of nowhere, mixed in with our bills and shopping catalogs.

THE PERFECT NANNY

With no return address or post office stamp to work off of, I had yet to learn where it came from. I quizzed each of our doormen as to whether they had seen someone slipping something into our mailbox. Ashton thought he may have seen someone, but he wasn't sure, and when pressed further, he couldn't recall a single thing about the person he may or may not have seen. We're talking about some highly useful information there.

I clutched the envelope close to my chest as I stepped into the elevator to ride the sixteen floors to our penthouse apartment. I was desperate to rip it open right then and there, but I stopped myself. There are cameras all over our building, even in the elevators. You don't have to watch Dateline to know no good comes in the form of an anonymous envelope stuffed into your mailbox. I instinctively knew this was no exception.

You read too many thrillers, I said to myself, trying to rein in my nerves on the slow ascent. It was probably just paperwork Chad's assistant dropped off.

I took a deep breath and stepped off the elevator, telling myself everything was fine. But, of course, it wasn't fine. And it would never be fine again after I found what was waiting for me inside.

I shake off the memory as I pull the five 8x10 pictures from the envelope. I run my fingers along a photograph, tracing the outline of Andrew's face. *How could he have done this to me?* I should have said something to him while I had the chance instead of burying his betrayal at the bottom of a drawer, leaving it to stew and fester.

You can't bury betrayal.

Not when someone knows your secret.

CHAPTER 16

MANY YEARS AGO

Judy insisted on staying put until my father got home from the hospital, where he was 'making arrangements,' or whatever that meant. What arrangements were there to be made at this point? My mother was dead.

And there wasn't a chance in hell my father was going to spring for a funeral.

Unless...did she mean arrangements for *us*?

"Come on," Judy said, pushing past me into our house. "I'll make y'all some breakfast and get you off to school." School? Was this woman out of her freaking mind? Our mother just died. Oh God, was I going to be the one to tell my brothers and sisters that our mother just died?

And what about our baby sister?

"The baby?" I managed. "What happened to the baby?"

"Oh, Isabella Grace is fine. Cute as a button, too. I think we'll call her Izzy."

My shoulders sagged with partial relief. But it was tempered when I thought of who would care for my cute-as-a-button baby sister, Isabella Grace, now that my mother was gone. And why was Judy gushing over Izzy as if she were her own child?

I watched as Judy's eyes busily surveyed her surroundings, almost like she was making some sort of mental itinerary. She'd been here dozens of times, but I swear, she was looking at things differently now. I could almost see the gears turning in her head, even if I had no idea which direction they were turning in.

I chased her gaze around the room, but all I saw was what had always been—ragged and worn furniture and stained carpeting. And now, what was no longer. My mother's absence was palpable, her presence still lingering in the room though not on the earth.

This couldn't be happening, could it? It felt like it was all a terrible dream.

But Judy made us a breakfast of eggs, bacon, and French toast, with real and intoxicating smells. It wasn't a dream. I watched as my brothers and sisters dug into the feast, unaware of how our world had just been turned entirely on its head.

"You need to eat, sweetie," Judy said, nudging the plate toward me.

"I'm not very hungry." I pushed it back, as far away from me as my arm could reach.

Judy rested a hand on my wrist and stared at me with her cat-like hazel eyes. Then she squeezed hard. Too hard. "I said eat."

I brought the fork to my mouth and forced a bite. I didn't feel much like eating, but something told me I should do as Judy said. And I'd admit, Judy was a phenomenal cook. She'd brought delicious casseroles, lasagnas, and pies through the years.

She dropped off a fresh batch of chocolate chip cookies for my mom just the other day. "Now, kids," she said. "You let your mother enjoy these." She placed the plate high on top of the fridge where none of us could reach it unless we dragged a chair over and climbed—considering the cracked, jagged tiles surrounding the fridge, that would have been a dangerous move.

"It's good, isn't it?" Judy's nails dug into my skin, bringing me back.

"It's good," I agreed.

"Take another bite," she ordered.

I looked around the table, watching my siblings dig in, oblivious to the fact that our mother was dead. Judy obviously hadn't told them yet.

"Cody?" My little brother glanced up at me, but didn't say a word. Judy shot him a stern look, and he continued tucking into a perfectly scrambled egg. Why wasn't he answering me?

Judy shifted her gaze back to me, an angry line forming between her eyes.

I took another bite. I didn't want to upset her. If her nails dug any deeper into my flesh, I was certain they'd draw blood. I couldn't stand the sight of blood after cleaning up my mother's.

Once my plate was clean and my stomach full, I attempted to stand from my chair to clear the table and wash the dishes before I left for school. But when I rose, the room spun, and my knees buckled beneath me, causing me to collapse back onto the chair.

"Oh my, dear. You don't look so well. I guess you won't be going to school today. I'm sure they'll be very understanding, considering."

Judy rubbed a hand across the back of my head and then yanked my hair, snapping my neck up to look at her. Her features swirled and danced like a Van Gogh painting. I found myself sinking into that angry crevice between her eyes.

"Let's get you to bed," she ordered, grabbing me forcefully by the elbow to steady me.

"But…but…"

"No ifs, ands, or buts," she told me in a too-cheery voice that didn't match the stern look on her face. I stared back down at the table, trying to anchor myself as my vision swam. I opened my mouth to say something, but the words stuck in my head. A strange sensation settled over me.

As if reading my thoughts, Judy said, "You're probably in shock." Her voice had a warbly quality, as if we were submerged underwater. "You've experienced a very traumatic event, sweetie. It's normal to feel untethered."

Was it? Because I felt more than just untethered. The air in the room was thick and heavy, almost as if trying to suffocate me.

With Judy's help, I somehow managed to rise to my feet. But moving them was another story that appeared out of my grasp. Judy pushed me forward, and I nearly fell, my limbs slow and sludgy as if attempting to wade through mud.

I'm not sure how we did it, but the next thing I knew, I was waking up in my bed. I glanced over at my window. The sun had taken on a muted quality, the brightness of the day fading away. It must have been late afternoon. I attempted to sit up in bed, but my head was pounding so hard I could hear it in my ears.

Panic quickly built in my chest as bile simultaneously rose in my throat. The first thing I did was lean over the side of the bed to dry heave. The second was I remembered what Judy whispered in my ear as I drifted into a dreamless sleep.

CHAPTER 17

Three days pass before I gather up the courage to leave our apartment. We're running low on just about everything, and I'm worried I may be developing a Vitamin D deficiency. No joke. According to Dr. Google, I have all the symptoms—fatigue, muscle weakness, poor sleep, you name it. Fortunately, I can gather all this information on my own without having to so much as step foot out the door. How in the world did people self-diagnose before the Internet?

Needless to say, Delilah has not left the apartment either. I know we have a nanny now, but until I uncover the mystery of my daughter's attempted abduction, Delilah is not going anywhere outside these apartment walls without me. Not unless it's an absolute emergency—and let's hope not, because I'm not sure my battered heart could withstand any more of those in the near future.

As tempting as it is, we can't stay cooped up here forever inside our Fifth Avenue bubble. The longer I stay, the harder it becomes to leave. The apartment still reeks of the burnt husk of an eggplant that we laid to rest. It's suffocating. Delilah could use the fresh air as much as I can about now.

Besides, there's something I need to do.

I invited Bree to come with us. Despite her emotional trauma and physical injuries, she's been great the past few days. She's constantly checking up on me, which I greatly appreciate but feel should be the reverse. *Right?* I mean, yes, I almost lost my daughter, but she almost lost an eye. The purples and blues have faded to a yellowy orange, like a sunset, but it's still glued shut.

I can't believe how annoyed I was with her for eating breakfast in her pajamas and borrowing my shoes. Sneakers! This woman saved my child from a near abduction and was nearly blinded. How could I be so incredibly superficial?

Bree said she'd prefer not to go out in public until her eye heals enough that she can mask the injury with concealer. She's going to be homebound for a while...

Honestly though, I'm relieved she turned down my invitation because I need to do this on my own. I'd rather not risk Bree slipping and telling my husband where we are going. Andrew would be all up in arms if I shared my plans for the day, especially in light of what happened at the park. That's why I didn't tell him or share any details with her.

I examine my reflection in the mirror, fixing myself up as best I can. I brush a light dusting of taupe shadow over my lids and line my eyes with a cobalt pencil. I dab a dollop of mauve blush on my cheeks before running a light pink gloss over my lips. A spot of highlighter skims the tip of my nose. I smile at myself because I don't look half bad. Jenna would be proud of me. Except, it's not Jenna I'm going to see.

There are two items on the agenda for today. First, I'm bringing Delilah down to the financial district so she can meet all my colleagues. With the unexpected turbulence at the park and the discord in my home, I crave the chaotic reassurance of my place of work. I let a few coworkers know that I'd be swinging by. I haven't been since my maternity leave, and everyone is dying to meet Delilah.

That brings us to the second item—Chad insisted on taking Delilah and me to lunch. Naturally, I accepted and then insisted we go to our old haunt—The Loungebook Pearl. I'm not sure what I'm looking for, but I hope to know when I find it. Chad was happy to oblige and said his assistant would make us reservations for noon at my favorite window table overlooking the Hudson River.

That matchbook has been all I can think about for the past few days, my mind turning it over and over just as my fingers did when Detective O'Brien sat across from me at my kitchen table. It couldn't have been a coincidence. I'm hoping someone at The Loungebook Pearl will remember something. Assuming, of course, they have a better grasp of details than our doorman, Ashton.

Speaking of whom—the elevator doors ding open, and Ashton pops into view. "Mrs. Douglass." He tips his hat as he greets me.

I respond with a stiff smile. "Good morning, Ashton." I'd hoped another doorman would be staffing the front desk today. I'm half expecting to return home to a pipe bomb presented by Ashton as a bouquet of flowers. Well, at least I know what he's getting for Christmas—a gift certificate to Warby Parker with a handwritten note about how handsome he'd look in glasses.

Ashton holds the door for Delilah and me as we press onto the sidewalk. My eyes ping pong across the street, but no one looks back at me. What was I thinking—someone was staked outside our building for the past three days, just waiting for me to step outside? That's ridiculous. Still, that prickly sensation crawls up the back of my neck as I push Delilah's stroller toward the subway station.

I stick a hand in the pocket of my linen pants and wrap my fingers tightly around the Mace I have hidden away. I didn't even know Mace existed until I moved into the city from my rural childhood home. Not until Andrew gave me a bottle of it on our first date. Romantic, right? I thought it was a bottle of perfume. I almost sprayed it on my wrists and neck. Thank God Andrew stopped me, or we would have spent our first date in the ER instead of the Metrograph Theater.

"It's so cute how innocent you are," he told me that night before he pressed his lips against mine. We had met earlier in the week in a sociology class at NYU. Jenna and I were huddled in the lecture hall's second row when Andrew inserted his head between ours. "Did you hear the one about sociology and biology?" he asked. Another student shushed him, so he lowered his voice to a whisper. "It goes—what is the difference between sociology and biology?"

"What?" I asked, not wanting to be rude.

"If a baby looks like the dad, it's biology. If he looks like the mailman, it's sociology."

A laugh escaped, and Jenna slapped my arm. She was *really* into the lecture, too busy ogling the professor to give Andrew the time of day. She had sex with him that night—the professor, that is. Andrew and I shared a bucket of popcorn, a kiss, and a can of Mace.

"Ma'am?" I pull the can from my pocket as I whip around, my thumb poised to press down on the trigger. The man standing behind me throws his hands up in the air.

"Don't!" he screams, drawing the attention of passersby on the sidewalk.

"Why are you following me?" I manage through gritted teeth. My hand is shaking, and my heart is pounding in my chest.

"Not. Following. You. You…You…" The man's face is bright red, magenta. "You dropped this." He trembles as he practically throws a set of keys at me. Sure enough, they're mine. They must have slipped from my pocket while I was fingering the Mace.

Oh, God. The Mace.

I drop my hand to my side. "I'm so sorry. I just thought—"

He shakes his head at me and raises his hands to stop me from moving any closer. "My parents said, 'Don't move to New York. That city will eat you alive, George.' Jeez. This is the last time I try to be a Good Samaritan." He says this as he's walking away from me.

Well, I feel like a real jerk now.

Seriously, what the hell is wrong with me?

Thank goodness, the rest of our journey downtown isn't nearly as eventful. It's about 10:30 when we descend the stairs to the subway station. We take the 3 train downtown to the financial district. Our subway car is surprisingly empty, which brings with it both a sense of relief and angst. My eyes shoot in each direction until I'm convinced no one looks suspicious. Only then do I allow myself to relax, just a little.

When we reach our stop, I wheel Delilah up the stairs. I focus on the wheels as they scale each step, my pulse quickening as I follow. A part of me has been putting off coming here. But now, there's no turning back.

As we rise from the concrete depths, we fall into stride with the dozens of people walking the same path as if on a conveyor belt. A few short blocks later, I'm standing in front of my building.

We made it here safe and sound.

So why do I still have a gigantic pit in my stomach?

CHAPTER 18

The Pearl Street building stretches thirty-two stories into the sky, its domed tip kissing the puffy white clouds overhead. I bring a hand to my forehead to shield my eyes as they travel up the length of the building to the twenty-eighth floor where our office lies. The sun shines brightly upon it, reflecting off the glass.

I pull my eyes from the building to glance at my watch. It's 11:15 a.m., which gives us around forty minutes to visit with my coworkers. Then, it's off to lunch. I should have us back tucked inside our apartment, with Andrew none the wiser, by four at the latest. Heck, I may even have time to cook us all dinner. On second thought, considering what happened last time...

Plus, after his oddly aggressive behavior last night, Andrew is the one who should be doing the buttering up, not me. But I won't hold my breath. He left without so much as a goodbye this morning. Well, that's not entirely true. I'm sure he said his goodbyes to Bree and Delilah, just not to me.

I take a deep inhale before pushing Delilah through the revolving glass doors. The sights and sounds of the financial world send a jolt of adrenaline through my veins. My legs propel me forward without thought, almost as if a magnetic force is pulling me deeper into the building.

I pause momentarily at the security desk, suddenly aware I've misplaced my identification badge. I typically wear it around my neck or wrapped around my wrist, but it's in neither of those places. I must have left it by the front door in my haste to leave the apartment.

Dammit. I dig through Delilah's diaper bag, searching for my license. I push aside bottles, binkies, and diapers—where the frick is my wallet? It has to be in here somewhere. I distinctly remember slipping it into my bag when I packed it this morning. I'm usually so responsible. But I suppose a near home-fire and attempted abduction over a twenty-four-hour span could throw anyone off their game.

A firm hand on my shoulder has me whipping around, my heart lodged in my throat.

"What the—"

Well, what do you know? Chad Morgan is standing behind me, his blue eyes sparkling as he grins from ear to ear. He's lucky I didn't reach for my Mace. I should have a sign on my back that reads: **Do not approach from behind, will Mace.**

"You made it," he says. I exhale the breath I knew I was holding. It feels like I've been holding my breath for days.

"What are you doing down here?" I ask, suddenly suspicious. "Shouldn't you be upstairs working?"

"I figured I'd wait for you. Good thing I did, too. It looks like someone lost her ID badge?"

My jaw drops.

"Kidding, kidding. I'm so happy to see you. And Delilah," he says.

Chad holds a hand over his mouth as he admires my sleeping baby. "Oh my goodness, Lucinda, she's gorgeous. Just absolutely perfect."

My shoulders relax. "Thank you," I say, meaning it. Delilah is absolutely, one hundred percent perfect.

"And you…you look good."

My eyebrows shoot up. "You're a terrible liar, Chad. What are you going to say next? I look rested?"

"Okay, okay." Chad throws his hands up in surrender. "Would you prefer, you look like shit? God, in all the time I've known you, I'm pretty sure I've never seen you look so bad. I mean, really, Lucinda, we're talking grotesque. Shall I continue?"

I playfully slap Chad on the chest. I don't look *that* bad. "I suppose not."

"I told you, you look good."

I roll my eyes. If there's one thing I've learned about men in this business, they always have to be right. You don't get to the top of the brokerage ladder by being wrong. Or playing fair, I remind myself.

"Well, we should probably get you upstairs, shouldn't we? Anita, in auditing, has been gushing all day about meeting Delilah. She may or may not have spent the last two hours constructing a gigantic diaper cake."

"Does it double as a hat? That'll make for an interesting subway ride home." I smile widely. It feels terrific to be back, better than expected.

"Steve, my man." Chad fist-pumps the security guard. "They're with me," he adds, motioning toward Delilah and me as if I haven't known the security guard for the past seven years. I've been on maternity leave for less than six weeks. I told Andrew two months is a lifetime in this business.

"Mrs. Douglass, it's so nice to see you." Steve grins widely, flashing a gold tooth.

"Just visiting," I say. "But back for good come October. It's nice to see you as well."

"That's wonderful. Just be sure to bring your ID badge next time—they're really starting to crack down here." He winks at me, and my cheeks go red.

I smile through the heat. "Of course, I'll do that. Thank you, Steve."

Chad leads me by the small of my back through the crowds toward the elevator. It's a chaotic time of day, with the early eaters pushing out of the building to visit street vendors or local restaurants like The Loungebook Pearl. The lump in my throat is back.

We squeeze into a crowded elevator. Delilah and I push into the back corner, with Chad standing protectively in front of us. After a few stops, the lift clears out, and it's just Chad, Delilah, and me riding to the twenty-eighth floor.

"Are you ready?" he asks.

I nod. "Of course I'm ready. Why wouldn't I be ready?"

The elevator doors ding open, and *surprise!*

CHAPTER 19

What in the world?

"Surprise!" Chad whispers into my hair.

There are pink balloons and pink streamers everywhere. A pink tablecloth covered with a tower of pink-frosted strawberry cupcakes. Another pink-blanketed table decorated with pink rubber ducks, pink pacifiers, and pink clothespins. Dear God, it looks like a Pepto Bismol bottle exploded in here.

I turn back to face Chad. "I can't believe you didn't tell me!"

"Tried to tell you on the phone," he grins. "Happy baby shower."

I was so *not* expecting this. I had heard rumblings of a baby shower before I set off on maternity leave, but then I left rather quickly, and I had chalked it up to just that—rumblings. Who knew you could have a full-on baby shower *after* having the baby? Well, apparently, everyone in this room knew except for me.

Delilah and I are engulfed within moments by my colleagues, each bearing well wishes and gifts. Seriously, more gifts?

"You shouldn't have," I say repeatedly, smiling so widely it feels like my jaw might get permanently stuck in the position. My cheeks actually sting.

"Speech, speech," someone shouts, banging a spoon against a glass jar of baby food, possibly the only baby-related item in the room that's not pink. A round of applause breaks out, and then the room goes quiet.

"Wow, thank you all so very much. This was so thoughtful and—" I clear my throat. "Unexpected. Really unexpected. I've missed you all, and this means the absolute world to me."

A loud pop causes me to jump. I glance at Chad to find him holding a newly uncorked bottle of champagne. He presses a plastic flute into my hand.

Aha, the benefit of having a baby shower *after* you've already had the baby. But still, I am breastfeeding, and I already had a few sips of wine the other day…

"I shouldn't."

"Don't be such a square, Lucinda. We all sometimes do things we shouldn't do, don't we?"

"But Delilah…" I look down at my daughter, who is wide awake. Her curious blue eyes are transfixed on all the oohing and aahing faces hovering over her stroller.

"Come on, Lucinda. At least a dozen people here would pay you to let them watch Delilah. And one drink is not going to kill you or her." He makes a very valid point.

But it's not the drink per se. It's more the dilemma of letting someone else watch Delilah after what happened last time. *Could I?* Of course, I could. I'm being ridiculous. I've known these people for the past seven years, working with them for forty-plus hours a week. Delilah is as safe here as she is at home with her father.

My stomach clenches at the thought of Andrew and how we left off last night. His words sting like a fresh wound. I don't want to think about my husband right now. Champagne suddenly sounds like the best idea ever.

As if on cue, Anita from accounting bends over the stroller and unstraps Delilah from her harnesses. "Oh, she's mine," she says, flashing her slightly yellow teeth with a smidge of pink lipstick. I take a deep breath. Anita has three grown children and seven grandkids of her own. She's perfectly capable of watching Delilah for the next half an hour while I mingle.

Before I can ask, Chad fills my plastic flute to the brim with sparkling champagne. I bring the cup to my mouth and savor a long sip. The bubbles tickle my throat, melting away all my pent-up tension.

I spend the next half an hour colleague-hopping. The vibe here is super chill. I'd be lying if I said I wasn't enjoying this—that I wouldn't like to bottle up this moment like that jar of mashed peas.

But alas, all good things must come to an end. Two flutes later, Chad is back by my side, telling me we must leave to make our lunch reservations. It's been fun, but Chad and I need to talk business. In a few short weeks, I'll be back here for good.

"I'll have all this stuff delivered," Chad tells me as I do mental gymnastics, trying to figure out how to manage a stroller and a five-foot pink balloon garland on the subway.

"Perfect, thank you." One less thing to worry about.

After prying my daughter from Anita's arms, I tell each colleague I can't wait to see them again on October 1st when I return full-time. So, I know I told Andrew that daycare was a hard no, but childcare is available in this building if things don't work out with Bree. And I'd have coworkers like Anita to check in on my little munchkin around the clock.

My head is all over the place. Why should I think things won't work out with Bree? She saved my child, for goodness' sake! I wish I could put my finger on what's bothering me. Because *something* is seriously bothering me.

The champagne sits like a brick in my gut as we leave the building and walk across the street toward The Loungebook Pearl. All the lightness I felt just minutes ago is gone.

"What's wrong?" Chad asks as we sit down at my favorite table overlooking the Hudson. The sunlight dances on the water, stretching out for miles, making it look like someone coated the entire river with glitter. "You seem distracted," he adds when I don't answer immediately.

"Champagne must be getting to my head." I force a smile. That's not the truth. And unfortunately, Chad has known me long enough to know when I'm not telling the truth.

"Lucinda, I can tell something is bothering you. What is it?"

"Do you really want to know?"

"Would I have asked if I didn't?"

"Fair enough." I take a deep breath before filling him in on the past few days. "I just don't know who I can trust anymore. It feels like I'm completely on my own."

Chad steeples his fingers under his chin. "You've had quite a week," he acknowledges. "But you're not alone. You have lots of people who care about you, Lucinda."

Do I, though? It doesn't feel like Andrew cares about me anymore. Outside of Jenna, I don't have many friends. I have my work colleagues and work husband, but it's complicated. Bree is my employee, and I've known her for a minute. My parents are long gone. All I have is Delilah.

And someone tried to take her from me.

No one is taking my daughter away from me.

Seriously, over my dead body.

CHAPTER 20

Twenty minutes later, I've talked myself off the ledge, and we've settled into the swing of lunch. "This is nice," Chad says as he digs into his tuna tartare. "I don't get out of the office much lately, what with all the extra work." He smirks.

"Well, don't you worry; I'll be back soon enough, and you'll be sick of me again in no time at all."

"If I'm not already sick of you after tonight."

"*Tonight?*" A crouton from my Caesar salad sticks to the side of my throat. I cough and then take a rather large, exaggerated gulp of ice water to wash it down. "What's tonight?"

"Marly and I are coming over for dinner. *Remember?*" Chad stares at me, eyebrows raised.

No, actually, I don't remember. It definitely sounds like something I *should* remember, but I don't know what Chad is talking about. Seriously, not a freaking clue.

"You're coming to dinner at my apartment? *Tonight?*"

Chad's eyebrows bend toward one another. He frowns. "You're scaring me, Lucinda. Marly said you texted her to invite us over." He checks his phone. "Yup, I have it right here." He points to the event on his calendar.

Did I? I pull my phone from Delilah's diaper bag and quickly read through my texts.

Well, shit. Apparently, I did invite Chad and Marly to dinner tonight. The time stamp shows I sent the text on Monday.

Me: Hey, lady, it's been too long. Are you and Chad free Friday to come over for dinner?
Marly: Love to! Let me know what we can bring.

There's more, but I don't bother reading through the rest, not with Chad staring at me the way he is. I'm sleep-deprived and under enormous stress, but how could I have zero recollection of an entire text exchange? Moreover, one in which I invited another couple to my home?

I shake my head. "Of course, Chad. I remember. I must have my dates a little mixed up. Baby brain." I shrug and wave off the oversight with a flick of a wrist.

If Chad thinks I'm lying this time, he doesn't say.

"Great. What can we bring?" he asks.

How do I answer that when I've no idea what I'm making because I had no idea they were coming over in the first place? I know what I'm never making ever again, but that doesn't help much, does it?

"Um...we should be all set, but I'll check with Andrew and let you know if we need anything. Okay?"

"Okkaayyy..." He pauses for an unnecessarily long while. "So, I'll just bring vodka, then?"

"Excuse me?"

"For Andrew. Vodka cranberry with a slice of lime, right? Not sure how or why I remember that, but..."

"Okay, sure. Bring vodka."

"Tito's?"

I nod my head even though Andrew prefers Absolut. I have more important things to worry about than Andrew's vodka preference. I've enjoyed this break from reality, but now I must rush home to prepare for the company I didn't know I was having. And Andrew won't be any help, that's for sure. If he didn't answer his phone when his daughter was nearly kidnapped, he's certainly not going to pick up to find out what crudités I'd like him to grab on his way home from the studio.

"Remind me what time I told you to come over."

"Five thirty. Some of us have to work on the weekends to pick up the slack for others." Chad winks.

Five thirty. Right. I'm sure that's somewhere mixed in with the texts with Marly that I don't remember sending. Did I even tell Andrew they were coming over? Probably not, since I don't remember inviting them. I'll likely spend a good two hours as a third wheel with Chad and his wife before my husband strolls through the door reeking of lacquer. Then he'll have to shower and change. I'll be lucky if he joins us before dessert.

Chad stretches his arms over his head. "I'm stuffed. I'm going to use the restroom, and then I should probably head back to work since I'm cutting out early."

"Sounds good." I fold my napkin neatly on the table. I've only eaten a few bites of my salad, but my appetite is gone.

Chad gets up from the table and heads toward the back to the restrooms. I pull out my phone and scroll through the rest of my text exchange with Marly. Sure enough, I told her five thirty and added in for good measure—**feel free to come earlier if Chad gets home before then.** Of course, I did.

Jeez, what was I thinking?

Taking advantage of the opportunity, I toss my phone back in my purse and approach the bar with Delilah in tow. Yes, I told Chad what happened at the park, but like Andrew, he does not need to know that I'm trying to track down our attacker on my own.

"Excuse me?" I bat my eyes at the bartender, a fit man in his late thirties.

"What can I get you?" he asks.

"Answers," I respond, hopefully.

"Answers... hmm...haven't heard of that one. It must be some new hipster drink. Do you know what's in it?"

Yeah, I can tell you what's in it. The words come tumbling out. "So apparently, someone followed me to Central Park, and they had a matchbook from this place. I'm just wondering if you've noticed anyone strange at the bar over the past few months. I'm guessing he'd probably be alone, watching the other patrons, maybe asking unusual questions. I don't know, just acting creepy."

"Lady, you just described almost every single male in here."

Ugh, he's right. My heart sinks into my feet. But I can't give up.

"Do you have a pen?" I ask.

He grabs a pen from behind the bar and hands it to me. I take a napkin and jot down my name and number. "Look, if you think of anything or anyone at all or notice anything that feels suspicious, please call me right away."

"Will do." He glances down at the napkin. "Lucinda Douglass." He crumbles the napkin and deposits it next to the register.

Not super optimistic.

Chad emerges from the restroom just as I sit back down at the table.

"All set?" he asks.

Not really, but, "Yeah."

"I took care of the check. I'll see you ladies out." Chad always gets the check. And he always makes sure I get where I need to go safely. It's part of his southern charm, from having grown up in rural Georgia. You'd never know it from his dialect, though. He has an uncanny ability to pick up and drop accents like haircuts.

We follow Chad outside The Loungebook Pearl onto Pearl Street. "See you tonight," he says, kissing my cheek.

"See you tonight."

My hands are gripped tightly around Delilah's stroller as I watch Chad walk across the street to our building.

I look down at Delilah, who is now out cold. All the excitement of this morning has tuckered her out. I'd feel the same if I weren't running on pure adrenaline.

"One more stop, sweetie," I tell my oblivious, sleeping baby. But really, we've plenty to do before five thirty rolls around. Not least, figure out why I invited the Morgans over for dinner tonight in the first place and why I can't remember.

CHAPTER 21

MANY YEARS AGO

It took some serious effort, but somehow, I dragged myself out of bed. It felt like I'd been beaten over the head with a baton. And my body hurt, too, a deep kind of hurt that was more than just physical.

I'd felt the raw pain of loss before. I was nine when our dog died. A puppy still. I remembered when Mom brought him home, a tiny bundle of ears and fur. "It was the strangest thing," she said, winking at me. "I was just minding my business walking out of the grocery store when I saw this woman with a litter of free puppies."

My eyes shot between her and my father. "Come on," she said, waving me toward her. "Do you want to hold him? His name is Buddy."

Buddy was a beautiful brown, black, and white beagle. I placed him on the kitchen floor and watched in complete awe as he padded around the room, his oversized ears sweeping our linoleum tiles.

Shockingly, Dad said we could keep him. But Buddy was my responsibility. I was the one who would feed him, make sure he always had fresh water, and let him out in our fenced-in backyard to pee. There were a few loose wooden slats in that fence—I took Dad's hammer and made sure they were securely in place before I ever let that beautiful ball of fur and ears out of my sight.

I took my job seriously and took *really* good care of Buddy. Luckily it was summer, and we were off from school. I spent my days moving from inside our house to the backyard. I didn't see any friends—not that I had any friends to see. Still, I never felt lonely once Buddy was around.

One afternoon, I heard my father screaming my name from inside. Buddy had an accident. It was rare—I trained him well and was with him all the time—but once in a while, it happened.

"You stay out here where it's safe," I told him. Buddy stared at me with his big brown eyes, head cocked to the side. He wagged his tail, oblivious to how pissed my dad was.

I ran into the house as quickly as possible, cleaning up the mess to get back to him. I hated leaving him alone, and I felt alone without him by my side. I wasn't sure how I'd manage to go back to school in September. I'd started researching homeschool options, though I doubted my dad would ever agree to something like that.

Mom had returned from the store while I was spraying the floor, so it was safe to bring him back into the house. When I opened the door and stepped back outside, I shielded my eyes to search for Buddy. Our yard was smaller than our kitchen, so he wasn't very hard to find. Buddy was curled into a ball under a large oak. It was the hottest summer day, and I thought maybe I had left him out there a little longer than I'd thought.

"Buddy," I called out as I closed the back door behind me. "Come here, good boy." Buddy didn't move from his spot. At first, I didn't think much of it—maybe he was asleep. But then, when I shouted, "Who wants some chicken?" and he didn't budge, I knew something was wrong. Very wrong.

I took off running. When I got within a few feet of Buddy, I noticed he was completely still. "Mom!" I screamed at the top of my lungs. Within seconds my mother was by my side, covering my eyes with her embrace.

But I couldn't unsee what I already saw.

I stayed in my room for the next few days, inconsolable. I heard my parents talking outside my door. "The vet said it was antifreeze. You wouldn't know anything about that, would you, David?" my mom asked.

"Why would I hurt the damn dog?"

"Not hurt, killed."

"Okay, Mary, why would I have killed the damn dog? We don't even have antifreeze."

"Well, I'm telling you, David. Someone killed that dog."

Those words replayed on a loop.

Someone killed that dog.

All these years later, tears welled behind my eyes at the memory. I was never the same after that day. It was never spoken of again in our home.

My mother was all I had left, and now I had nothing.

I creaked open the door to my room. Building up courage, I poked my head into the hallway, hoping Judy had returned to her home next door. My eyes swept across the empty space. It was awfully quiet. No signs of life, quiet.

Maybe she had left. That would have been great, wouldn't it? But where had everyone else gone?

"Hello?" I called out into the silence, my voice crackling like the embers of a fire. My throat was raw and dry, my tongue as scratchy as an emery board. I desperately needed something to drink.

More than that, though, I needed to find my father—to tell him what Judy whispered in my ear. He may not have wanted me, but my father loved my mother. He would never do anything to hurt her. He certainly wouldn't have just let her die as Judy claimed. *Would he?*

No, no, no. Judy was a big fat liar.

I tiptoed down the hallway, waiting for the voices of my siblings to float up the stairs. At first, it was silent—no cries, shouts, or squeals of laughter. But then I heard Judy, and I froze in place at the edge of the top step.

"I'm worried about her, David."

"Worried?"

"I know she's upset about Mary, but she was saying crazy things."

"Like what, Judy?"

"She had this dazed look and was mumbling something about them all being better off dead. I think you need to have her evaluated. I'm worried she's a danger to herself and others."

"She's harmless, Judy."

I pressed myself tightly against the wall as I heard the loud footsteps of my father pacing around downstairs. I felt sick to my stomach again. I held a hand over my mouth as it clicked that Judy was talking about me. But I didn't do those things. I didn't say anyone would be better off dead. *Did I?*

"You say she wouldn't go to school today?"

"I tried to get her to go, David. I really did. But she downright refused. She made quite a scene, too. She was kicking and screaming. I didn't want the younger ones to get upset. I want to help you, but I don't know if I feel safe living in this house with her."

My head spun. Was I *living* in this house with *her* now? Oh God, what was happening here? What was Judy talking about?

"Come here, baby. It'll be okay, I promise. We got what we wanted—to be together, right?"

"You know I want to be with you, David. It's just…"

"I'll take care of her, okay?"

So what Judy said was true. He wanted my mother gone. He let her die.

And if that was the case… Was I next?

CHAPTER 22

I don't have much time.

Three hours to get to the store and back home, with dinner cooked and the place all tidied up and sparkling. And that's if Chad and Marly don't show up early, which I so readily suggested, apparently. I smack myself on the forehead.

Once settled on the subway, I pull out my phone and search for recipes to impress last-minute guests. They are last-minute guests. For me, at least.

Hmm. What to make?

Chad had fish for lunch, so he won't want fish again tonight. Andrew won't eat meat, though he did eat pork the other night, whether he realized it or not. That leaves…pasta. So, I settle on a simple but sophisticated-tasting pasta dish (at least according to the Epicurean reviews).

After the subway pulls into our station and I ascend the stairs, I walk briskly to the nearest bodega. I immediately start filling my cart with the ingredients for a white pesto dish. I grab some walnuts, creamy ricotta cheese, salty parmesan, and lemons. I purchase a premixed salad to save some time and garlic bread that comes pre-prepared in a cylinder of foil that you stick in the oven for twelve minutes and serve (can't mess that one up, can I?).

Then I hurry back home.

The apartment is pin-drop quiet when we walk in. I pause with the stroller outside Bree's room on my way to Delilah's but don't hear a sound. The poor thing is probably napping. She's been through the wringer. I'm sure a black (and yellow and purple and blue) eye was not how she expected to start her tenure here. Of course, you do run the risk in childcare of being hit with a wayward toy now and again, but fighting off a child's would-be abductor and taking an adult-sized elbow to the face?

My phone rings loudly in my pocket, and I quickly push past Bree's door as I fumble to silence the call. Thank God Andrew isn't home right now. If he catches me loitering outside of Bree's door again, he'll think I'm a stalker.

I'm not a stalker.

Though I do believe I have one.

I push Delilah's stroller into the nursery and shut the door behind us before accepting the call.

There's a ton of background noise on the other end, and I can just barely make out Jenna's voice. "Lucy, Lucy… Can you hear me?"

"Where are you?" I ask, whispering.

"You have to speak up; I can't hear you, Luc."

Why am I whispering in my own apartment?

"Hey," I say, louder this time. "Where are you?"

"I'm at a bar on 53rd and 3rd. Third and Long. Can you come meet me for drinks?"

Jenna must have had quite a bit to drink if she thinks I can, spur of the moment, drop everything and meet her at a bar for drinks. I'm a mother now.

"And how am I going to do that? Remember your goddaughter, Delilah?"

"Remember your nanny, Bree? Can't she watch Delilah?" She's right, I realize. Bree could watch Delilah. But no, I can't meet Jenna; our company will arrive in less than two hours.

"I wish I could, Jenna, but we have dinner plans."

"Oh." I can hear the disappointment in her voice, and my heart sinks into my stomach. I hate disappointing my best friend. I haven't seen her since the park, and I'm sure there's lots she wants to catch me up on. Like, for one, that date I didn't know she was going on. I chew on my lower lip, an idea forming.

"Listen," I say. "Why don't you come here and join us? It's just Chad and Marly coming over. I'm making pasta. Chad is bringing vodka. I can go downstairs and grab a bottle of wine. What are you drinking?"

"Red, and I'm on my way."

"Feel free to bring a date," I add quickly before hanging up. Knowing Jenna, she will eagerly take me up on my offer. All she has to do is bat her eyelashes, and whoever she's standing next to is a goner. He'll most certainly have his heart broken, but I can't worry about everything, can I?

Besides, at least I feel better about dinner now. The thought of playing the third wheel to Chad and Marly is painful, even if they are 'like our really good friends,' as Andrew pointed out. At least now, I'll have Jenna as a buffer until my husband gets home. Hopefully, she'll bring a date, and we can all focus on her flavor of the week instead of the tension rising within these walls.

But I will have to bite the bullet and wake Bree to pull this all off. I do not have the time or energy to drag Delilah into a liquor store, make dinner, and then attempt to clean with a newborn glued to my breast. So, I pad down the hallway and knock gently on Bree's door.

"Yes?"

"It's Lucinda, Bree. May I come in?"

I listen to Bree shuffling around before she opens the door a crack. I'm staring at a blue eyeball; presumably the one not glued shut. Why is she only opening the door a crack? Is she hiding something in there? *Someone?*

"Hey, Lucinda. What's up?"

I try to peek into her room, but her body fully blocks the door, and I can't see a thing.

"Um, could you possibly watch Delilah while I run to the store to grab some wine and cook dinner? We have company coming over this evening."

"Right," she says, blinking her eye. "Andrew mentioned something about that."

Andrew mentioned something about that. *To Bree?* It's bad enough that I don't remember inviting Chad and Marly over. Now I can add not remembering the conversation in which I told my husband about our plans to my list of forgotten things.

I feel the heat rising in my head. I bite the inside of my cheeks. "Would you mind?"

"Of course not." Bree opens her door fully. My eyes quickly flit around the room. It's empty. No sign of my husband. *What was I thinking?* Of course, Andrew is not in her room.

"Thanks, Bree."

Bree smiles at me, but it doesn't reach her open eye.

"Well, hello there, little cutie pie." She pulls Delilah's stroller into her room and closes the door, leaving me standing in the hallway, more confused than ever.

I desperately need to talk to Jenna. What will she make of all this?

Well, at least I won't have to wait very long to find out.

CHAPTER 23

I pour over the vast selection of red wines in the liquor store two blocks from our apartment. Just as Jenna knows my tastes in coffee, I know hers in wine—the beauty of friendship at its finest. Jenna certainly enjoys the finer things in life, but if her slurred voice on the other end of the line is any indication, she won't be able to tell the difference between a vintage pinot noir or a price-slashed cabernet tonight. I can't spend too much time here debating pedigree and prices anyway.

I select a Prisoner Red Blend along with a Mascota Vineyards Malbec. I'm handing over my credit card to the cashier when something catches my eye outside the shop. Rather, *someone*.

"Can you hold on to this for a minute?" I ask, dropping my card on the counter. I don't wait for him to answer—I've already got one foot out the door.

My thoughts are frantically whirling. It's as if I'm spinning inside a clothes dryer set on high as I follow the person I spotted from inside the liquor shop for an entire city block. Almost eight and a half million people live in New York City. It couldn't possibly be her, could it? It looks so much like her, but at the same time, not at all like I remember her. Something about the resemblance is unsettling enough though to make me abandon my wine to find out if I'm right.

"Ms. Randall? Is that you?"

The woman whips around at the touch of my hand on her shoulder. At first, she looks confused, but then her face changes as recognition sets in.

"Just a second," she says sweetly to the towheaded toddler she was pushing in a stroller a moment ago. "Ms. Randall is just going to talk to her friend for a moment."

She turns to me. "Well, hello there, Mrs. Douglass. You startled me, dear."

"I'm so sorry, I just...I wasn't sure if it was you. You look so *different*." Different is the understatement of the century. Ms. Randall's silver hair is styled loosely over her shoulders in waves. She's dressed in jeans and a fitted T-shirt with walking shoes. Walking shoes! Surely this is not the same woman who interviewed with me for a nanny position. Where's the twinset? The pearls? The hairspray?

"It's me," she says cheerily, smiling.

I'm sorry, but Ms. Randall doesn't smile. It's as if I've stepped into some alternate universe.

"You look confused," she says, a slight frown beginning to form. "Are you okay?"

"You were so prim and proper when we met. I just..." I just don't know. Something isn't sitting right with me, though I can't understand why that's the case. Why should I give a shit about what Ms. Randall looks like? She's not my nanny.

I don't know why, but I do. I *really, really* do.

"Um, well, I guess it doesn't hurt to be honest with you now since you already decided not to hire me." Ouch.

"Honest? What do you mean?"

"I received a phone call about an hour before our interview."

"A phone call? From who?" I interrupt.

"She said she was from the nanny agency."

"What nanny agency? I didn't go through a nanny agency. I found you on Facebook."

"Yes, but I also worked with an agency. I had lots of interviews. And I just assumed when they mentioned you that you were using them to find a nanny. Anyway, the woman told me you

THE PERFECT NANNY

were looking for a no-nonsense nanny— 'Mary Poppins on steroids,' she said. So, I tried to make myself as no-nonsense, 'Mary Poppins on steroids' as possible. Oh my gosh," she continues, realization setting in. "Was that why you didn't hire me? Was I too over the top?"

"Thomas?" I ask, my voice lodged in the back of my throat.

"Oh, I made him up, darling. I would never dream of making a child suck on a bar of soap." She shakes her head. "That's just barbaric. And besides, *A Christmas Story* is my all-time favorite movie. That bar of soap turned Ralphie into a blind pauper."

That only happened in his fantasy, but it's beside the point. I'm suddenly extremely dizzy, my vision swimming. Someone called Ms. Randall before our interview. But *who* and *why?* Did Bree have something to do with this? Is it farfetched to think she contacted other nannies off the Facebook group on the off chance that they were interviewing with me? Why would she go to so much trouble to get a job in my home?

I think about how Bree saved my child, and once again, I feel like a horrible human being for doubting her. Maybe Ms. Randall has her interviews confused.

"Are you okay?" Ms. Randall has a hand on my shoulder. "You don't look well, dear. Come, let's get you sitting down."

"No, no, I'm okay, but thank you." I'm definitely not okay, but that's also beside the point. I need to get back to my apartment.

"Well, it was nice running into you."

"If I ever need an extra hand, could I give you a call?"

"I'm delighted with this little angel here." She beams at the little boy with a finger wedged so deeply up his nose I'm worried he may give himself brain damage. "But feel free to call anytime."

I quickly say goodbye and head back to the liquor store to collect my wine. I have zero intentions of hiring Ms. Randall for anything—I mean, the woman lied about making a child suck on a bar of soap. What kind of maniac says something like that to get a job? But I need to keep the lines of communication open. It doesn't take a pescatarian to know something fishy is happening here.

I grab my credit card and shopping bag from the liquor store clerk and hightail it to my building. I'm in a full-blown sweat by the time I make it back to the apartment. The unexpected Ms. Randall sighting cost me a good twenty minutes I didn't have to spare. It may also have taken a few years off my life.

I'm fumbling for my keys in my purse when I catch a whiff of something intoxicating sifting from under my apartment door. For a moment, I'm wondering if I could have started dinner before I left and forgotten. But no, despite the texting incident, that doesn't seem likely at all. My culinary alarms are on high alert after the eggplant fiasco.

But my nose is not deceiving me. Something is cooking in there. And it smells freaking phenomenal.

And then I hear voices, and I freeze. My keys fall from my hand to the floor. As I bend down to scoop them up, the door swings open.

Well, look who decided to come home early.

CHAPTER 24

"What are you doing here?" I stare at my husband in startled shock as I rise to my feet.

Andrew starts to run a hand through his hair but stops himself. Egad, he has it pulled back in a man bun—when we have company coming over in an hour, no less. At least he's traded his paint-splattered jeans for a pair of non-paint-splattered jeans.

"Why do you look so surprised? I live here, Lucinda."

"Duh, I know that," I say, brushing the lint from the hallway carpet off my pants. "But it's like four something in the afternoon. You usually don't roll in until seven or eight."

"What—and miss our company?" Andrew's jaw twitches as he says this. He's got a crazed look in his eyes. Oh boy. Is he mad *I* didn't tell him that we are having company? Or is he emphasizing that *he* didn't tell me we are having company? But why would he not tell me that Chad and Marly are coming over?

It's all so strange. I swear, there's Twilight Zone music playing somewhere right now. I can practically hear it.

I have so many questions, but I don't know where to start. On second thought, dinner is as good a place as any. "Well, I guess it all worked out. Thanks for starting dinner."

Andrew's eyebrows shoot up. "I'd love to take credit, but I didn't start dinner."

Then who started dinner?

My husband moves out of the way so I can enter our apartment. Naturally, I go straight to the kitchen, where Bree is standing by the stove, stirring the fragrant sauce I smelled from the hallway with a wooden spoon.

Our television, catty-cornered in the kitchen, is turned on and, well, what do you know—I did hear the theme song for The Twilight Zone. I stare at the screen, momentarily frozen in place, as Rod Serling introduces the sixth dimension. At least I haven't gone completely crazy.

But this situation here? *This* is crazy.

And it's about to get crazier.

"What are you doing, Bree?"

Bree flips around and—*oh my*—she's wearing Andrew's apron. That apron was an anniversary gift. I bought it for my husband when we celebrated two years of wedded bliss. It's a gag apron that reads, "Once you put my meat in your mouth..." I'll admit it was funnier before Andrew swore off meat, but still, it has special meaning to us.

Bree places the wooden spoon on a paper towel and wipes her hands down the front, leaving a smear of cream.

Did Bree help herself to the apron? Or did Andrew tell her she could wear it? I don't know why I'm so bothered. It's just an apron. And no one is putting any meat in their mouth tonight. I made sure of it when I pieced together the menu.

"Oh hey, Lucinda," Bree says casually. "You're back."

I stare at her, waiting for an explanation for—I don't know—why she's in my kitchen, cooking my dinner, wearing my husband's apron. And where in the world is Delilah?

Her face falls. "Oh no. I've upset you, haven't I? I'm sorry I overstepped. It's just—you seemed so overwhelmed before you left, I figured I'd help you and get dinner started."

"But my recipe—"

"*Recipe?*" Bree raises an eyebrow. "Come on now, Lucinda, everyone knows how to make a simple white pesto pasta sauce. It's like Cooking 101."

I regard her suspiciously. "How did you know I was making a white pesto pasta dish?"

Bree rolls her eyes and throws back her head with a laugh. "What *else* would you be making with these generic ingredients?"

Generic ingredients? My cheeks turn the color of beets.

"Delilah?" I ask through gritted teeth. Where is my daughter while the woman who's getting paid to watch her cooks my dinner and flirts with my husband?

"Oh, Delilah Bear is fast asleep. I'll feed her when she wakes up so you can enjoy your guests."

Delilah Bear? Wow, what a great nickname for someone else to give my daughter. Seriously folks, I just can't.

I clench my jaw so tightly my teeth hurt. Then I walk over to the kitchen island to deposit the plastic bag housing the two bottles of wine I picked up while Bree was busy hijacking my dinner. My hands are trembling, and I'm worried I might drop them to the floor, where they'll shatter and bleed all over our white marble tiles.

"This smells amazing," Andrew chimes in. "May I?" He walks over to the stove, motioning toward the simmering sauce. It does smell amazing. I wish it didn't smell so freaking amazing.

"Of course, you can. I'd love a chef's take on it." *A chef?* Jeez, the guy made her pancakes, like once, and now he's a chef? Andrew is beaming. If his ego gets any bigger, he won't be able to fit through the door, especially with that odango on his head.

I examine Bree's face. The way she's batting her eyelashes at my husband—I bet she doesn't mind his man bun at all. Heck, she'll probably fawn over that next.

I watch Bree dip the spoon back into the pot, blow on it, and then hand it to Andrew. I'm surprised she doesn't physically feed the sauce to him herself. Perhaps she would have if I weren't here watching. Oh gosh, is this *toned down*, Bree? If that's the case, I should probably install cameras in every room of this apartment.

Andrew carefully licks the white pesto off the wooden spoon and lets out a groan of pure pleasure. "Man, oh man, that's good. You'll have to give Lucinda your recipe."

He has to be fricking joking.

Bree smiles widely. She picks up a paper towel from the countertop and casually dabs the corner of his mouth. "Missed a drop."

I'm going to be sick.

I open my mouth to protest, but Bree doesn't give me the chance.

"By the way," she adds, pulling her eyes from my husband. "I hope you don't mind, but I made a mixed greens salad and garlic bread from scratch while you were out. I mean, plastic bags and foil wrap for entertaining?" She shakes her head in disapproval.

Salt, meet wound.

Then Bree takes an exaggerated breath as if I've personally offended her with my attempt to cut corners. The way she's acting, you'd think I was hosting the president and first lady or foreign dignitaries for dinner.

Bree removes Andrew's apron and drops it into my hands. "I guess you can take over from here. Just don't forget about the garlic bread, okay? I'd hate for you to have a repeat of the other night, if you know what I mean." She places a hand momentarily on Andrew's chest, and they both laugh.

Did I miss something here? When did Andrew and Bree become so chummy? Seriously, why is my nanny's hand on my husband's chest?

"Oh goodness, I almost forgot, someone left this for you at the front desk." Bree walks to the opposite end of the island and grabs an envelope. As she slips it into my hand, my stomach drops. I think about the last time I got an envelope like this—no return address and no stamp—just my name scribbled across the front in the script.

Is Andrew cheating on me, again?

"Ashton brought it upstairs and asked me to give it to you, seeing as how we're sisters and all." She winks, and my cheeks flush scarlet. Then she flips her hair over a shoulder and struts out of the room, leaving Andrew and me alone in the kitchen.

I push two fingers into my forehead, trying to remember—was Ashton even working today? I'm not sure. He might have been. The day has become a complete blur.

It doesn't matter, I suppose. What matters is that I can't open this right now—not with dinner already cooking on the stove and Andrew eyeing me suspiciously.

A knock at the front door makes me jump. No one called up from the front desk. Ashton is definitely working. I stick the envelope in my back pocket. Whatever is inside will have to wait.

Because apparently, our company's not going to.

CHAPTER 25

Please be Jenna, please be Jenna, please be Jenna.
"Chad, my man," I hear Andrew say from the entryway.
Darn. Not Jenna.
"Marly, you look beautiful as always."
Marly giggles. "Oh, stop."
Andrew can be smooth as silk when he wants to be. He can also be as abrasive as a Brillo pad.
I glance at the clock on our kitchen wall—4:55 p.m. Why oh why did I tell Chad and Marly to come early? Dinner isn't ready yet. Jenna's not here yet. God, what's taking her so dang long?
As my husband and guests continue exchanging pleasantries, I quickly pull the envelope from my back pocket and rip open the seal, unable to wait another second to find out if Andrew is cheating on me again.
What the...? My heart drops into my stomach. I'm initially relieved to find it's not a picture of Andrew canoodling like the other ones I received. But what is *this?* I stare at the image of Chad with his hand on my lower back. I recognize from our outfits that it's from earlier today as we walked from our office building to lunch. I flip the picture over, discovering a handwritten message scrawled across the back.
It's all coming out.
Well, that's cryptic.

I stuff the picture back into the envelope, stick it in a random drawer, and rush back to the stove just in time so as not to get caught red-handed. I can hardly explain what I don't understand. Namely, who took this picture and why?

And the ones that came before...

Hand-delivered images of Andrew getting too cozy with a paralegal from his former law firm.

Now you know the reason our marriage has come to resemble War of the Roses. Andrew cheated on me with his paralegal! I mean, can you get any more cliche than that? I was fully planning on confronting him when I first received the pictures. I was going to leave him. But then, I found out I was pregnant. I couldn't let my daughter grow up in a broken home like I had. I had no choice but to forgive him.

But I haven't forgotten.

"Lucy!" I flip around at the sound of my name, and wow, Andrew was right—Marly does look beautiful. Stunning. She's dressed in a trendy romper with her jet-black hair pulled back in a sleek ponytail. Her legs are tan and taut, the combination of genetics, yoga training, and no kids. Chad wanted children, but I guess motherhood is not for everyone.

"Marly!" I attempt to place the stirring spoon on the counter but realize that in my haste to look natural, I plum forgot to pick it up in the first place. "It's great to see you! It's been forever!"

I walk over to hug her, hoping she didn't notice my momentary brain freeze.

"Hey, Lucy." Chad waves across the island, where Andrew is pouring him a cocktail with the bottle of Tito's he brought. I wonder if Andrew is disappointed that it's not Absolut. Oh well. You know what they say about payback.

The picture burning a hole in the kitchen drawer may not be of Andrew, but it's brought back to the surface what he did to me. I need to pull myself together or one of us may be hanging from a chandelier before the night is through.

I take a deep breath and return the wave. I'm about to say, *Long time no see,* but I didn't tell Andrew we went to lunch in the first place. I don't want to start anything that'll ruin our perfect dinner party. The perfect dinner party I didn't know we were having.

"Can I get you something to drink, Marly?"

"Oh, I'd love a glass of wine if you're having." Her eyes settle on the two bottles of red I bought for Jenna sitting on the countertop. How odd—I don't even recall taking them out of the bag.

"Of course!" I open a drawer, pushing the envelope aside to pull out our bottle opener. The kitchen drawer is probably a horrible place to keep the envelope. I'll have to move it to my nightstand to join its friends once our little party has shifted into another room. Unfortunately, I realize that doesn't seem to be happening any time soon, as Chad makes himself comfortable on a barstool.

I pour Marly and myself each a generous glass of the Prisoner Red Blend.

Marly takes a long sip. "So," she says. "Chad tells me you're coming back to work soon."

"Sure am." I smile, then take a sip from my glass.

"Good thing. Maybe then my husband will get home at a reasonable hour. He's out so late; I swear, I'm starting to suspect he's having an affair."

I spit my wine across the island dramatically.

"Lucinda!" Andrew scolds, rushing to grab paper towels to clean our countertop, which now looks like a bloody crime scene.

"It's her fault." I point at Marly. "She made me laugh."

"There's nothing funny about an affair," Marly says, shrugging her shoulders, her face serious. She has a point.

I, of all people, should know as much.

Well, this is uncomfortable. I just assumed Marly was joking around. I guess we should add affairs to the list of things you don't talk about with company—right up there next to politics and religion. And now, it feels like they're all staring, waiting for me to say something.

But then, by what I can only imagine is divine intervention and an abnormally ineffectual doorman, there's a knock at the door. Yep, Ashton is one hundred percent working the front desk. This time, though, the knot in my stomach loosens.

"What do you know? Jenna must be here." I clap my hands together. Then I abandon my wine to let her in. "Keep stirring the sauce," I call to Andrew over my shoulder.

I swing open the front door just as Jenna is poised to knock again. "Finally," I say, pursing my lips. "I was starting to think you weren't going to show."

"And miss a fun and incredibly awkward dinner with Chad and Marly? Wouldn't dream of it."

"Sshhh." I bring a finger to my lips. "They're in there." I point behind me toward the kitchen.

Jenna's not a big fan of Marly. I'm pretty sure it's an alpha dog sort of thing, though it's never seemed worth the effort to dig. I mean, they see each other twice a year, if that.

Like I said, Jenna doesn't like many people. While I'd rather she not insult my nanny, husband, or houseguests, it does make me feel incredibly special.

"You look amazing," I say, admiring Jenna's skin-tight tank paired with a flowy skirt, the studs of a Valentino slide peeking out from underneath its hem. I think of Marly in the other room in her cute little romper, and it feels like I'm hosting auditions for a fashion magazine cover.

As Jenna walks into the apartment, I poke my head out in the hallway, looking around. "Where's the date?"

"Well..." She waves her hand around. "We had a little argument on the cab ride over, and I told him to get out."

"Really? Was he angry, Jenna? He knows where I live!"

"Oh, Lucy, you need to relax. Do you think he's going to come here and murder us all because I rejected him?" When she puts it that way, it does seem unlikely. Though considering what almost happened to Delilah earlier this week...

"Don't worry. He stuck his tail between his legs and got out of the cab. He probably went back to the bar. Come on, let's share that bottle of wine you picked up."

I guess I won't be breastfeeding my daughter at all tonight, or quite possibly for the next twenty-four hours.

I feel guilty, but thankfully, I have probably a year's worth of frozen breast milk in our laundry-room fridge. "You're like an actual cow," Andrew told me the other day while he searched the freezer for some Bubba burgers. I couldn't tell if that was a compliment or an insult, from the mouth of a vegetarian.

In any event, I'll have to pump and dump tonight. I'm not sure what's gotten into me today. Starting tomorrow, no more alcohol (said every breastfeeding mom ever)! Just my nutritious and delicious Mother's Milk tea.

But for tonight, when in Rome…

CHAPTER 26

Thankfully, my other guests have vacated the kitchen, leaving Jenna and me to sip our wine and catch up in peace.

"Was it the guy from the park?" I ask, rubbing the tannins from my teeth with a finger.

"Was *who* the guy from the park?"

"The guy you were with at the bar, Jenna. The one you threw out of a moving cab on your way over here."

Jenna throws her head back and laughs. "The cab wasn't moving, silly. We were stopped at a red light. But no, it was a different guy."

It's a wonder how she keeps track.

I shake my head in mock disapproval and head over to the stove, where I put a pot of water to boil for the pasta. I double-check that the water is at the right level so it doesn't boil over like the last time. To be safe, I move the salad as far as I possibly can from the stove. Then I discreetly set a timer on my phone so I don't accidentally evaporate all the water and burn down the place.

Once everything is in order on the dinner front, I tell Jenna, "You should probably go say hello to everyone."

"Right," she says, looking less than pleased. "Do I have to? Can't we just hang out in here?"

I shake my head at her. "Sorry, my friend, you know I'd love to, but that would be rude."

Just as I pick up my glass of wine to lead Jenna into the living room, her phone vibrates loudly on the counter. She glances down at the screen and then back up at me.

"You go ahead. I'll be there in a minute. I have to take this." She brings the phone to her ear.

I wonder if it's a legitimate phone call or if she sent one of those 'help me' texts that elicits a fake call. I've received plenty of those texts from Jenna.

Whatever—she can't hide out in the kitchen forever.

I leave her behind and head to the living room where—surprise, surprise—Bree has joined our intimate dinner party. She's standing in the middle of the room, cradling my baby. I stop short in the archway, unable to move my feet. Bree is in the middle of the story recounting how she single-handedly, heroically saved Delilah at Central Park. If you didn't know better, you'd think she was the mom and I, the help. The policeman at the park certainly thought so.

They're having a grand ol' time here without me. I watch as Chad pulls out two pink cigars and a matchbook. My eyes key in on the matchbook in his fingers as he lights Andrew's cigar. The Loungebook Pearl. My knees go weak.

"Oh hey, Lucinda," Bree says as she notices me awkwardly watching them. "Sorry to interrupt your party. I just figured your friends would want to see Delilah Bear. That's the real reason you're all here, right?" She winks at Chad and Marly with her good eye.

Marly smiles widely. "Bree is a real hoot, Lucinda. Is it weird that I want her to live with us even though we don't have a baby?"

Yes, it's weird, Marly. Incredibly freaking weird.

"She was just telling us how she came to Delilah's rescue. You have a real-life superhero at your disposal. Talk about hitting the nanny jackpot!"

I purse my lips, forcing a tight smile.

"Sure did," I say. Then, "Thank you, Bree. I can take over from here."

As I reach out for Delilah, Bree pulls her tighter into her chest. She takes a step back, away from me. "Do you think that's a good idea, Lucinda? You've clearly had too much to drink."

"Excuse me?" I've had two glasses of wine—okay, and the drinks earlier today, but only Chad knows about those—and, NO, it shouldn't matter because Bree is not *my* nanny! She works for me.

"You know, I think she's right, Lucinda," Andrew adds, because of course he does. Apparently, Bree is Andrew's new best friend. My face feels like it's been set on fire. "Why don't we let Bree take Delilah back to her room so we can hang out properly with Chad and Marly?"

"And Jenna!" I whip around, my body relaxing. Thank goodness she's off the phone. Now this awkward scene can come to an end. I give Jenna 'the' look. "The water is boiling, Lucy," she announces. "You can start the pasta now."

I owe you, I mouth. And then I stomp out of the room like a cartoon character with smoke blowing from my ears.

But don't worry; the party goes on without me. Andrew doesn't check to see if I'm okay. Then, why would he? He's too busy picking sides with our nanny.

I straighten out my shirt and refocus. Revenge is a dish best served cold. Or, in this case, revenge is the perfect dinner to remind my husband and friends of how wonderful I am. Since Bree moved in, it seems I've been forgotten. If this nanny situation is going to work out, *that* is going to change.

I throw on Andrew's apron, which still smells of our nanny, and get to work. I check on the garlic bread—which, I'll admit, has all the right seasonings in all the right places and a generous amount of butter. While the bread is still baking, I gently pour a bag and a half of gourmet farfalle into the pot of boiling water.

Then I watch and wait.

And try not to think about the incriminating picture in our kitchen drawer.

CHAPTER 27

MANY YEARS AGO

Judy kept me at home where she could 'watch me.'

It had been weeks since my mom died, and I had not left the house. My siblings were all back at school and in daycare. At least, I assumed so. Come to think of it, I hadn't seen much of my brothers and sisters since Hurricane Judy ripped through our house.

"You could homeschool her," I overheard my dad tell Judy one night when they thought I was asleep.

Judy tutted, "Homeschool her? Are you kidding me, David? I don't know how much more of this I can take. She's a nightmare."

A nightmare? Me? Why in the world did Judy hate me so much?

"She's just a kid. Come here, baby. I'll make it all better."

I hated when my dad called her baby. But Judy seemed to like it. The complaining stopped, and soon after that, the sex started. My dad and Judy were so loud, I swear, they could have started a two-person band.

I wasn't faring nearly as well as both of them. My skin was pale, almost gray, from the lack of natural light. I barely had the energy to get out of bed. And although Judy had been forcing me to eat, I'd lost weight that I couldn't afford to lose. I looked like a ten-year-old boy, not like a high school girl.

One could surmise that I took my mother's death the hardest as the oldest child. Or one could surmise something different altogether. Dad didn't want CPS to come poking around and asking questions. Why his mind went straight to CPS spoke volumes about the deterioration in our home after Mom died.

It felt like we were stuck in a powder keg, just waiting for it to explode.

Tick. Tick. Tick.

It was time to get out. I knew I had to go back to school. I tried to look on the bright side—anywhere was better than here. I didn't have any friends at school, but in all fairness, I was awkward. Mom called me her swan. Well, she *used to* call me her swan. To everyone else, I was nothing more than an ugly duckling.

I stared in the mirror that morning, determined today would be the day I would figure a way out of my house. But I couldn't go to school like this. I smelled awful and looked wretched to boot. Two weeks' worth of sweat and tears had made my white pajamas start to yellow.

I turned on the faucet in the bath to start the shower. The door swung open, and I tried to cover myself from Judy. "What do you think you're doing?"

"I need to shower before school," I said as defiantly as I'd dare.

"No, there's not enough time. What you need to do is get your skinny ass in the car. Or should I call your dad?"

The witch wouldn't even let me run a brush through my hair.

I scrambled to slip my clean clothes over my dirty body. We weren't even late. To add insult to injury, even after dropping my siblings at daycare and school, we were still the first vehicle in the high-school carpool line.

As we sat in the car, waiting for the doors to open, I ran my fingers through my hair, trying to tame it. I felt Judy's eyes bore into me.

"If you're so concerned about your hair, maybe we should chop it off."

My fingers instinctively flew to my lap.

She wouldn't do that to me, would she? Oh God, she probably would.

I sat stock still as Judy grabbed her purse from the back seat. I prayed, *please let the first bell ring, please let the first bell ring*. Why did we have to be so dang early?

It didn't ring.

And then I saw the glimmer of carbon steel as Judy pulled a pair of scissors from her purse. Yes, actual scissors. Judy was a hairdresser. But I didn't want that woman anywhere near my head with something so sharp.

"Turn," she instructed.

I thought about grabbing the scissors from her hand and burying them into her chest.

But I couldn't bring myself to do it. Not when there were so many witnesses around.

I looked her in the eyes, pleading, "Judy, please. I'll do anything you want. Please don't cut my hair. That's all I have left..." *Of my mom.* She knew exactly what I was going to say. I had my mom's hair.

Judy grabbed a chunk of hair and ran her scissors across it. For five minutes, I listened in horror to the sound of cutting. *Snip. Snip. Snip.* And then the bell rang. But the damage was already done.

As I placed my hand on the door handle, barely breathing, Judy grabbed me by the arm. She ripped down the passenger side mirror.

"Look," she ordered with an evil smile playing on her lips.

It was worse than I ever could have imagined. Worse than if Judy had shaved my head. My hair was cropped above my shoulders now and uneven, hairs sticking out in every which direction. I swallowed my tears and got out of the car.

I don't know what I expected, but school was not quite the reprieve I had hoped for. It felt like all eyes were on me, not in a good way. It was as if I had some contagious, terminal disease. "Take a bath," a fellow upperclassman sneered as he smashed me into a locker. "Ever heard of a brush?" a girl whispered loudly to her friend as they passed me in the hall.

THE PERFECT NANNY

Someone lined my seat with ketchup packets in biology class so that it looked like I had gotten my period when I stood up. I walked around all day like that.

I was the laughingstock at school, and the punching bag at home.

There was only so much one person could take before—well, that remained to be seen.

CHAPTER 28

With Delilah tucked away for the night with Bree, I'd say our dinner calls for some fine china. I dust off our cobalt-rimmed Vera Wang plates, polished silver flatware, and crystal water glasses. I plate the salad neatly in the matching salad bowls that Jenna bought us for our wedding gift. Then I scoop a cup of pasta at each table setting, coating it in the creamy white pesto sauce. I position the sliced garlic bread in the center of our eight-seat table and light a candle at each end.

I pause for a moment to admire my handiwork.

Then, I ring the dinner bell to call our guests to the dining room. Just kidding—we don't have an actual dinner bell. I call out, "Dinner's ready," and then wait for everyone to join me in the dining room. I wish I had a camera to capture the reactions on their faces when they bear witness to this masterpiece I pieced together.

Okay, dinner is not technically my masterpiece since Bree is the one who prepared it. But no one knows that other than Andrew. Hopefully, he'll keep his mouth shut.

I chew on a nail as I wait, and then my guests trickle into the dining room one by one. Their reaction is even better than expected.

"Wow. You've really outdone yourself. It looks amazing in here," Marly gushes.

"And smells," Chad adds. "It smells amazing. My mouth is literally watering right now."

Andrew smirks at me, but thankfully, exposing my secondary role in dinner is not on his agenda. Instead, he quizzically looks at the place settings and asks, "What about Bree?"

"What *about* Bree?"

"You didn't set a spot for her." He motions around the table, set for five.

"And why would I set a spot for her? She's watching Delilah." The color rises to my cheeks.

"She needs to eat, too, Lucinda."

He's making me sound like some wicked human being who starves her help. And worse, all eyes in the room are laser-focused on us. I turn to our guests, plastering on my best Stepford wife smile. "Please, dig in before it gets cold. Andrew—could I speak with you for a moment in private?"

Andrew rolls his eyes but nonetheless follows me into the kitchen.

"What is going on with you, Lucinda?" he asks before I have a chance to speak.

"I think a better question is, what is going on with you, Andrew, and our nanny? And go…" I roll my wrist, giving him the go-ahead to attempt to explain away his odd behavior.

"Look. You're the one who wanted to hire a nanny in the first place. You're the one who invited her to live with us without even consulting with me. Your exact words were, 'She'll only be a stranger at first, but then I bet she'll become like family.' And now—it's you who hates her for no reason. It feels like we're living in a war zone."

"You're not the one dodging Bree bullets, Andrew. I am."

"What's really going on here, Lucinda?"

I sigh audibly. "I don't hate Bree, Andrew. But I also don't appreciate how flirty she is with you and you with her."

"So that's what this is about. You think something is going on with Bree and me?"

Do I? "I'm not sure what I think. I just know I don't like it."

His expression softens. "I'm sorry I've made you feel that way. I'm just being friendly. Warm and welcoming. The way I assumed you're supposed to be when you invite someone to live in your home and take care of your child. I will be more mindful moving forward, okay?"

"Thank you. And I'll try to be more conciliatory with Bree, okay?"

"Okay."

Tell him. Tell him you know about the affair.

"There's something else, Andrew. I—"

Something stops me. Rather, *someone*.

It's Chad. He's screaming at the top of his lungs from the dining room.

"Marly? Marly!"

"What's wrong with her?" Jenna shouts. "What can I do?"

"Grab her purse. Check the label on the nuts Lucinda used. Call 9-1-1. Get Lucinda. *Lucinda!*"

Jenna doesn't have to get me because I sprint into the dining room.

Oh. My. God.

Marly is sprawled out on the dining room floor with her head in Chad's lap. She's shaking. I rush to their side and drop to my knees. Poor Marly. Her breaths are coming in wheezy gasps, almost like a gurgle. It's as if she has fluid in her lungs.

And her face. Oh my. It's lined with angry, red welts. She opens her mouth, and I see her tongue visibly swollen to at least twice its normal size.

"What was in the pesto sauce, Lucinda?" Chad doesn't look so hot, either. He's broken into a cold sweat. His normally steady hands are shaking.

This is bad. *Really, really* bad.

I start rattling off the recipe, but then I remember Bree made dinner. She didn't follow the recipe.

"Walnuts," I add lastly. "I specifically bought walnuts because I know Marly is allergic to pine nuts. But…" I pause for a split second. "I didn't make dinner. I came home and Bree was already cooking…"

Andrew materializes in the dining room, waving a plastic container of near-empty nuts. "I found these next to the stove."

Chad grabs it from his hands. "Oh God, Lucinda...Did you buy *these*? *These* are *not* walnuts!" He throws the container at me.

I scoop it up from the floor, staring at what are unquestionably pine nuts. "No, of course not. But I told you, Bree prepared the sauce." I hang my head, mortified.

Chad wrinkles his nose at me. His wife is in anaphylactic shock, *and* I took credit for someone else's sauce.

But I suppose we have bigger problems here as Marly's eyes roll into the back of her head, and she goes completely still.

CHAPTER 29

She can't be dead. She can't be dead.

This repeats on a loop as I watch a group of paramedics get to work on Marly. She's already had two epinephrine shots, and now someone is performing CPR on her. The defibrillator panels are out and ready to go. It looks like they're filming a scene from Chicago Fire in my dining room. The only thing missing is Taylor Kinney. Now that would have been a scene I'd rather enjoy. But *this?*

Jenna slips a protective arm around my shoulders. "Well, this turned out to be quite the dinner party," she whispers in my ear.

"Really, Jenna? Not the time." I shake my head at her.

"I'm sorry. I was trying to make you feel better. Marly is in good hands, Luc. Look—" She points to Marly, who seems to have regained consciousness. "Her eyes are open."

Oh, thank God. So I didn't kill our dinner guest. But Bree almost did. Was this merely some freak coincidence? Bree couldn't possibly have known that Marly is allergic to pine nuts. *Could* she? As far as I know, they had never met before tonight. And even if they had, why would Bree want to poison our guest?

The only thing I'm certain of at this moment is that there should not have been pine nuts in that sauce.

But there were. One look at Marly's bloated, splotchy face and—clearly, there were.

"I'm going to talk to Bree," I decide, slipping out of Jenna's embrace. "I totally get it if you want to split. I'll text you later once things calm down here."

Jenna flashes a sympathetic smile. "Go ahead. I completely understand. Love you, Luc."

"Love you more."

I start walking to Bree's room, but a hand on my arm stops me. I flip around to find Andrew glaring. For a moment, I wonder if he's choking again—because his face is that same deep purple color. "Where do you think you're going, Lucinda?"

Nope, he's not choking. Just angry.

"I'm going to talk to Bree. I don't understand how pine nuts wound up in that sauce. I don't even keep pine nuts in the cupboard in the event Chad and Marly come over. So where did they come from, Andrew?"

"I eat pine nuts, Lucinda. They may have been mine. Have you considered the possibility that Bree grabbed them because she thought pine nuts would fare better in a pesto sauce than walnuts? I'm sure this is all just some unfortunate accident."

Could he be right? Were the pine nuts in our cupboard all along?

No, no, no. Absolutely not.

"No Andrew, I deep cleaned the cupboards the other day. I'm one hundred percent certain there were no pine nuts in there."

Andrew huffs and throws his hands in the air. "Okay, so let me get this straight... Are you suggesting Bree somehow knew about Marly's allergy and intentionally grabbed a hidden stash of pine nuts to—what—*poison* her? Do you have any idea how utterly ridiculous that sounds? Are you seriously about to go accuse our nanny of attempted murder?"

"Well, what would you call it? And whose side are you on here anyway, Andrew? You and I both know it was Bree who made the sauce. Bree decided to make dinner without asking if I wanted her to. Bree went rogue and decided to use her own ingredients, evidently. I'd say this is her fault, wouldn't you?"

"She was trying to help, Lucinda. It isn't anyone's fault. Like I said, it was an unfortunate accident."

~~Was it?~~ ~~Detective~~ O'Brien's words flash through my mind—"I don't believe in coincidences." And yet we're to believe Bree just so happened to have a container of pine nuts stashed away in her room for a special occasion like this?

No one is that naive. Well, other than my husband. Apparently, he is that naive.

Andrew follows me like a shadow to Bree's room. Despite our conversation in the kitchen, it's as if he doesn't trust me to be alone with her. What exactly does he think I'm going to do? Pull her hair? Make her cry?

A woman—a friend—almost died in our apartment. All I know is I didn't buy the pine nuts, and I certainly didn't use them to make the sauce. Because again—I didn't make the freaking sauce!

Andrew stands a few steps behind me with his hands on his hips. I bang loudly on Bree's door. She cracks it initially but then fully opens the door when she sees me standing there. It's so *not* what she did the last time I knocked, making me wonder if she also sees Andrew standing behind me. God, this girl will do anything to look good in front of my husband. And it seems she'll do just about anything to make me look bad.

Including poisoning one of our dinner guests?

"Hi, Lucinda," she says before I have a chance to open my mouth to confront her. "I'm sorry about what happened before. I didn't mean to make a scene and embarrass you. It's just—well, you were a little wobbly, and your speech was slurred, and I know you would never forgive yourself if something happened to Delilah. I figured I'd give you the night to have fun and relax while I took care of her. I can't stop thinking about the look on your face when you stormed off..." She closes her eyes and shakes her head as if traumatized by the image. "Anyway, I'm sorry. I should have spoken to you in private."

Okay, maybe she didn't mean to humiliate me in front of my husband, work colleague, wife, and best friend.

But the nuts.

"Thank you," I say stiffly. "Not sure if you heard the commotion out there, but—" How could she *not* have heard the commotion out there? Wouldn't any normal person come running to make sure everyone was okay?

I continue, "Marly went into anaphylactic shock from the pesto sauce. She's severely allergic to pine nuts. Why did you use pine nuts in the sauce, Bree?"

"I used whatever nuts *you* bought, Lucinda."

"I bought WALNUTS, Bree. There were *pine* nuts in that sauce."

"If you didn't buy them, where would I have even gotten pine nuts from? I haven't left the apartment in days." True, but…

"Are you positive, Bree?"

Bree tucks a loose strand of white-blonde hair behind her ear and looks down at her feet. "I'm so sorry about Marly. I just used what was out, Lucinda. And now…You think this is my fault, don't you?" Her lip quivers like she's going to cry. "I was just trying to help make things easier for you, and now I've embarrassed you, and your friend is sick."

"My friend is not just *sick*, Bree. She's in anaphylaxis en route to the emergency room. Because there were pine nuts in the sauce you made."

Andrew pushes me out of the way. "Enough. She said she used the nuts you bought, Lucinda. You must have accidentally bought the wrong nuts. End of story."

He places a hand on Bree's shoulder. "Bree, we don't think you did anything wrong."

We? Like hell, I don't think she's done anything wrong.

I'm so angry I could punch someone. Instead, I turn from them and walk away.

My husband may have fallen for Bree's sweet-girl, innocent act, but I don't believe a word she says. Jenna was right—me and my good feelings… Well, now I know. Something nefarious is going on here. I'm going to figure out what that something is.

I need to find the walnuts I bought for the white pesto sauce. The container should be full, since Bree didn't use them. Then I can show Andrew that I bought the right nuts and Bree is lying. I'm not the crazy one here. He'll have no choice but to believe me.

I'm his wife. He should believe me over some woman he's known for less than two weeks. *Shouldn't he?*

Before commencing my search, I grab my phone off the island in the kitchen and shoot Chad a text.

I'm so, so sorry. Is Marly doing any better?

Chad immediately reads the text, and I watch three dots pulse on the screen. But then, they disappear, and after standing with my phone in my hand, just staring at it for a few minutes, it becomes clear Chad is not writing back.

I'm sure he's busy taking care of his wife.

I place my phone back on the countertop and get to work. First, I search the grocery bags and pantry for any sign of the walnuts. Then, I sift through the garbage can and the recycling bins. It's in none of those places. I search the sink next, digging in the garbage disposal with my bare hand to see if Bree attempted to pulverize the evidence. That's clean, as well.

The nuts have to be here somewhere. She never left this apartment. She may be manipulative, but she's not a magician.

Unless, could they all be right? Could I have accidentally bought the wrong container of nuts?

I dismiss the possibility as I continue to search the cabinets one by one and then the drawers. I stop short when I open the last drawer where I stashed the envelope earlier. In all the commotion with Marly going into anaphylaxis, I completely forgot about it. The envelope is still there, but it's not how I left it. The picture of Chad and me is now sitting out on top.

I examine the photo more closely. Whoever took this picture did so at the very worst moment—it actually looks as if Chad's hand is resting on my ass. Or the very *best* moment?

Now it's lying out for anyone who opens the drawer to see.

Oh, God. Someone else who was in this apartment saw this.

Bree? Marly?

Or was it Andrew? Is this what has him so angry?

I throw a hand over my mouth and run to the sink, where I vomit up all the red wine I drank on an empty stomach. I clutch the sink tightly with both hands so I don't collapse to the floor. The walls dizzy and begin closing in as if trying to swallow me whole.

Someone has to be fucking with me.

CHAPTER 30

I pace the kitchen, debating what to do with this. Do I bring it to Andrew's attention, tell him someone is out there trying to make it look like there's something going on between Chad and me? Considering how hot and cold we've been, would he even believe me? And, am I ready to tell him that I know about him and his very young former paralegal? I was a breath away from telling him before, but then Marly went into anaphylaxis.

If I open Pandora's box, there's no closing it. And then I'll have to ask myself the question: Do I want to leave Andrew and raise Delilah on my own? The truth is, I don't have an answer. As much as I want to hate him, a part of me still loves my husband.

I have to do something though. I can't ignore this picture like I did the last batch hoping it will just—*poof*—disappear.

I take a screenshot of the image. Then I pull up the text exchange with Chad on my phone and hit send. Maybe this picture will get his attention. Although, to be fair, the last time we talked about "us" didn't go very well.

When I said things were "complicated" between me and my work husband, I meant it. Chad has wanted more from our relationship for almost as long as I've known him. I would never dream of doing something so hurtful to my husband, but then I saw those pictures of Andrew and his paralegal and…

I let Chad kiss me. It was a horrible, selfish thing to do, and I immediately regretted it. It never happened again. But not from a lack of trying on Chad's part. If anything, after that kiss, Chad's courtship grew bolder.

I flash to our last conversation when I made it crystal clear that there was no romantic future for us.

"Think about Marly," I whispered, after Chad slipped a key on my desk for a room at the Wall Street Hotel.

"What about Marly?"

"She's your wife, Chad. Think of how she would take this. We're all friends."

"You're the one I want, Lucinda. You."

"I'm pregnant, Chad."

Chad's eyes grew wide.

I shook my head, refusing to let my eyes meet his. We had already taken things too far, crossed a line that never should have been crossed. "You have to stop. We are work colleagues, maybe even friends, but nothing more. And we will never be anything more. I'm sorry, but if you continue to pursue this, I'm going to have to tell my husband. And your wife."

Chad's expression hardened. He stormed to the door of my office, gripped the knob, and turned back to face me.

"You're going to regret this, Lucinda."

Then he walked out, slamming the door behind him.

Okay, so I realize how ominous that sounds. But truly, when we returned to work the next day, everything was fine. Nothing about us pursuing an affair was ever mentioned again.

But standing here now, staring at the picture of Chad and me walking toward The Loungebook Pearl, I wonder if things really were fine between us. What if Chad was still upset about my rejection and looking for a way to blow my marriage apart?

And what about the pictures of my husband? Could Chad have had something to do with those as well?

But *who* took the picture of Chad and me together? It's not as if Chad could have taken it as his hand was inching dangerously close to my ass…

I stare at my phone, willing it to ring. After several minutes of agony, the three dots reappear. So I was right about sending the picture. It definitely got his attention.

I tightly grip the phone in my hands, transfixed on the response coming through.

You conniving bitch.

My heartbeat quickens in my chest. What in the world does he mean by that? Oh gosh, perhaps I was wrong. Maybe Chad didn't know about the picture. Does he think I'm *threatening* him?

Me: You've got this all wrong, Chad. This was anonymously left with the doorman of my building. I don't know by whom. I thought you should know that someone was following us. I'm worried Andrew might have seen this and suspects there's something going on between us.

I chew on a cuticle as I wait for his response. And when it comes, my phone drops from my hand.

Don't ever text my husband again.

Marly? Is *she* the one behind this?

I think about what she said about suspecting Chad of having an affair. Did she already know about our kiss?

Well, she definitely knows now.

CHAPTER 31

By the time I've composed myself and cleaned up the mess from dinner—at least in the literal sense—it's gotten very late. The sky is pitch black, and our lights set to timers in the living room and hallways have kicked over to night-light mode.

I've finally given up on searching for the missing walnuts. At this point, I don't know what happened to them. All I know is that they didn't sprout legs and walk out of this apartment. *Did I accidentally buy the pine nuts in my frenzied state to prepare for the company I wasn't prepared for?* I find that possibility highly unlikely. Marly and her pine nut allergy are like Marly 101, as Bree would put it.

I could check the receipt to be certain, but then I remember the bodega man yelling after me, "Hey lady, you forgot your receipt," and me waving away his reminder because I was too busy to take the five seconds to walk the ten steps back to the counter to retrieve it. Well, that one bit me in the ass.

I'm ninety-nine percent certain I did not buy pine nuts, even if Andrew thinks I did.

Does Marly think I did as well? I recheck my phone for another text or the three dots that appeared earlier. Nothing. I guess that friendship is over.

How have things gone so horribly wrong?

I grab a notepad and a pen from a drawer and start making a list. I've got lots to do tomorrow, the first of which is attempting to talk to Marly. I need her to know I had nothing to do with what happened to her tonight. I need her to know there is nothing going on between Chad and me.

And, I need to know if she shared her suspicions with my husband.

The second thing I need to do is give Detective O'Brien a call. I was wrong that there was no one who I could think of that might wish to hurt me.

I jot down a few more to-dos, and then I flick the switch in the kitchen, plunging the room into darkness.

The pit grows in my stomach as I approach our bedroom. I'm half expecting to find Andrew's side of the bed empty. After everything that has happened over the past week—let's just say I wouldn't be shocked.

Still, my stomach settles slightly when I spot the silhouette of my husband's body alone in the darkness, his chest gently rising and falling. Of course, he's in our bed. Did I believe he'd be sleeping with Bree?

That's the problem with trust. You know, once it's broken…

I peel off my clothing and slip silently into bed beside him. I close my eyes, but I'm too riled up to sleep. I toss and turn, sitting up to take a long swig of tea. My heart pounds in my chest, and I remember the other reason I don't drink like this.

I cover my head with a pillow and try to force my mind to quiet. But it's so fricking noisy in here. What's that awful sound? Good God, did Andrew always snore this loudly? It's like I'm lying in bed next to a jackhammer.

I throw off the pillow and duvet and jump out of bed with a *hmph*. Andrew lets out a snort. I roll my eyes and let myself out of our room.

Go straight to the living room. Do not pass go. Do not collect two hundred dollars.

As I pass our guest room, I fight the temptation to break down Bree's door. Because what would that accomplish, really, other than a broken door in my apartment?

Except, I don't have to break down her door because I find it wide open as I pass her room. The shades are pulled up, the moon illuminating the space. Delilah is fast asleep in a bassinet in the corner of the room. And Bree is fast asleep in her bed, her hair spread around her head like a halo. The irony!

I don't consciously plan to walk into her room, but my feet seem to have a mind of their own. And my eyes are drawn to the object sitting on her nightstand, a mere two feet from her head.

Bree's cellphone.

I tiptoe closer until it's within reach. Then I quickly snatch it and attempt to calmly walk out of her room.

I said *attempt*. So maybe I'm not so calm. I've never taken anything that doesn't belong to me—okay, with the exception of stealing a kiss from Marly's husband—I'm feeling like a bit of a criminal here. But desperate times…

I can't let Bree or Andrew catch me with her phone. I lock myself in the powder room and flick on the light switch. I press my finger down against the side of the phone, holding my breath as it comes to life.

I can't believe I'm doing this—breaking into my nanny's phone. But given my growing suspicions about the woman living in my apartment, what other choice do I have at this point?

CHAPTER 32

Houston, we have a problem. Like half the population, Bree's phone is password protected. And unlike in the movies, where I'd have some 'aha' moment enabling me to crack the code, I've got nothing to work with. That's not to say I don't still try.

After getting locked out for the umpteenth time, I finally give up. I've been at it for so long, the sun is already rising. I'm good with numbers, but not the kind that involves hacking into a phone, apparently. I creep down the hallway, breathing a sigh of relief to find Bree still out cold. I tiptoe over to her nightstand and place her phone back where I snatched it from.

As I lift my trembling hand, Bree's eyes shoot open, and she jolts upright in bed. I freeze in place.

"Lucinda—" she utters accusingly. "What are you doing here?" Our eyes meet on my hand, hovering above her cell phone. Talk about being caught red-handed (insert emoji hitting herself in the forehead here).

"I…I…" I can't think of a damn thing to say. "Delilah," I stammer. "I've come for Delilah."

"Okay, but—" Bree leans back against the headboard and pulls the covers up to her neck. "Delilah is sleeping over there." She points across the room as if I've never seen a bassinet before. "So why are you over here, looking at my phone?"

"I wasn't. I mean, I was, but it's not what it looks like. Your phone buzzed, and I didn't want it to wake you up after all the excitement last night."

"I see." Bree's eyebrows bend toward one another as she regards me skeptically. "I guess I must have left it on last night. Although that's strange, considering the last thing I do before bed every single night is turn off my phone."

She doesn't believe a word that's coming out of my mouth. In all fairness, though, I'm stammering and don't sound very convincing. And she's right—not that I'd admit as much—her phone was turned off.

I shrug. "Weird. Anyway, I will bring Delilah to my room now so you can go back to sleep."

Bree narrows her eyes at me. "Are you sure that's a good idea? I mean, after last night, you don't look like you've slept at all."

Gee, thanks.

"I feel great," I lie. "Look, I appreciate how helpful you've been, but Delilah is my daughter. I want to spend some time with her. I'm going back to work soon, and I want to soak up every moment I have right now." I scoop Delilah from her bassinet, pulling her as close to my chest as humanly possible. She lets out a gentle moan, and my heart squeezes.

Bree has already rolled over in bed with the covers pulled snugly over her head. I hope she sleeps through the next two weeks.

I draw the blinds and shut the door behind me as I leave the room.

I jump at a loud bang from somewhere in the apartment. My heart thumps in my chest. Am I hearing things? *Crash.* No, I'm sure I heard that one. It's coming from the kitchen. Has someone broken into our apartment?

I cautiously make my way down the hallway, cocooning Delilah with my body. I turn the corner into the kitchen, and—*oh my*—Andrew is shirtless in his apron, scrambling eggs. And bacon, I smell bacon sizzling on another burner. My vegetarian husband is frying bacon.

"Andrew?"

He doesn't answer or turn around to look at me, for that matter. Wow, he must still be really angry. But he's dancing, so he can't be that angry. Wait, now he's singing, too. He's actually like the opposite of angry.

My, my—someone is in an awfully good mood, considering what went on here last night. It almost makes me wonder if he had something to do with sabotaging the dinner plans I still don't remember making.

But why poison Marly? It's not like I cheated on him with her.

Suddenly, Andrew flips around, one hand wrapped around the spatula, the other pressed against his chest. "Geez, Lucinda. How long have you been standing there? You scared the crap out of me!" He pulls an AirPod from his ear.

"Sorry, I called your name."

Andrew pulls out the other AirPod. "Right," he says, a smile forming on his lips.

"What are you doing here, anyhow?" I check the clock on the wall. It's 7:00 a.m., on a Saturday, no less. My husband is usually *extra* inspired on the weekends. "Shouldn't you be at the studio already?"

"I decided to take the morning off. I was hoping we could spend some time together as a family."

Spend time together? As a family?

Who are you, and what have you done with my husband?

"So you're not mad?"

"Look, last night was intense," Andrew admits as he turns off the burner. "I said some things I shouldn't have said. And I certainly shouldn't have been more worried about Bree's feelings than yours. But, you've just been so ornery lately…"

I laugh out loud. "Did you just call me ornery?"

He smiles widely. "I know, I probably shouldn't say that to a new mom with all those hormones flowing, but honestly, it feels like we're walking on eggshells around one another."

"Here," he continues. "I'll take Delilah. Please sit down and enjoy the breakfast I made for you. And tea." He places a steaming mug of tea on the table. "You'll need to replenish that milk supply after last night."

"Oh, what a night."

"Marly will be okay," he says, placing a reassuring hand on my shoulder. "Chad said they're releasing her from the hospital this morning."

"You spoke to Chad?"

"Yeah, we were texting all night."

Oh.

I take a large swig of tea, a forkful of bacon and eggs, and then change the subject.

"What did you have in mind for this morning?"

Andrew winks. "You'll just have to wait and see."

CHAPTER 33

Thirty minutes and a quick shower later, I've packed all of Delilah's stuff and am ready to go. *Where?* Of that, I'm not so sure. Andrew has flat-out refused to tell me what the big surprise is. Should I be excited? Afraid? I can't say why, but my stomach is a tangle of knots.

Andrew holds the door open for me, then locks up as we leave the apartment. Today he's trying to woo me. Last night he wanted to kill me. And the guy says I'm moody.

We step into the elevator, and I stare at Andrew's back. He's wearing his paint-splattered jeans (of course), but he has them paired with a form-fitting black tee that showcases the muscles lining his shoulders and torso. It's a shirt you might wear to tend bar or work out. Oh God, is he bringing me on a date to the gym? Is *that* the big surprise? *Heavens no!*

I take a deep breath as the elevator descends to the lobby. As soon as the doors open, I spy Ashton deep in conversation with—*is that?*—I blink my eyes rapidly, convinced I'm seeing things.

Detective O'Brien? What is he doing in the lobby of my building, interrogating my doorman? Okay, so I don't know for a fact he's interrogating him, but still. What am I to think?

We live in an upscale building. There's no crime here—at least, not on the actual premises as far as I know, and not if you consider what happened to Marly last night an accident.

Could I have accidentally bought pine nuts? After thinking about it *all* night, the answer is yes. I guess anything is possible, and I have been discombobulated lately. But, I can't shake the thought that pine nuts are tiny and flat and smooth. Walnuts are like giant, deformed pine nuts. There's really no mistaking one for the other.

Andrew's eyes are glued to his phone, so he doesn't see the scene unfolding. His fingers move rapidly across the screen as he texts with someone. All I have to say about that is it better not be Bree. Though last I left her, she was fast asleep in bed.

I rub a hand across Andrew's back. I'll meet you and Delilah outside in a minute. Okay?"

"Okay, but don't take too long. Your surprise awaits..."

"Can't wait." I try to feign enthusiasm. I wouldn't say I like surprises, especially given the events of the past few weeks. I wish Andrew would just tell me where we're going already. My husband seems to be the only one enjoying this twisted game of foreplay.

Andrew nods and heads out the revolving doors of our building. I march straight over to Ashton and Detective O'Brien.

"Ah, Mrs. Douglass. Just the person I was looking for."

Just what I wanted to hear from a detective, said no one ever.

I look to Ashton for some information or validation—any form of 'ation'—but he shrugs and disappears behind the front desk. Apparently, the king of erroneous observations suddenly has nothing left to say.

"Are you here to see me, Detective? Has there been a development in our case?"

"Yes, I am here to see you. But no, not exactly."

"Okay..."

"A report came in about an event at your apartment last night. I wanted to make sure you and your daughter were okay."

The tension drains from my shoulders.

"How very kind of you," I say. "Our guest—friend—went into anaphylactic shock. It was quite scary, as you might imagine." I'm not sure why I need to keep emphasizing the fact that Marly is our friend. I mean, *is* she? Do you kiss a friend's husband?

"Yes, I imagine it must have been. Were you aware before last night that she had a nut allergy?" Detective O'Brien pulls a notepad from his pocket as he asks this.

So *that's* what this is about. It's not a kindness call. It's a 'did you knowingly or unknowingly send your "friend" into anaphylaxis' visit. Well, shit.

Sweat beads pop along my forehead. I wish the floor would open up right now and swallow me whole. Why am I so gosh darn flustered? Last I checked, serving homemade pesto sauce for dinner guests is not a crime. Especially when you're not the one who made it.

Why oh why did Andrew have to go vegetarian? None of this would ever have happened if I'd just grilled us all a steak. No one in their right mind uses pine nuts to season a steak.

I focus my attention back on Detective O'Brien. "We knew she had an allergy, but I was unaware that we even had pine nuts in the house, let alone used them in the sauce. So, yes, I'd say the whole thing was a very unpleasant surprise. If that's all for now, Detective, my husband is waiting for me with our daughter outside."

"For now." Detective O'Brien jots something else down in his notebook. "I'll be in touch."

The hairs on the back of my neck stand up.

"I hope with some useful information about who tried to abduct my daughter." I turn on my heels and exit my building as quickly as possible. This encounter has me extremely unsettled.

Andrew is waiting outside, as oblivious as ever.

"Everything okay?" he asks.

"Yeah, can we go? I can't wait to see what this big surprise is that you have in store for me."

"There are some ground rules," he tells me as we stand outside our building.

"What kind of ground rules?"

"Well, for starters, you will be blindfolded."

"Blindfolded? You can't be serious."

"As serious as the flu, Lucinda."

THE PERFECT NANNY

I shoot Andrew a side eye. "Fine, blindfolded. Anything else?"

"You have to promise to be one hundred percent completely honest."

A shiver runs down my spine. I nod, fully knowing I can never be one hundred percent completely honest with my husband. Not unless I want Andrew to file for divorce, take me to the cleaners, and fight to take away our beautiful daughter. Nope, that's not happening.

"Well, now that we have that all settled." Andrew lifts a hand and hails a cab. It pulls to the corner, and I slip inside onto the worn leather seat with Delilah. My husband slides in beside us and then passes a piece of paper to the driver with an address on it, I presume.

Then he pulls a blindfold down over my eyes.

CHAPTER 34

We ride to the destination 'who knows where' in mostly silence. And darkness. Complete darkness. Well, I ride in darkness. Andrew can see just fine without a blindfold covering his eyes.

Is this *really* necessary?

The taxi reeks of cigarette smoke, and something sharp is poking me in the back. The driver is speaking to someone in another language. He blabs away, apparently oblivious to the fact that there's a blindfolded passenger in his car. I could literally be getting kidnapped, for goodness' sake!

Worse, we're stuck in some major New York City traffic. The cab jerks back and forward repeatedly, at one point swerving so abruptly that I collide with Andrew. He doesn't ask if I'm okay, which seems odd. Then, what about this current scenario doesn't seem odd?

It isn't easy to gauge how long we're in the cab. Depending on the day, traveling a city block could take between two minutes to two hours. It does feel like a while, though.

I'm starting to get incredibly antsy when the loud squeak of brakes and the impact of tires brushing a curb indicates we've arrived at our destination. I reach up to remove my blindfold, but Andrew stops me, his hand wrapping around my wrist.

"Not yet."

"Seriously?" I ask.

"Seriously. Just a little longer. You trust me, don't you, Lucinda?"

I don't know. *Do I?* Did my husband not sleep with his paralegal?

Andrew pulls Delilah from the cab and slips his hand into mine to guide me onto the sidewalk. He presses his fingers into my back and propels me forward.

"Our first stop, my lady."

Andrew slips the blindfold down my face. It takes a minute for my eyes to adjust to the sunlight. My heart hitches in my chest. *This* is the big surprise? Surely this must be some sort of sick joke.

When I don't say anything, Andrew breaks the awkward-infused silence. "You've been under so much pressure lately. I thought you could use a little R & R."

"At the Wall Street Hotel?"

He smirks. "I booked you a massage. Didn't you used to get massages here when you were working?"

Well, I definitely told him I've gotten a massage here while working. But nope, I've never had one here in my life. In fact, the only time I've been here was when I almost let my anger lead me into making the worst mistake of my life with Chad. I don't know what to say, so I nod and force my lips to form a half-smile.

"This was so thoughtful of you." I nearly choke on the word thoughtful. Because, really, *what* was he thinking? Does he know it was outside this hotel where Chad kissed me? Where we walked hand and hand through the door before I decided I couldn't go through with it, turned back and walked away? Is this the part where I'm supposed to be one hundred percent completely honest?

Andrew glances down at his watch, a Rolex I bought him for our first anniversary as husband and wife. "Massage starts in twenty minutes. You better get in there." He slaps me playfully on the rear, and I jump.

"Wha...what about you and Delilah?"

"I'm going to walk around with her, and then we'll swing back to get you in ninety minutes. Surprise—it's a ninety-minute massage. Already paid for in cash, tip covered."

"Wow, Andrew, thank you. This must have cost a small fortune." I want to ask where he got the cash to pay for this, considering I get an alert for every credit card transaction and ATM withdrawal either of us makes, but I don't.

"We'll pick you up at eleven for surprise number two."

My eyes widen. "There's more?"

"Sure is. Oh heck, I'll tell you that one—lunch at The Loungebook Pearl."

I'm sure all the color drains from my face. I might pass out on the spot.

"What's wrong, Lucinda? Chad told me you love that place."

Oh, did he?

It feels like Andrew knows. Did Marly tell him? Has he known all along?

I take a deep breath. "Really, Andrew, this was so sweet of you to do for me. I can't wait to have lunch with you and Delilah after my massage."

Andrew reaches into Delilah's diaper bag and pulls out my Stanley. "Here, you need to stay hydrated. You should probably drink this before the massage and then ask them to fill it up after."

"Wow, you thought of everything."

"Oh, just one more thing. There must have been something wrong with the computers because they had no record of you in the spa when I came by to book the appointment. So…"

I swallow against the giant lump in my throat.

"The man at the front desk remembered you, though. He said he'd make sure you are well taken care of." Andrew winks, and then his face turns to stone.

Am I imagining things, or did a muscle in his jaw twitch? I bend down and give Delilah a soft kiss goodbye. "Thanks for doing this for me," I manage as I lean in to hug my husband. It's like I'm hanging on a statue.

He pats me on the back, "Enjoy."

I swear, there's something ominous in his tone. As I turn and walk away, I feel Andrew's eyes boring into my back.

How the heck am I supposed to relax now?

Well, at least I've got ninety minutes to figure a way out of this.

CHAPTER 35

My face is pressed into the massage table as a stocky woman named Inga kneads her fists into my back.

"So much tension," she complains in a thick accent. I can't quite place it—Croatian, maybe? Russian? Something Eastern European.

I open my eyes momentarily, staring at her thick-soled, stark white shoes. I bite back a grunt of pain as her thick fingers circle my scapula.

"Inga will get these knots out in no time."

I wish Inga would ease up a little. At this rate, I might not live to see this alleged knot-free existence.

"What kind of massage did my husband book for me?" I ask politely. A finger on the back of my neck confirms now is not the time to be confrontational. Inga could probably pick me up and toss me across the room. Her hands are freakishly strong.

"Deep tissue," she says as she plays my spine like Beethoven on the piano.

"Oh?"

"You no like?" Two hands grip my waist, thumbs poking like knives into my pelvis.

"No, no. I like, I like."

Inga continues rubbing away, and I try to relax. I've never had a deep-tissue massage. It almost feels like a punishment. For the next ninety minutes, Inga pokes and prods me like I'm a practice dummy.

"You come back and visit me again." Inga slaps me on the back. I guess that means the torture is over.

"Yes, most definitely."

Most definitely *not*. Inga couldn't pay me to let her give me another massage. Although, I will say I'm pretty loose right now. But dang, that was painful.

I get dressed and find Inga outside the room, holding my Stanley.

"I filled with water. Drink," she tells me. "A lot today."

"I will."

"You take care." Inga looks like she's about to say something else, but she stops herself. "I go now." She turns away from me and disappears down the hallway.

Well, that was weird.

I find Andrew and Delilah waiting for me in the hotel lobby.

"How was it?" Andrew asks.

"I'm pretty sure at least half of my body is covered now in bruises."

"So, good then?"

I eye him quizzically. "Since when do I get deep tissue massages?"

Andrew chews on his lower lip. "I thought that was what you liked."

"Well, thank you. I do appreciate it." I appreciate the gesture, but I will be whispering Swedish in Andrew's ear while he sleeps so I don't get another one of these bad boys for our anniversary.

"Are you hungry?" he asks.

"Starving, actually. You?"

"Famished. Delilah and I must have walked fifty blocks while you were in there. Well, I walked—she got to enjoy the ride. Didn't you, little munchkin?" Andrew smiles at Delilah, and my heart melts as I watch her smile back. I'd love to tell Bree what she can do with her gas right about now.

Despite the agony I felt while on the massage table and the trauma of last night, I'm feeling somewhat relaxed now. I hope Andrew left Inga a nice tip. And if he didn't, let's pray I never run into the woman in a dark alley.

"Shall we?" Andrew asks, motioning toward the awning at the front of the hotel.

"Does Delilah need to eat?" I check the time on my watch—11:10 a.m. Delilah usually nurses at eleven on the dot. But she seems awfully content right now.

"I gave her a bottle so we could enjoy our lunch. Now let's go."

He really did think of everything.

I follow Andrew from the hotel onto the sidewalk, my husband pushing the stroller. We're about to cross the street when his arm slaps back against my chest. A car speeds through the intersection, nearly running me over. It honks its horn loudly as I jump back onto the sidewalk. And there goes the relaxation. My heart threatens to rip through my chest.

"Holy crap," I say as I gasp for air. "I literally almost just got hit by a car."

"That was close," Andrew agrees. "Remember what Detective O'Brien said? You really need to pay attention to your surroundings, Lucinda."

"I do? But I was—"

"You had your face buried in your phone." He motions toward the phone in my hand that I don't recall taking out.

Good God, what did Inga do to me?

The crosswalk turns green, and we walk uneventfully across the street. When we arrive at The Loungebook Pearl, my heart rate has almost returned to normal. Andrew holds open the door for me and then pushes Delilah through the frame.

Wild, it was just yesterday that I sat here with Chad. Before the incriminating picture showed up on my doorstep, before Marly went into anaphylaxis, before the threatening texts from Chad's phone…

Speak of the devil. I scan the restaurant, and—what do you know—Chad is sitting at our table by the window overlooking the Hudson River. His eyes lift from the menu, and he waves us over.

Um, did I miss something here? I look at Andrew, like, *what the heck?*

"Oops. Did I forget to tell you I bumped into Chad while Delilah and I were walking around? I invited him to join us for lunch. You don't mind, do you?"

Yup. Completely forgot to tell me.

I shake my head because what the hell am I supposed to say? Chad is just about one of the *last* people I want to see after last night.

"What's up, man?" Chad fist pumps Andrew and then motions to the seat across from him. Andrew sits down while I awkwardly lean my hands on the stroller. I know what I said before, but *I* would pay a million dollars to be back on Inga's table.

"Hey, Chad. How is Marly doing?" My voice comes out as a squeak.

"She's resting. Naturally, she had to cancel all of her yoga classes for the day. The doctors said she was fortunate. It was one of the most stubborn cases of anaphylaxis they'd ever seen. Must have been a heck of a lot of pine nuts in there." He narrows his eyes at me.

"The recipe called for a quarter cup, but I didn't make the sauce, so I have no idea what was in there." I jut out my lower lip. How many times is this guy going to make me admit I didn't make the sauce?

"Right," Chad says. "Anyway, she should be okay physically, though she's pretty traumatized, as you might imagine."

I nod my head in understanding. "I'll reach out to her later to check in."

"Yeah, about that—"

"What is it?"

"Marly is pretty upset. I don't think you're the person she wants to hear from. Give her some time."

I think about her texts from last night, and then I look at my husband with a hand curled into a fist on his lap.

Because if Marly knows…

CHAPTER 36

Lunch is incredibly awkward—for me, at least. Andrew and Chad chat while I pick at my Caesar salad, moving the lettuce and croutons around on my plate like a sand mandala painting.

I get this strange feeling that someone is watching me. I glance up from my impressive, green-leafed creation to find Chad and Andrew staring—not at me, but at each other.

Someone is watching *me*, though. I'm sure of it. My gaze flicks around the restaurant. I'm not imagining the creepy sensation crawling up my spine.

No, really, I'm not. The same bartender from yesterday has his gaze steeled in my direction. He's just staring at me. But then he waves me over to the bar, so it's a little less creepy. Slightly.

"I'm going to go grab a drink. Do you guys want anything?"

Andrew and Chad shake their heads and continue discussing the latest Star Wars release. Chad pulls up his sleeve and points to the small Chewbacca tattoo he got inked during a blackout-drunk night in college. We should be okay so long as he doesn't pull down his pants and flash the one on his left butt cheek. *Men.*

My legs tremble as I make my way to the bar. The bartender obviously remembers me from yesterday. Why else would he wave me over?

"Lucinda Douglass, right?" he asks as I approach the bar.

"In the flesh." I laugh, but it comes out more like a strained cackle. It's not funny that he remembers me. And I'm about to find out just how unfunny it is.

"I was hoping you'd come back. I wanted to talk, you know, about what you asked me."

Every muscle in my body instantly tightens—like a full-body charley horse.

He continues. "I'll admit, I was skeptical yesterday, when you approached me. But, it turns out you were right. Not more than a minute after you left, a man sitting at the bar started asking questions about you."

My jaw drops, but no words fall out.

"I got a picture on my phone. It's not great, but would you like to look?"

My eyes widen as I nod. Of course, I want to take a look. That goes without saying, doesn't it?

The bartender grabs his phone off the cash register. He flicks through a few pictures and then hands it over to me.

He wasn't kidding that the picture isn't great. It's super grainy and blurred, as if the man in it was jogging in place while the bartender captured his image. While I don't think I've ever seen him before, I can't be sure. Because again, the picture is *that* bad. All I can make out is a mop of brown hair and dark orbs for eyes.

This is not helpful at all. It's like the opposite of helpful. Still, I zoom back out and take one last look at the picture.

And that's when I see it. Well, *her*. A chill runs through me, turning the blood in my veins to ice. The phone slips from my fingers, landing face-up on the bar top.

I may not know the man asking the bartender questions about me. But I do know the person sitting two seats down. Why did Bree follow me here yesterday? And then claim she never left the apartment?

Did *she* take the picture of Chad and me?

I take a deep breath and pick the phone back up. The bartender reaches out to grab it, but I stop short of giving it back to him. My legs wobble beneath me, and I collapse onto a barstool, still gripping his phone tightly in my hand. I blink my eyes rapidly as if to reset, to prove to myself that I'm not seeing things. I kind of wish I were. But, I'm not. I'm most definitely not. The photo is still there, exactly as I saw it the first time around.

Bree was in this restaurant watching me while I ate lunch with Chad.

"Would you mind if I sent myself a copy of this picture?"

"Just do it quickly," he says. "I need to get back to work." He motions with his chin toward a businessman at the opposite end of the bar with his arms crossed angrily in front of his chest as he waits for a drink.

I hit the send button and type in my phone number. I thank the bartender profusely and try to compose myself as I walk back to the table.

My insides are shaking. What should I do? Is this the point that I tell Andrew?

My husband looks up as I approach the table, and I want to confide in him; I do, but—

"Where's your drink?"

"My what?"

"Your drink...the one you went to the bar ten minutes ago to get." He crosses his arms across his chest.

What was I thinking? I can't tell this guy anything.

Jenna. I need to talk to Jenna. She'll say, *I told you so*, and probably gloat for a hot minute, but at least I can trust her. I certainly can't trust either of the two men staring at me, waiting for an answer.

"I drank it at the bar. Figured I'd let you two enjoy your journey to outer space together."

Andrew rolls his eyes. "Well, we've just arrived back on Earth, so your timing is impeccable."

"I got this," Chad says as he pulls out his wallet.

"Are you sure? It feels like we should be treating you after last night. Like we owe you a meal." Andrew gives me a side eye as he says this.

For the love of God, I didn't make the freaking sauce!

"Stop, it was an accident." Chad slips his credit card into the leather bill holder and hands it to the waiter who has come to refresh our drinks. I wish I had *actually* gotten one at the bar.

"Well, thank you, man. It was nice seeing you. Please, send Marly our best."

"You know I will."

I offer a weak smile. "I hope she feels all better soon."

"I'm sure you do." Chad's voice drips with sarcasm. The guy actually thinks I tried to poison his wife. It shouldn't be awkward at all when I go back to work.

"Lucinda?" Andrew's fingers dig into my elbow. "Who are you talking to?"

"What?"

"You were saying something." Andrew's eyebrows bend toward one another as he regards me quizzically.

"I…I…"

"Let's just go," he says, shaking his head.

I'm so confused. *Was* I saying something?

I nod anyway and follow Andrew out of the restaurant. He hails a cab, but he doesn't bother with the blindfold this time. The honeymoon phase of this date seems to have come to an end. Oh who am I kidding? One could argue it ended the minute Inga pressed a knuckle into my cervical spine.

I take a long swig of water as I stare out the window of our yellow cab.

I wonder where he's taking me now.

But more than that, I can't help but wonder why I was talking to myself.

CHAPTER 37

MANY YEARS AGO

My home life was awful, but school had become downright unbearable. Over the course of a few weeks, I had single-handedly become the butt of everyone's jokes. It was almost as if the school board called a meeting at which they gave the students and teachers carte blanche to torture me in any way they could.

It wasn't like I was popular in any capacity before I came back to school. But at least back then, I was invisible. When you're invisible, you're off the radar. I could live with being off these people's radars instead of being the at the center of their ridicule.

The rumors flying around were ridiculous, one crazier than the next, yet no one seemed to be doing anything to stop them. A few: I talked to myself (and answered), I had lice and scabies (or cooties as some of the kids called it), and—this one was my personal favorite—I was running a meth lab from my home. I swear, kids stared at me in the hallways as if I was the bearded lady at a carnival.

And the teachers. It was as if they were afraid of me, all because of those stupid little rumors and the horrible haircut Judy gave me (she should definitely quit her day job) that lent me the appearance of a horror movie doll. Think Annabelle meets Chuckie.

It wasn't just the rumors, though. It was the suggestions (threats). I should disappear. I was better off dead. I should kill myself. Maybe one day someone would do me a favor and kill me themselves. I was beginning to think they were right. Everyone at school hated me.

I started carrying a pair of Judy's scissors in my backpack for protection. I wondered if she noticed they were gone. If she suspected it was me who had stolen them. The way she looked at me, I'd guess that the answer to both of those questions was yes.

Judy was watching me like a freaking hawk.

My father, meanwhile, seemed to be avoiding me like the plague. I couldn't get him alone, no matter how hard I tried. And I tried. I really tried. Somehow, Judy was always there.

But then, when I couldn't take another minute of it all, I met Dougie. I noticed him staring at me one day in the cafeteria, but not in a, *you have bugs crawling in your hair*, or *I'm looking to score meth* sort of way. Those were the looks I'd grown accustomed to. This was different. Dougie looked like he actually wanted to talk to me.

And then he did.

The bell rang, and Dougie approached my table, where I was *shockingly* sitting alone.

"Are you busy?" he asked.

I shook my head, unable to find my voice to answer him.

"I've seen you around. Do you talk?" The corners of his mouth lifted into a smile. I never noticed how incredibly good-looking he was, though every other girl in the school had if one were to judge by the etchings on the toilet stalls in all the girls' bathrooms.

"Yes, I talk," I managed.

It didn't matter what I said because I must have been dreaming. The hottest guy in our school, talking to me. *Me.* I so did not want to wake up from this dream like ever.

For some stupid reason, I pinched my arm, but to my surprise, Dougie was still standing there with a hopeful grin on his face.

"So what do you say?"

Not a daydream. Dougie was definitely talking to me, and I definitely wasn't listening. But I couldn't exactly admit that to the football team's quarterback, could I?

He probably asked for my help with homework. That was the only reason this guy would talk to me. I was such a loser, I must have been brilliant, right? Truthfully, I couldn't have cared less if that were the case. Dougie could have asked me to streak across campus, and I'd probably have done it. He was that hot, and I was that lonely. "Um, sure."

"That's great," he said, smiling at me with perfectly straight teeth. I smiled back, waiting for him to give me a clue as to what I just agreed to. "So I'll pick you up around seven?"

"Seven is perfect." I scribbled my address on a cafeteria napkin. Dougie gave me one long, last, lingering look before walking away.

I was filled with a sense of both excitement and dread. Was I going on an actual date with Dougie? Or would I be doing his homework tonight? And how would he react to discovering I was not nearly as bright as he thought I was?

Oh God, what did I just agree to?

CHAPTER 38

We are standing outside Andrew's building on Astor Place. I've been here twice since Andrew signed the lease. One of those times was when Andrew signed the lease. Well, technically, when I signed the lease.

And the other time is now.

It was not for a lack of interest, initially. I asked Andrew multiple times if I could come take a look around when he first opened up shop. But he was never 'ready' when I broached the subject of coming to visit his studio. So, I eventually stopped broaching it.

I guess he's finally ready. My husband has been hot and cold today, but this is a lovely gesture. It's been a whole year since he embarked on his artistic adventure, and this is literally the first time he's expressed any interest in sharing his work with me.

As I push Delilah's stroller toward the front door of the building, I stop in my tracks. I hear the distinctive crunch of glass beneath her Bugaboo tires. My eyes find the concrete. There's broken glass everywhere.

"Andrew?" My husband is busy fumbling around in his pockets for his keys. His paint-splattered jeans have an excessive number of pockets, like clown pants.

"I'm working on it," he says, sounding annoyed.

"Look down."

He looks up at me. *I said down!*

"What now, Lucinda?"

"Look down, Andrew. There's glass all over the sidewalk."

Andrew looks down, surveying the shards of glass scattered on the sidewalk. There's no broken bottle or anything else obvious to explain its presence. My husband's eyes scan the area, then shoot back up to the front of the building as he searches for the source.

"Holy shit. Look." His finger stretches up to the awning of his building.

And there it is—the source of the glass. The camera and lights above the entryway are completely shattered, as if hit with a baseball bat.

"The security camera?" I ask, eyeing Andrew suspiciously. I mean, *is* he surprised? Is this why he so willingly passed the information about his building having security cameras along to Detective O'Brien? Because his activities literally couldn't be verified, but couldn't *not* be verified at the same time. How convenient.

Maybe Andrew wasn't at his studio all day when Delilah was almost abducted. But then, where was he? *Who* was he with?

No, that's crazy. Someone would have swept up the glass over the past week. Wouldn't they? My eyes dart to the neighboring building on the left. There's no glass there. And to the right—as clean as a New York City street can be.

My head is spinning. Like, I'm actually dizzy. Inga warned me I needed to drink after the beating I took at her hands. I take a long swig of water.

"What do you think happened?" I ask.

"Probably some drunk homeless guy thought it would be funny to knock out some lights."

"And a CCTV camera?"

"Why are you fixated on the camera, Lucinda?"

Hmm, let's see…because I fear my husband is hiding something from me? There are plenty of people married to sociopaths who are none the wiser. Could I be one of them? Crime Junkie could run a podcast on this. No one's dead (yet), but Marly almost died last

THE PERFECT NANNY

night. And doesn't it seem like we're headed in that direction? *Ashley Flowers? Britt?*

"Fixated? It's a question, Andrew. Do you have any idea how much those security cameras cost?"

"Not now, Lucinda. NOT NOW," Andrew says tightly. Geez, it was just an observation.

Every fiber in my being is screaming to hail a taxi or call an Uber and get out of here. But then, Andrew finally fishes the keys out of some hidden pocket and unlocks the lobby door.

"Shall we?"

I peek into the building before stepping inside. It looks untouched—just a small, well-worn entryway with mailboxes leading into a narrow hallway with apartments on either side.

Maybe it was just a drunk homeless person wreaking havoc outside the building...

I follow Andrew to his studio at the rear of the building. I don't know why, but my heart hitches in my chest as his key turns in the door.

And then he opens it.

And...

"Oh, my God." I freeze in place, my legs unable to move. I've never seen anything like this. There are pictures of *me* wallpapering all four walls of Andrew's studio. Photos I don't remember taking because I didn't know they were being taken. There are pictures of me on the street, subway, in Central Park, outside The Loungebook Pearl, and, coming in and out of the Wall Street Hotel.

Andrew's studio looks like the home of a stalker. Or a serial killer. Or a jilted husband who is both of the above.

I'm going to be sick. I hold a hand over my mouth and gag, but nothing comes up.

Andrew reaches out, and I jump back. He flicks on a light switch, illuminating the small space. Good God, I'm *everywhere*. There are even pictures of me lining the ceiling. He would have had to have used a ladder to reach the ceiling.

It gets worse, if that's even possible. There are pictures of me with Chad—walking too close, hugging, kissing. Andrew knows. He's known all along. And now he's going to…

Do nothing, apparently.

I caution a glance at my husband. He's staring at the walls with the same dumbfounded expression I must have.

"What is this?" I manage.

"I have no idea."

"Don't you?"

"You think I did this to my *own* studio?" He advances farther into the room, surveying the pictures on the walls, which have been smeared with—oh jeez, is that blood?

"Who else did this? You want a divorce? Fine. I'll give you a divorce. Seriously, whatever you want. This is just…*sick*. You can keep the apartment, but please don't hurt me and Delilah." I instinctively position myself in front of Delilah's stroller and raise my arms to protect my head and face.

Before I know it, Andrew's hands are on my shoulders. On my neck. Oh God, he's going to strangle me. He's literally going to strangle me to death. I'm going to die in a room while I watch myself dying in a room because I'm freaking everywhere.

I start hyperventilating. I can't catch my breath. It's as if I'm inhaling through a straw.

"Don't do this," I gasp. "Please, don't do this."

"Lucinda, calm down. I'm mad as hell right now, but I'm not going to hurt you." Andrew drops his head into his hands. "I don't understand how you could do something like this to me. And with Chad of all people."

I guess he's not going to kill me. Well, that's a relief.

"It's not as bad as it looks," I say. "And if you want me to be one hundred percent honest with you, you're going to have to do the same. Starting with telling the truth…Do you promise you didn't do this?" I motion around the room.

"I promise I didn't do this."

My pulse slowly returns to normal

He didn't do this.

So who did?

CHAPTER 39

MANY YEARS AGO

When I was about nine, Mom taught me how to sew. We started with a traditional needle and thread but worked up to a sewing machine. I was surprisingly good at it, too. Mom trusted me enough to let me hem all my siblings' pants. With so many siblings, as you might imagine, it kept me quite busy.

Mom wrapped up her sewing machine on my eleventh birthday and gifted it to me to keep in my bedroom. She bought me an overflowing box of fabrics and threads and told me to have at it. I spent six months making anything I could think of—pillows, teddy bears, Barbie Doll clothes, you name it.

I thought of her all these years later as I sat on the closet floor making a dress. Because—wait for it—Dougie asked me out on another date. Not just any date. But to prom! Little old me was going to the prom with the hottest guy at my school. I know, right? I couldn't believe it either.

In all fairness, I would have preferred not to make my own dress. Who wants to make their own prom dress, right? Okay, someone might want to make their own prom dress, but not me. I wanted to buy something sparkly and get my makeup and hair (which had somewhat grown back) done. You only get asked to prom by the hottest guy on the planet once in a lifetime if you're lucky.

But of course, Judy had other ideas. I overheard her saying as much to my dad. "David, something is seriously wrong here. How do you not see it?"

"See what, Judy?"

"Why would the football captain, who could have any girl he wanted, ask her to prom?"

"I guess he likes her."

"Likes her? Please, do you honestly believe that he likes her? No one likes her." Ouch. "I'm telling you, I don't feel good about this."

"I can make you feel good, baby." Cue the part where I threw up in my mouth.

Judy refused to participate in this 'charade,' as she called it, so I was on my own preparing for prom. She had tossed most of Mom's stuff when she died, but I had a secret stash of dresses that my mother gave me to always remember her by (as if she knew something untoward might happen to her). I picked a pink satin dress and spent all night nipping and tucking.

When I slipped the dress over my head, it fit like a glove, hugging my chest and hips, with a large slit exposing one long leg. For the first time, possibly ever, I looked good. Like really good. So good, I would date me.

People were beginning to notice, too. Girls started talking to me (instead of making fun of me) at school. And the boys were all looking at me differently as if overnight I'd transformed from an ugly duckling into a beautiful swan, just as my mother had said I would.

Dougie sat with me every day at lunch. We talked about school (not once did he ask me for help with his homework!) and the prom. He was even more excited than I was.

"Did you get a dress?" he asked one day as I picked at my cafeteria lunch of peas and carrots.

"I did." Naturally, I didn't mention the part where I made it myself.

"What color is it, you know, so I can get a matching tie?" I noticed him folding his hands in his lap. It occurred to me that I didn't know Dougie's favorite color yet. Things were so new between us.

Should I have asked him before I said yes to (making) the dress? Oh boy...

"Hot pink." I gritted my teeth, worried he would disapprove.

Dougie breathed a long, deep sigh of relief. "As long as it's not red. I hate the color red.

So did I, ever since I cleaned my mother's blood off our living room carpet and got my ketchup period that day at school. I wondered if he was thinking the same thing—the second part, at least.

"Well, do you like hot pink?"

"I love hot pink. I'm sure you'll look beautiful."

"If you keep talking like that, my cheeks may match my dress."

Dougie laughed and slipped his arm around my shoulder. I could feel all eyes in the cafeteria on us as we stared at one another.

Was this the moment? Would Dougie lean in and give me my first kiss?

My heart raced in my chest, so powerful I could feel it in my neck.

Thump. Thump. Thump.

I licked my lips and tilted my head slightly back—signs, I read, that you wanted someone to kiss you. And I wanted Dougie to kiss me. Oh God, did I want him to kiss me.

His face inched closer to mine, hovering above my lips. I closed my eyes as he leaned in, but then out of nowhere, he abruptly pushed me back.

What the...

I opened my eyes, which had instantly filled with hot tears. Dougie was staring down at the table now, refusing to meet my gaze. I looked up and immediately saw what had him spooked.

The principal stood inches from us with her hands on her hips. "I'm going to need you to come to my office," she said, eyes laser-focused on me.

"To your office? But why? I didn't do anything," I protested. At least, I didn't do anything *yet*. I wasn't sure what the rules were on PDA in the school cafeteria, but nothing had happened, thanks to her untimely interruption, so it seemed like a moot point.

"I don't think you want to do this here." The principal spoke through her teeth with her jaw clenched tightly.

"But, but—"

She rolled her eyes. "I guess you *do* want to do this here. I searched your locker on a tip."

"Okay? And?"

"We found the knife."

I nearly choked on my saliva. "I'm sorry, did you say *knife?* There must be some sort of misunderstanding. I don't have a knife."

She shook her head at me, her expression cold and hard. "Do I need the school resource officer to escort you to my office, or are you going to come willingly?"

I looked over to Dougie to explain, but he was gone.

"Okay," I said, rising on shaky legs from my seat. "Let's just go."

CHAPTER 40

We realize quickly that it's not blood, despite the multiple gouge wounds in the wall that according to Andrew weren't there before. Yes, you read that correctly—there are literal gouge wounds in the wall. I'm no Dexter, but it looks like the assault weapon was some sort of knife. And whoever did this grabbed a can (or three) of red paint and went to town. The whole scene is very Carrie meets the Manson Family. I wrap my arms around my body and shiver.

"Don't touch anything," Andrew says. "We need to call the police. This is a crime scene."

Sure as hell looks like one.

My fingers instinctively find Detective O'Brien's card in my pocket. As much as I did not appreciate his intimations about my dinner party earlier, I believe he's best equipped to investigate this vandalism. The events of the past two weeks are obviously connected. Someone is clearly out to get us. Or maybe just me.

Who? Why? Million-dollar questions.

I regard my husband carefully, examining his face. I'm not going to lie—a part of me hopes that if Andrew wasn't in his studio the day Delilah was abducted, Detective O'Brien will put two and two together when he sees the damage done to the CCTV camera.

Not that my husband would have tried to stab his own studio to death. *Would* he?

He'd have to be pretty mad. *Wall gouging by reason of temporary insanity?* My eyes hone in on a picture of Chad and me outside the Wall Street Hotel with his arm swung around my shoulders. Yeah, I'd say Andrew must be pretty mad.

How mad? I'll leave that to the detective to figure out.

I hand the business card to my husband. "Here, call Detective O'Brien. His cellphone number is on the back."

Andrew nods and takes the card. As he punches the numbers into the phone, he tells me, "You should take Delilah home. I'll deal with this. We can talk about what's going on with you and Chad when I get home."

"There's nothing going on with Chad and me. I swear, Andrew, it was one kiss. A stupid mistake. I saw the pictures of you and your paralegal and I just... I lost it, okay. But nothing else happened between us."

Speaking the words out loud unleashes a giant weight from my shoulders. Unfortunately, it settles on my chest.

"Pictures of me and my paralegal?" Andrew's eyebrows shoot up. "Like from our website? What the hell are you talking about Lucinda? God, for once in your life can you please just take responsibility for your actions?"

I open my mouth to speak, but Andrew isn't done.

"You're my wife and I love you, but I cannot stand to look at you right now. So please, just leave." He turns his back to me. His shoulders are shaking.

He seriously thinks I'm going to just *leave*? I narrow my eyes on him. No, sir, I am not going anywhere. Other than outside to make a call.

When I'm safely out in the open outside of Andrew's building, I pull out my cell phone and hit the speed dial. Jenna's phone goes straight to voicemail.

So, I call the next person on my list. Thankfully, she picks up after the first ring.

"Hello?"

"Hi, it's Lucinda. I need a favor. I'm down at Andrew's studio. We're dealing with something here. Could you possibly come grab Delilah?"

"Of course, I can. Address?"

I give her the address and details.

Twenty minutes later, Ms. Randall shows up at Andrew's building.

Come on; you didn't think I would actually call Bree?

"Hi, dear," she says, smiling widely as I open the door to the building. "Well, hello there, little cutie pie." She trains her eyes on Delilah.

"Thank you so much for doing this. I can't even begin to tell you how much I appreciate it. I will pay you well for this."

Ms. Randall tuts, "I don't care about the money, dear. After everything you've been through. I feel terrible for you. I'm just glad I had the day off."

"So am I, Ms. Randall, so am I."

Even though I said I wasn't going to, I called Ms. Randall after our chance encounter in the street. I filled her in on our current nanny situation and Delilah's near abduction. She told me to let her know if I needed anything. It turns out she meant it.

"I'll take her back to my place, and you just call me when you have everything sorted out here."

I pass her Delilah's diaper bag. "Really, thank you. From the bottom of my heart. You're a real-life Mary Poppins."

All that's missing is the umbrella. I kiss Delilah goodbye and close the door behind them.

I pause in the hallway and pull out my phone to try Jenna again. I haven't heard from her all day. It goes straight to voicemail again. I leave her a message:

Where are you? I'm starting to worry. Call me when you get this. It's important.

I walk back into the studio to find Andrew slumped in the corner of the room, his knees pulled tightly into his chest.

"Andrew?"

He starts at the sound of his name. Then he looks at me and shakes his head. "This whole situation is so fucked up."

Is he talking about Chad and me, his studio, or a combination of the two?

I move closer cautiously. Someone stabbed the walls. And Andrew sure does have an awful lot of pockets in those pants. Could he be carrying a knife? "Incredibly disturbing," I add.

He nods in agreement, looking incredibly disturbed.

You'd have to be an actual psychopath to do something like this. I've known Andrew for fifteen years. You can't very well hide psychopath, can you? If his inability to hide his affair is any indication...

I take a seat next to my husband on the floor. "What did you want to show me since it obviously wasn't this?" I gesture a hand around the room.

"I finally finished the project I've been working on. And the big surprise is that I have an exhibition at a gallery in Soho tomorrow night."

"Shut up!" I slap Andrew on the chest.

His lips turn up. "I saw the look on your face when I told Bree I'd bring her to the studio. I felt bad. I never offered to bring you to my studio. But it's not what you think. The truth is your opinion mattered to me more than anyone's. I just wanted everything to be perfect. Things have been so tense between us, I wanted you to be proud of me."

It's the most beautiful thing my husband has ever said to me. But, "*Mattered*?"

"I'm not sure how I feel right now."

He can't be serious. Andrew is the one who cheated first. Does he honestly think I have no idea?

I guess he's not thinking about that right now as his fingers trace a photo of me French kissing Chad. It's a closeup. Whoever took this must have used a telephoto lens. Oh God, you can actually see our tongues.

"So, how *do* you explain this, Lucinda?"

I swallow the lump in my throat. "I can explain..." said every philandering spouse ever.

"I'm listening."

I'm about to lay it all on the table but am interrupted by the front door buzzer. Saved by the bell, though, the truth is quite literally staring us both in the face. There's no more stuffing our issues in a drawer, where we don't have to talk about them.

"I'll get it." I scramble to my feet. I'm not staying alone in this room. It's creepy as hell.

I find Detective O'Brien standing outside the building with his eyes trained on the awning where the CCTV camera used to be. As I open the door, he lowers his gaze to meet mine.

"Twice in one day," he says. "You are certainly keeping me on my toes, Mrs. Douglass."

He isn't kidding.

"I'd rather not be keeping you on your toes," I reply, stating the obvious.

Detective O'Brien nods in understanding. "So what do we think happened here?" He points to where the camera used to be and then down to the ground, where glass and metal fragments litter the sidewalk.

"I was hoping you could tell me, Detective. It's a hundred times worse inside."

Detective O'Brien pulls his cellphone from his khaki pants and snaps pictures of the building and sidewalk. "Okay, let's see what's happening in there."

"Can I ask you a question first?" I ask.

"Have at it."

"The security camera. Were you able to view the foot—"

"Detective O'Brien." I freeze mid-sentence. Damn it. Talk about impeccable timing.

"Mr. Douglass."

"You've gotta take a look inside, now. You're not going to believe this." Detective O'Brien shrugs and mouths *sorry*. Then he follows Andrew into the building and down the hallway to his studio.

My lingering questions about my husband will have to wait.

CHAPTER 41

"So let me make sure I have this straight. You're telling me this is *not* your doing?"

"Of course not. I've already told you that like twenty times." Andrew paces his eight-by-eight studio, raking a hand through his hair. "Someone broke in here and defiled my studio."

Detective O'Brien walks the room's perimeter, pausing at the door. He slips on a plastic glove and runs a finger along the wood before bending down to examine the lock. "There are no signs of forced entry whatsoever, Mr. Douglass."

Andrew's face turns bright red, and a rather large vein throbs in his neck. "Maybe I forgot to lock the door?"

"How long have you lived in the city, Mr. Douglass?"

"I don't know, like two decades or so."

"And you forgot to lock the door to your ground-floor studio apartment?"

"Okay, fine. I probably locked the door to the apartment. But I have no idea how someone could have gotten in."

"Does anyone else have a key?"

Andrew's face goes sheet white as he turns to look at me. Detective O'Brien follows suit.

"Lucinda," Andrew says through gritted teeth. "Lucinda has a copy of the key."

Both men stare at me as if I'm the one who broke in, posted incriminating pictures of myself all over the studio, splatter-painted them in what looks like blood, and then stabbed the walls for good measure. We can't forget about that. "You think *I* did this? Why the hell would *I* do this?"

"I'm not sure what I think yet. But I would like to see your key."

"Fine, of course. Whatever I can do to help." I reach for my bag but remember I don't have it. "Shit, I don't have my bag. My babysitter took it."

Detective O'Brien consults his notes. "Miss Bree Miller?"

"Well, no…"

"What do you mean *no*?" Andrew interjects. "I thought you sent Delilah home with Bree. Who has our baby, Lucinda?"

"Relax, Andrew. Her name is Ms. Randall. She's one of the nannies I initially interviewed."

"One of the nannies you initially interviewed and *didn't* hire," Andrew tuts. "Oh God, is that the soap lady? You gave our baby to the soap lady?"

"Who is the soap lady?" Detective O'Brien asks, but neither of us is listening to him.

"It is, but she's not a soap lady. Not actually, anyway. Someone called her before the interview and told her I wanted someone super strict. It's a long story. Anyway, I know you don't want to hear this, but I suspect Bree was behind it. I don't know why she wanted to work for us so badly…"

Andrew throws his hands up in exasperation. "*Bree?* Why would Bree engineer a soap story? Seriously, what the hell are you talking about? I'm really starting to question your judgment, Lucinda."

"Says the guy who may have left the door of his ground-floor studio apartment in Greenwich Village unlocked."

I take a long sip of my drink, aware that Detective O'Brien's eyeballs are ping-ponging between me and my husband. He does not look pleased. "Should I leave you two alone, or do you want to let me do my job and try to figure out who did this?"

My cheeks redden. "Of course. I'll call, okay?"

I dial Ms. Randall's number and put the phone on speaker.

"Hello?" she answers on the second ring. I immediately hear Delilah cooing happily in the background. I breathe a sigh of relief.

"Sorry to bother you, but I may have left my keys in Delilah's diaper bag. Would you mind checking for me?"

"Of course not, dear. Hold on a second."

There's the shuffle of feet and what sounds like the contents of my diaper bag being poured out on a table.

"Are you there, Mrs. Douglass?"

"Yes, I'm here. Do you have the keys?"

"I'm sorry, but they're not here. I dumped the entire bag and checked every pocket."

"Well, thank you for looking. I'll let you know when I'm en route to collect Delilah."

"You be safe, Mrs. Douglass."

"I'll certainly try."

I hang up the phone and shrug my shoulders.

"Where are your keys, Mrs. Douglass?" Detective O'Brien taps his booted foot on the floor. *Tap. Tap. Tap.* It's as if we're at a dance recital. I'm not the only one whose patience is wearing thin.

"I honestly have no idea where my keys are."

"Could you have mistakenly left them at home?"

I mull that over momentarily and then shake my head. "No. They are always in my diaper bag. I don't typically leave the house without Delilah."

"Who could have accessed your keys since you last had them?"

I consider my company last night. "Chad, Marly, Jenna, Bree, and Andrew."

Andrew crosses his arms across his chest. "Really, Lucinda? Why would I take your keys? That's the most absurd thing I've ever heard. I have my own keys."

"Detective O'Brien asked who had access to my keys. You were in our apartment last night, too. Weren't you?"

"This is ridiculous. I can't with you."

"You can't with me?"

"Enough!" Detective O'Brien's deep voice reverberates in the small space. Andrew and I both go completely silent. "I don't want to hear another word from either of you."

He unclips a walkie-talkie from the waistband of his pants.

"Detective O'Brien here. I need a forensics team down on Astor Place ASAP." He rattles off the address and then reaffixes the walkie-talkie to his pants next to his big, black gun.

"While we wait," he tells us, "I would like to interview each of you individually. Mr. Douglass, can I ask you to step outside the building while I speak with your wife?"

"But this is my—"

"We can do this the easy way, or I can take you both down to the station. Your choice, sir."

"Fine." Andrews stomps out of the studio and down the hallway onto the street, leaving me alone with Detective O'Brien.

"Before you start interviewing me, can we finish the conversation we were having outside before my husband interrupted?"

"Go ahead."

"Were you able to access the footage from the security camera the day Delilah was almost kidnapped? I don't think Andrew had anything to do with it, but..."

"But what, Mrs. Douglass?"

"Well, seeing the camera destroyed like that just made me wonder, is all. I guess I'm becoming a bit paranoid." I laugh unconvincingly.

"No, I don't believe you are paranoid at all. I spoke to the landlord, and that security camera has been inoperative for months. He said most, if not all, of the tenants were aware of this."

So Andrew knew all along that there would be no footage.

The room spins. And then it all goes black.

CHAPTER 42

MANY YEARS AGO

"I'll go much easier on you if you're honest. Why did you bring a knife to school?"

I sat in the principal's office with my arms wrapped tightly around my body. She had begun questioning me after calling my father and then, unable to reach him, Judy. According to the principal, Judy was on her way to get me. My cooperation in this matter could mean the difference between suspension and expulsion.

My status at school was the least of my problems. I shuddered to think of what Judy would do when she got her hands on me. She butchered my hair just for running my fingers through it to dislodge a knot. The woman was mentally deranged.

Still, I hadn't done anything wrong. Certainly not what they were accusing me of.

"I swear, I did not bring a knife to school. Where would I even get a knife?"

The principal raised an eyebrow and leaned across her desk. "I don't know. Maybe your kitchen?"

Thanks, Captain Obvious.

"I'm just saying I did not bring that to school. I promise you. Things have been going really well for me lately. I'd have no reason to hurt anyone."

"Are you saying you had a reason to hurt someone before things were going quote-unquote really well for you?"

She was twisting my words. "No, that's not what I'm saying. I'm just—I'm happy. Happiest I've ever been. Happy people don't carry around kitchen knives."

"If you didn't bring the knife, how did you know it was a kitchen knife?"

"Didn't you just say—"

She cut me off, no pun intended.

"We cannot afford to treat matters like this lightly. You brought a weapon to school. Someone could have gotten seriously hurt, regardless of your intentions."

"But I didn't—"

"The knife was in *your* backpack in *your* locker. Are you telling me someone planted it there and then tipped us off? Do you honestly expect me to believe that?"

"Yes, I honestly expect you to believe that, because it's the God's honest truth!"

A knock on the door interrupted our conversation.

"Mrs. Wallace?" The principal's secretary Rhonda stuck her chubby face through the door frame. I'd seen quite a bit of her this past year. More than I'd liked. I was somewhat of a fixture in the principal's office, much like a potted plant. "I have someone here to see you. Her name is—"

"Judy. Tell her it's Judy."

"Judy."

My stomach tightened.

"You can send her in, Rhonda."

Mrs. Wallace rose from her desk, smoothing her sensible, gray pencil skirt.

I stared at the floor as I listened to Judy's footsteps approaching. My insides crawled as I felt her hand on my shoulder. "What have you done this time?" she hissed.

Mrs. Wallace reached into the top drawer of her desk and pulled out a chef's knife. "We found this in her locker."

Judy shook her head at me, her face filled with disgust. Then she turned her attention to the principal. "I'm so sorry about this, Mrs. Wallace. I completely support your decision regarding her tenure at your school."

"Yes, well, it would be helpful if she would admit to bringing it."

Judy's nails dug into my skin. "Tell her you brought the knife."

"But I didn't—"

"Tell her you brought the knife."

I looked Mrs. Wallace in the eyes. "I'm sorry. I must have brought the knife."

She nodded in approval. "Well, I think a two-week suspension is fair, so you have the time to think about what you've done. I expect you to keep up on your work, and if anything like this is ever to happen again…"

"It won't," I promised. And I meant it. I wouldn't be leaving the house again without thoroughly checking my bag.

I studied Judy's face as we drove home in the car. She looked proud of herself. I knew exactly how the knife got in there and, on top of that, who provided the anonymous tip. It couldn't have been any more obvious than if Judy had flat out admitted she did it. She was slowly building a case against me. She wanted everyone to think I was crazy—especially my father.

Judy needed to be stopped.

"So," she said as she checked her reflection in the mirror. I hadn't noticed how put together Judy looked today—very professional, unlike her usual hair salon uniform of too-tight jeans and crop tops. The woman was like a chameleon. "What are we going to do with you?" She tapped a finger on the steering wheel, pretending to contemplate an appropriate punishment.

"Except you know very well I didn't do this. Seriously, why would I bring a knife to school? I'm not stupid."

"Stupid, no. Crazy, yes. It doesn't look like your father will need much more convincing."

"What do you want from me, Judy?"

Judy looked me dead in the eyes. "I want you gone. Out of our house. Out of our lives."

Well, we had one thing in common.

"He won't believe you, you know."

Judy threw her head back and laughed. "Oh, dear, a man always believes a beautiful woman. You, on the other hand." She looked at me with disgust. "Well, sorry, but I don't think your dad will believe a word you have to say. Especially now that they've suspended you from school for bringing in a weapon."

She was right. No one would believe me over her.

I stared out the window as Judy drove back to the house. It was a good thing Mrs. Wallace did not return the knife. Because all I could think about at that moment was plunging it into Judy's chest.

CHAPTER 43

I awake with a start to the crack of smelling salts beneath my nostrils. I find Detective O'Brien staring at me, his face wrinkled with concern.

"Are you okay, Mrs. Douglass? You gave me quite a scare, there."

"I think so." I try to sit up, but a searing pain knocks me back. I touch the base of my head, where a rather large nodule is beginning to form. It feels like I was hit with a jackhammer.

"You banged your head pretty hard there. We should probably have you evaluated by a medic."

"No!" I say a tad too forcefully. My skull throbs. "I'm not going anywhere."

"Are you dizzy, nauseous?" He rattles off a list of concussion symptoms.

"No," I lie.

"Fine. Well, let's at least get you something to drink."

I motion toward my Stanley in the corner of the room, right next to a picture of Chad with his hand brushing against my bottom. Detective O'Brien retrieves the mug, pausing to examine the picture.

Oh, dear.

By now, I've managed to sit up, propping myself against a wall for support. Detective O'Brien leans down to hand me my drink. I suck down the remainder of its contents in one extra-long gulp.

"I guess this is as good a place to start as any." He pulls out his notepad and gestures toward the pictures. Judging by the expression on his face, by 'this,' he means Chad.

"It's not what it looks like, Detective."

"And what is it you think it looks like?"

My cheeks grow hot. "It looks like we are having an affair. Whoever took these pictures clearly wanted it to appear that way."

"I see." Detective O'Brien's eyebrows bunch together as his eyes scan the room. They stop on a picture of Chad and me locked in a kiss. "So if you're not having an affair, how do you explain kissing someone who is not your husband?"

"It happened one time. I told him it would never happen again. And I meant it."

Detective O'Brien nods his head, his expression even. I can't tell if he believes me. Why shouldn't he believe me? I'm telling the truth.

"Who is the man in these pictures?"

"Chad Morgan. We work together."

The detective flips back a few pages, consulting his notes. He raises his eyebrows.

"Chad Morgan? As in the husband of Marly Morgan, the woman who almost died in your apartment last night?"

"Yes, that would be him. Listen, I know this doesn't look good. But I swear to you, I did not try to poison Marly. I consider her a friend."

Of course, I can't say she feels the same after her angry texts last night. I can't say I blame her for hating me, either.

"And as for the kiss, I never meant for it to happen. It was a mistake."

"Does he think so?"

"Does he think so, meaning what?"

"That it was a mistake?"

"Well, no, I don't suppose he does. Chad said he wanted more. He wanted me to leave Andrew, and he wanted to leave Marly so we could be together."

"And your husband, how long has he known?"

I dig my nails into my palms, motioning with a hand around the room. "I'm honestly not sure. I mean, obviously he knows now." I shake my head.

"So let's see—we have a jilted lover, a jilted husband, a jilted wife who almost died of anaphylaxis in your apartment, and a baby who was almost abducted. Any other details you'd like to add?"

"A nanny who I suspect wants to steal my husband."

"I see. So plenty of people around you with motive."

"Correct."

Detective O'Brien leans down so we're face to face. His eyes are less hazel and more of a sea green-blue. One has a speck of gold in it. Something clicks.

I gasp loudly, drawing a hand to my chest. "I remember something. About…about…" I struggle to get the words out. "…the man at the park," I manage.

"What is it?"

"He had a tiger's eye—a stripe of gold cutting through the brown of his right eye. I don't know why it didn't register at the time. Maybe I was in shock. But I can picture it vividly now. Do you think that could help narrow down a suspect?"

Detective O'Brien regards me sympathetically. "I have a theory, Mrs. Douglass."

"I'm listening, Detective."

"Someone paid that guy to spook you. There's no chance a random stranger is behind all this." He fans his arms around the room. "This right here is as personal as personal gets."

I think about the pictures here and at home, of Delilah's near abduction, and nod because he's right—this *is* as personal as personal gets.

"I'm still sifting through the video footage from the park, trying to locate the attempted abductor. Regarding your husband—there are 18,000 CCTV cameras in New York City. If Mr. Douglass left his studio that day, I will find out."

"I don't believe he would do something to hurt us, but—"

"But?"

"I don't believe that he was in his studio all day. The truth is, I don't know what my husband does all day."

"I'm not ruling anything out at this point. I'll be in touch, Mrs. Douglass. I'm going to ask Mr. Douglass some questions now."

Detective O'Brien extends a hand and helps me to my feet. "Thank you, Detective."

I walk outside to grab Andrew, panic building in my gut. He's pacing back and forth, mumbling something to himself.

"Andrew?"

He looks at me. "I gotta go." His hand reaches into his pocket then pulls an AirPod from his ear. Well, good, at least he wasn't talking to himself.

"Who were you talking to?"

"As if you have the right to ask me any questions. You gave that up when you stuck your tongue in Chad's mouth."

My face flames. I lower my eyes to the glass on the sidewalk, unable to look at my husband. But then I remind myself of what he did. And while I do feel guilty for my actions and how I've hurt Andrew, I'm mad. I'm fucking mad.

"What about *you*, Andrew?"

"*Me?* Godammit, Lucinda. I'm not the one who cheated on you."

I clench my hands into tight fists at my side. So, apparently, we're doing this.

"Like hell you aren't. It may be pictures of me all over your studio, but I've seen the ones of you. I should never have let Chad kiss me. It was a huge mistake. But the only reason it happened was because of what *you* did! Was it worth it, Andrew? Ruining our relationship and your career over some young blonde floozy?"

Andrew's jaw drops. "You're out of your mind, Lucinda. Out of your freaking mind."

He doesn't answer my question. Instead, he shakes his head and then pushes past me into his building. He slams the door, shaking it on its frame, leaving me alone on the sidewalk.

Except, it doesn't feel like I'm alone. In fact, I've never felt *less* alone. The hairs on my neck shoot up as my eyes dart around the sidewalk and across the street.

Sure enough, someone is standing across Astor Place, watching me.

CHAPTER 44

I dart onto the street, weaving in and out of traffic. Horns blare, and a taxi driver gives me the finger. I narrowly avoid becoming roadkill.

"What are you doing here, Bree?" I gasp, trying to catch my breath as I stumble onto the sidewalk.

"Hey, Lucinda." Bree offers a slight wave.

"*Hey?* That's all you have to say to me?"

She looks genuinely confused. "What do you want me to say?"

"Maybe you could start by filling me in on what you are doing here, following us, watching me from across the street like a stalker."

Bree steps back as if afraid I might reach out and grab her. She raises an eyebrow. "I was just about to cross the street, and I didn't follow you here. Andrew told me to come. He wanted to surprise you."

"*Surprise* me?"

"He asked me to scoop up Delilah so he could be alone with you."

Oh God, so that he could *kill* me? She's lying. She has to be lying.

"Look, I don't know what I did to upset you, Lucinda, but whatever it is, I'm sorry. I really do care about you and this job. I love Delilah Bear. I want to make things right between us." Bree reaches into the diaper bag I bought her for when she ventures out alone with Delilah. Which, at this rate, should be—let's see—um, never. She pulls out my backup Hydro Flask, filled with— "...your favorite Mother's Milk tea."

She hands me the drink while I stand silently, staring at her. She couldn't possibly be telling the truth, could she?

"You say you want to make things right, Bree. That's easy enough. Show me the text."

"What text?" Bree wrinkles her forehead.

"The text Andrew sent telling you to come here."

"He didn't send me a text. He asked me last night."

"Is that so?"

"It is so. You can ask him. Where is he?"

Inside his studio, getting interrogated by a detective.

"Fine." I grab Bree by the elbow. "Let's go ask him."

"Ow!" She pulls back her arm. "What in the world has gotten into you?" As she says this, the sidewalk and street momentarily swim. I wonder if I do have a concussion.

"I'm sorry." I throw my hands up in the air. "Can I just—can we sit down for a minute?"

Bree nods and signals to an empty bench upon which I collapse. I fight a wave of nausea threatening to drown me on the spot.

"Are you okay? You don't look well."

"I hit my head earlier. I'm just a little off."

"Oh no, you poor thing. I may have an ice pack in here." Bree must read the look of confusion on my face because she adds, "I threw a first aid kit in Delilah's diaper bag. After that day at the park, I figured you never know when you might need one."

She empties the bag's contents onto the bench between us—diapers, wipes, burp cloths, an extra onesie, an insulated bottle holder, and finally, the first aid kit. A glint of brass at the very bottom of the bag captures my attention.

Keys.

Only, they're not mine.

Where the hell is my set of keys?

Bree pulls an ice pack from the first aid kit. She cracks it and begins to shake. After thirty seconds of shaking, she hands it over. "Here, hold this on your head."

It's almost as if she genuinely cares. My nanny could be an award-winning actress. She could play the role of a nanny out to steal her employer's husband. She's incredibly well-researched on the part.

"Look—" Bree pulls me from my thoughts, her finger outstretched across the street. "There's Andrew with some guy. Is that a cop? Where's Delilah?"

Despite my suspicions, I don't have the heart to tell her I sent my daughter home with another nanny. I still haven't decided what to do with Bree. "Jenna," I say quickly. "I sent her home with Jenna. Andrew didn't mention anything about you coming, so..."

"That's odd." She chews on a fingernail.

That is odd, isn't it? Why wouldn't Andrew mention Bree was coming to get Delilah? Unless she's lying, but that would be dumb since Andrew could easily confirm one way or the other.

Bree replaces all the items in her bag. "Do you think you can get up now? Walk?"

"I think I'm okay." I rise to my feet, still slightly shaky. I glance across Astor Place, watching Detective O'Brien walk away from Andrew and disappear down the street. Well, he's not taking him away in cuffs. So there's that.

"Andrew!" Bree starts waving wildly to my husband as she crosses Aster Place, with me trailing closely behind. The girl looks like she's having a seizure. Not quite the enthusiasm she showed me.

"Hi, Bree." Andrew kisses her on each cheek. Did I miss something? Were we somehow teleported to France? "Thanks for coming."

"Of course. Anything for you." Bree giggles, tucking a strand of hair behind her ear.

"What did Detective O'Brien say?" I ask, interrupting their special moment.

Andrew pulls his gaze to mine. The corners of his lips dip. "He's going to meet us at the gallery in Soho."

"Why in the world is he meeting us *there*?"

"I think he wants to make sure that the exhibit was not targeted as well. He said something about 'gathering evidence.'"

"Well, when is he meeting us?"

"Now."

I turn to Bree to tell her she can have the rest of the day off. But I don't get the chance because Andrew invites her to join us. "You should come and see my exhibit."

"Well, I'm not doing anything since Lucinda called another sitter." *Does she know I was lying about Jenna?* Bree and Andrew look at me like I'm guilty of ordering a hit on someone instead of arranging for childcare. "I'd love to join you."

"Wonderful." Andrew's smile is back, so big and bright; I wish I hadn't left my sunglasses in my diaper bag.

Andrew waves an arm through the air and hails us a cab. Bree slides in first, placing her diaper bag by the window behind the driver's seat. Andrew slips in next to her. That leaves no room for me in the back seat. As if to emphasize, my husband slams the cab door shut.

I reluctantly open the passenger side door and plop beside the driver. He hits the gas before I've even fully closed the door. I stare out the window as we make the short trip from Astor Place to the Jennifer Homestead Gallery on Wooster Street. I don't understand why Detective O'Brien would want to see Andrew's exhibit. The only conclusion I can draw is that the detective suspects Andrew is lying about something. But what will his exhibit show other than his affinity for tinkering with trash?

So why are my fingers and toes tingling?

This sudden exhibition has come as a complete surprise. Not once has Andrew mentioned securing an art gallery or an agent. Doesn't that seem like something worth mentioning?

I flip around in the cab, opening the money depository in the bulletproof partition. "Hey, Andrew?"

Andrew holds a hand to his ear as if he can't hear me. Geez, it's bulletproof, not soundproof. This guy must take me for an absolute idiot.

"Dude, I know you can hear me."

"What's up?" he asks coolly.

"How did you manage to line up an exhibit?"

"I got a call about a week ago from the gallery manager. He said someone had recommended my work."

"Who, Andrew? *Who* recommended your work? Who has even seen your work?"

Last I heard, Andrew was running a solo operation in the back of the building studio that no one ever visited. Maybe I don't know as much about my husband as I thought.

"Does it matter, Lucinda? I swear, it's like you want me to fail."

Andrew and Bree stare at me with matching looks of disgust. Then Bree leans forward and presses two fingers into the plexiglass, pushing the money repository shut and cutting me off from them.

CHAPTER 45

I stew in the front seat for the remainder of the cab ride, not turning back once to look at my cagey husband and shady nanny.

I wish Jenna were here. I fire off a text to her.

Seriously, where are you? Call me the second you see this!

I wait for the delivered message to pop up, followed by three dots, but it doesn't. Is Jenna's phone off? That's incredibly weird. Jenna never—and I mean, never—turns off her phone.

So now, I'm actually starting to worry. Jenna is flighty, yes. She's been known to go home with a random guy (or two), sure, but she always responds to my texts. Not hearing from my best friend all day is completely out of character.

I'll stop by her apartment after we visit Andrew's exhibit. I have a spare key to her apartment. Wait, make that had. I *had* a spare key to her apartment before my keys went missing. Whatever, I'll figure something out.

The cab screeches to a halt in front of the Jennifer Homestead Gallery, thrusting me into the glove compartment. My teeth sink into my lip as my forearm smashes against the dash.

Don't worry, folks; I'm okay! Not that my husband or nanny stick around to ask.

Andrew and Bree casually step out of the cab, leaving me to pay the bill. Except, I don't have my wallet. I'm about to scream for my husband, who's walking side by side with Bree into the gallery, when Detective O'Brien materializes at my window. "How much?" he asks the cab driver as he hands over his credit card.

Once that's all settled, Detective O'Brien helps me out of the cab.

"You didn't have to do that," I say gratefully. "But thank you. My wallet is in my diaper bag, which—"

"Is with the other babysitter who is not your nanny," he finishes.

"Correct."

"I'm getting a sense that there's a complicated backstory here." He motions toward the gallery, where Andrew and Bree are now standing so close together that he might as well be carrying her on top of his shoulders.

"They've gotten quite friendly, I'll admit. Much closer than I'm comfortable with."

A serious expression settles on his face. "You're probably not going to want to hear this, Mrs. Douglass, but have you considered the possibility that your husband and nanny are having an affair and trying to get you out of the picture?"

When he says it like that, my life sounds like a soap opera gone terribly wrong.

"I have. But the Marly part doesn't make any sense. How would poisoning Marly help get me out of the picture?"

"If Marly died, and you were the one who prepared the food with prior knowledge of her allergy, you could be charged with murder."

"With *murder*?"

"As it is, if she wants to, she can still accuse you of attempted murder." *Attempted murder?*

"But I didn't make the sauce…"

"It's your word against theirs."

I'm going to be sick. Is my husband sleeping with our nanny? Are the two of them framing me for attempted murder? Well, I'll give it to Andrew and Bree—watching them from outside the gallery, they do make a very handsome couple. No, this is ridiculous. She's our *nanny*, for Christ's sake.

Still, I don't want to leave them alone together for another second. For all I know, they're in the gallery plotting their next move against me. "Could we just go inside now, please?"

Detective O'Brien nods and holds open the door to the gallery. As I step inside, the hairs on my neck prickle. A ladder is painted above the door on the inside of the gallery so that you are quite literally walking under a ladder. I don't know much about art, but isn't that bad luck? Like black cats and breaking mirrors bad luck?

Well, at least Bree now has it too.

Because things appear to have been going very well for her until now, judging by Andrew's hand on the small of her back, leading her through the studio. Looking at the pair of them gives me a roaring case of déja vu. It's as if I'm staring at the picture of Chad and me crossing Pearl Street as we walked to The Loungebook Pearl.

Coincidental? Or is my husband giving me a taste of my own medicine?

Andrew's free hand is animated, pointing to paintings on the wall and a sculpture of what looks like a penis on a pedestal. *A penis on a pedestal?* What kind of gallery is this? As if I wasn't anxious enough about seeing the display I only just learned about.

Detective O'Brien and I follow Andrew and Bree down a narrow hallway into a large, open room. I nearly fall to my knees as the illuminated walls and ceiling appear.

It's…it's…beautiful.

There are pictures of me everywhere, just like in Andrew's studio. But thankfully, these are less of the stalker variety and more life's captured moments. There are pictures of me sleeping when I had no idea Andrew was taking pictures of me sleeping, but at least they're tasteful. I mean, my tongue is not in another man's mouth. So there's that.

The exhibit consists of more than just pictures. A variety of metal sculptures sits on pedestals throughout the room. And there are no penises. I wasn't joking about repurposed trash, though—in one sculpture, I'm pretty sure Andrew constructed my head out of an empty soda can and rusted hangers. Still, there's something organically beautiful about the whole thing, and I feel a swell of pride for my husband.

Apparently, Bree does as well. My eyes find her with a hand on Andrew's back.

Detective O'Brien clears his throat loudly. Andrew whips around as if caught in the act.

"Oh, hey, I hadn't realized you'd come inside yet."

"So sorry to surprise you like this, Andrew. I was in the same cab, you know. Unless you forgot when you left me in there."

Andrew ignores the jab. "Well, what do you think?"

I think I'm so mad I could scream! "I think you should cover all these pictures of me with pictures of Bree since you seem so fond of one another."

Andrew's eyes widen, and the room quietens. You could hear a pin drop or Detective O'Brien clearing his throat again.

"Miss Miller," he says, moving his eyes away from the painfully awkward standoff between me and my husband. "I'd like to ask you some questions. Could we step outside?"

"Okay," Bree says nervously, tucking a strand of loose hair behind her ear. At this point, it's anyone's guess why she doesn't throw it up in a freaking ponytail.

Detective O'Brien leads the way, and Bree follows him from the room, leaving Andrew and me alone.

Well, here we go.

CHAPTER 46

We stare at each other in silence for a painfully long while. Finally, Andrew breaks it. "How could you, Lucinda? I know things haven't been great between us, but *Chad?* I found that picture in our kitchen drawer last night—with his hand groping you." Andrew eyes me with disgust. "What is that? Some sort of memento? As if what you did wasn't bad enough—you need a reminder of it? Are you in love with him?"

"A *memento?* Seriously? Did you read what it said on the back? Someone brought that picture to our building, Andrew. I didn't even know it existed. We were literally just walking to lunch. And no, I'm not in love with him."

Andrew's shoulders sag with what I can only imagine is partial relief. But this isn't over. Far from it. "I'm not going to say I haven't made any mistakes, because I have. But maybe now you know how I felt when I saw the pictures of you with your paralegal."

"What in God's name are you talking about, Lucinda. *What pictures?"*

Maybe Andrew should star in a movie as well. He's a truly amazing actor. He can play the love interest of our nanny, Bree.

"As if you don't know, Andrew. Apparently whoever was following me was following you as well."

"I seriously have no idea what you are talking about, Lucinda."

"Let me refresh your memory. That twenty-one-year-old blonde you hired a year or so ago. What was her name? Clementine? Cherry?"

"*Cheryl?*"

"So you admit it?"

Andrew pulls at his hair. "Admit what?"

"Admit that you were sleeping with your paralegal. I can't believe you would take advantage of a young woman like that. I can't believe you would cheat on me, Andrew."

"That's good you can't believe it, because it didn't happen. You hear me, Lucinda? I. Did. Not. Cheat. On. You. I trained her, yes. But other than a few work lunches, I never once saw her outside of the office."

I momentarily freeze in place. *Could Andrew be telling the truth?* I think about the pictures, and while they look bad, my husband isn't actually doing anything in them. I mean, his tongue isn't shoved down her throat. They look as incriminating as hell, but so does the picture of Chad and me, and we were only walking to lunch. Sometimes lunch is just lunch.

Why would someone want me to believe my husband was cheating on me?

All of a sudden, it's extremely hot in here. I feel like I might faint.

All I had to do was ask. Instead... *What have I done?*

"I'm sorry, Andrew. I truly believed you had betrayed me and..."

"And what?" he asks, closing the space between us. "You wanted to get me back? By sleeping with my friend?"

"I didn't sleep with him, Andrew."

Andrew lets out a small laugh. "Really, Lucinda? I'm supposed to take your word. With how you've been acting? Is—" he stops midsentence.

"Is what?"

"Is Delilah even mine?"

I gasp, completely taken aback. "How could you even ask me that?" My eyes well with a wall of tears that threatens to collapse at any moment.

"Right." Andrew folds his arms across his chest. "I want a paternity test." Oh God, it feels like I've been stabbed with a knife in the heart. I have actual physical pain.

"Delilah is your baby, Andrew. I swear."

It's clear from the pinched expression on his face that he doesn't believe me.

Andrew begins pacing around the room. He closes the space between us, raising a hand as if he's about to slap me across the face. I wince, but the hit doesn't come. Instead, he swings his arm, knocking his tin can sculpture of me to the floor. Strands of rusty hair fly everywhere while my orange Fanta head rolls dramatically to a corner of the room.

"It's all a big lie. Our marriage. Our family…"

"It's not a lie, Andrew. Please, you have to believe me. We loved each other once. We can find that again."

"I don't know that we can, Lucinda. I honestly don't know that we can."

On that note, footsteps break our conversation. I wipe a hand under my eyes to dry the tears. Then I turn toward the sound, expecting to find Detective O'Brien and Bree. Except, Detective O'Brien is alone.

"Where's Bree?" Andrew asks because of course, that's what he cares about.

"Miss Miller went back to your apartment. She was quite disturbed when I filled her in on what was found in your studio, Mr. Douglass."

"She doesn't think I did it, does she?"

I roll my eyes. Who cares what Bree thinks? Right, Andrew. Andrew cares about what Bree thinks. Perhaps it's not about Chad. Maybe Andrew thinks he's found more of a match in Bree. But where does that leave me? Delilah?

"I can't speak for her. But I can tell you that she was distraught."

"Well, that's just great," Andrew seethes, throwing his hands up in the air.

"I'm going to head back to your studio, Mr. Douglass, so I can walk the perimeter again and try to pull some CCTV footage from neighboring buildings. I've seen and heard enough here."

A part of me wonders if he came here just to watch us implode.

"Fine, whatever," Andrew huffs.

"Mrs. Douglass? Could we have a word before I go?"

I hazard a glance at my husband, but I might as well have already left. Andrew is busying himself in the corner of his exhibit, attempting to reconstruct my head. He's got a tube of Gorilla glue in his hand and a harried expression on his face.

I follow Detective O'Brien outside the building. The sun is blaring, almost angry. How apropos, considering.

"How are you doing?" he asks as he signals to a bench for us to sit down.

"As well as can be expected."

Detective O'Brien scratches his chin. He's got at least two days' worth of stubble. And now that I'm sitting close to him in the light, I notice the purple bags circling his eyes. It looks like I'm not the only one who has lost sleep over this.

"I overheard some of your conversation. Your husband sounds pretty angry."

Biggest understatement *ever!* "You could say that."

"Angry enough to do all this, though?"

"I don't know *who* would do all this, but whoever it is is clearly not operating with a full deck."

"Here's the thing, Mrs. Douglass." Detective O'Brien tightens his gaze on mine. "When I was talking to Miss Miller, she expressed concern about whether *you* are operating with a full deck. We talked about the dynamic in your home, and she questioned your current state of mind."

"My what? You have got to be kidding me! She's known me for two weeks, and did you see how she was fondling my husband? That girl's got some nerve."

"I don't disagree with you, but—"

"But what?"

"I'd like to bring you in for a voluntary drug test. Miss Miller told me she suspects you may be abusing drugs. She said your behavior has been erratic. She seems to think you may be responsible for all this." Detective O'Brien pulls out his notepad. "And I quote—'she forgets things, like a lot. Like, she bought pine nuts at the store to make her friends a pesto sauce but then insisted she never bought pine nuts. I caught her in my room when I was sleeping, too—just watching me. It was alarming. She also tried to rip her daughter from my arms when she was fall-down drunk or hopped up on whatever it is she's been taking.'"

"She said *what?*" I bring a hand to my jaw to ensure it hasn't fallen to the floor. "She said I'm on drugs?"

This girl has gone too far.

"Look, I'm not saying I believe her, but I must take this accusation seriously. And your husband alluded to the same thing. Mr. Douglass and Miss Miller have discussed having an intervention and getting you into rehab." That would certainly be one way to get me out of the picture. "If you willingly submit to a drug test, we can put this speculation to rest and focus on determining who tried to abduct your daughter and who vandalized your husband's studio. Technically, I should be alerting CPS, but I believe you are a victim here."

That's nice because my husband believes I'm a drug addict.

I cross my arms angrily across my chest. "Fine."

"I'll let the department know you'll be coming by."

"And you?"

"As I said, I'm going to do a deep dive around Mr. Douglass's building, and I also need to interview Chad and Marly Morgan."

I take a long breath. Drugs? Really? I'm nursing my one-month-old daughter. What kind of monster does Bree take me for?

She takes me for a monster who would take drugs while nursing her one-month-old daughter, apparently. And worse, she now has my husband believing it as well.

CHAPTER 47

MANY YEARS AGO

While I was getting suspended at school that day, Judy installed a lock on my bedroom door. A padlock on the *outside* of my bedroom door. "To keep us all safe," she told me, a wicked grin spreading across her face as she imprisoned me in my room like an inmate.

When Judy smiled, her eyes transformed into dark slits. It was some serious Pet Sematary shit. And further validation of my suspicions that she planted the knife in my backpack.

After coming home from school, I lay on my bed staring at the peeling paint on my ceiling until the sun dipped in the sky and then disappeared altogether. When I was younger, my mom painted a mural of a sky with bright blues and puffy white clouds. Over the years, the paint had chipped and peeled, revealing a darkness underneath resembling a storm.

My eyes were heavy and beginning to droop. But then, an unfamiliar noise ripped me from that semi-conscious state between wakefulness and sleep.

Tap. Tap. Tap.

I blinked my eyes a few times, making sure I wasn't dreaming or hearing things that weren't there. But nope, lo and behold, there it was again.

Tap. Tap. Tap.

I pulled my covers up to my neck, my eyes darting nervously around the room.

Tap. Tap. Tap.

The window. It was coming from the window. I jumped out of bed and pulled open the shades.

I could barely make out the figure in the darkness. "Dougie?" I cracked the window, letting in the warm night air. "What are you doing here?"

"I wanted to make sure you were okay. Mrs. Wallace was a real bitch to you today."

"She sure was. So you believe me?"

"Of course, I believe you."

My stomach did a flip. Dougie believed me. That was all that mattered.

"She suspended me for two weeks, you know. I'll be back at school just in time for—"

"Prom," he finished.

"That is if you still want to go with me."

"Of course, I still want to go with you."

My insides smiled, despite, well, everything else going on in my life.

"I have a crazy idea," I said.

"Try me."

"What do you have planned after prom?"

"I haven't really thought much about it. I mean, there will probably be a party or something. You know Nolan loves to throw those ragers when his parents are out of town." I did know, having heard kids talking about it at school, but he never personally invited me to one. Or to anything, for that matter. "Why do you ask? What are you thinking?"

"I'm thinking we run away together."

Dougie laughed, but I was as serious as a heart attack. He opened his mouth to answer, but then, out of nowhere, the floodlights flashed outside.

"I better get out of here," Dougie said, backing away from the house. "I'll see you soon."

He quickly ran off into the night. I watched him until he disappeared into the blackness. I lingered for a moment in the window, replaying our conversation.

Things weren't so bad. He hadn't said no, had he? We could run away together, leave this godforsaken place, and never look back.

Unless Judy tried to commit me or kill me, both definite possibilities. I needed to bide my time and survive the next two weeks. After prom, this nightmare would be over.

I jumped at the sound of a key turning in the door and leaped back into bed under the covers. I closed my eyes, feigning sleep. Judy's heels clicked on the wood floor as she approached my bed.

A chill crept up my spine. I gripped my duvet tightly in my fingers. Did Judy see Dougie outside my window? Did she hear us talking? I clenched my teeth, riddled with fear.

I felt her hovering over me. My hand searched for the scissors I kept hidden beneath my mattress. My fingers brushed against the cold steel as my heart thudded in my chest. Judy was so close I could smell the tequila on her breath— tequila and bad decisions.

Could I do it? Stab her if she tried to attack me? A better question, perhaps: Could I stop myself?

The seconds dragged on like hours. I tightened my grip on the scissors. Three, two, one…

"Judy? What are you doing?" My father's voice broke the silence, and my hand instinctively relaxed. The last thing I needed was to be caught with stolen scissors in my bed after getting caught with a stolen kitchen knife in my locker. I might as well have held up a giant sign that read: **Danger to others.**

"Oh, David. You startled me. I…I was just checking on her. She had a rough day at school."

"Kids being assholes again?"

"No, it's not that. I don't know how to tell you this without upsetting you, but they found a rather large knife in her locker."

"A knife?"

"Yes. She stole it from our kitchen and brought it to school. I noticed it was missing when I went to prepare dinner. I shudder to think of what she was going to do with it. Look," she continued. "I know she's your daughter, and you love her, I do, but one day she's going to slaughter us all in our sleep."

My father chuckled. "No more Dateline for you, missy."

"You're laughing now, but mark my words, David, this isn't going to end well. She's suspended for the next two weeks. She's lucky they didn't expel her from school. They wanted to, but I convinced them to let her stay."

That liar. That skinny, little liar.

"I'm sorry I wasn't here for you, Judy. I should have been the one to go to the school, not you. Come here, baby. I'll deal with her in the morning." My father had chosen sides—the line drawn in the sand.

I chewed the inside of my mouth as Judy's heels clicked out of my room and disappeared into the hallway. She slammed the door behind her and locked it.

I squeezed my eyes shut for a while after Judy left, though I was very much awake. Finally, when I was certain she wasn't coming back, I jumped up from my bed, grabbed a suitcase from my closet, and began to pack.

Judy was right about one thing and one thing only—this would not end well. I needed to leave before something really bad happened.

Two more weeks and this would all be over.

CHAPTER 48

I hail a cab outside of the Jennifer Homestead Gallery on Wooster Street.

Except, I'm not going to the police station as I told Detective O'Brien I would. Not yet, anyhow. There's something I need to do first. Something that can't wait.

I need to find Jenna.

"West 4th and Jane Street, please," I tell the driver as I collapse into the backseat of the cab. This day has been exhausting to say the least. And it's not even dinnertime yet. My breasts ache, reminding me that Delilah will be hungry soon. I text Ms. Randall.

How is Delilah doing? Do you have enough milk to hold her over for a while longer?

Unlike Jenna, Ms. Randall responds right away. Ironic, since Jenna is the one whose phone is typically glued to her face.

She's great. Such a pleasure. Take as long as you need.

I exhale a sigh of relief. I'll need to pump soon or I'll become engorged. But I can't worry about that right now.

I text Jenna again.

Where are you? I'm on my way to your apartment.

The questions pelt me like a hailstorm. Why is Jenna ignoring me? Was it something I said? *Did?* Is she okay? Is she *not* okay? And the one I can't even bear to consider: Could my best friend have had something to do with this? It's an impossibility of epic proportions, but then, so is everything that has gone on over the past two weeks.

THE PERFECT NANNY

You can't make this shit up. I mean, obviously you can, but who would believe it?

I shake the thoughts as we pull up in front of her building, a restored brick walk-up with renovated apartments and balconies that overlook an exquisite flower garden. It's the perfect place for someone like Jenna, who makes a living off of her pictures.

I knock on the plexiglass divider as the cab comes screeching to a halt. "Excuse me?"

The driver turns around. "Yes?"

"I need to run upstairs real quick. Could you possibly keep the meter running and wait?"

He scowls at me. "*Wait?* How do I know you'll come back down?"

Good point. But I've got nothing on me. No purse, no money, no...

"Phone," I say. "You can take my phone, you know, as collateral."

The driver nods without hesitation, and I pass him my phone, praying he doesn't decide to drive off with it. He'd certainly make more off an iPhone 15 than he'll make off my fare. Assuming I'm in and out as I plan to be.

Find Jenna. Figure out what the f*ck is going on.

I inhale a deep breath as I step out of the cab onto the sidewalk. I'm still feeling dizzy from knocking my head and woozy from the day's events. As I stand outside her building, it occurs to me how foolish it is for me to go *anywhere* right now with no way to call for help. But what choice do I have?

Just as I approach the door, a young man exits, holding it open so I can step inside. He must not be from around here. Who lets a complete stranger into their New York City apartment building? This is *precisely* the reason I told Jenna she needs to live in a doorman building.

The door slams shut behind me, and I draw a deep breath. I should feel better now that I'm inside, but instead, I'm filled with an overwhelming sense of dread.

D.L. Fisher

A chill snakes up my spine as I walk the four floors to her apartment. I'm unsettled in a way I can't explain. And the feeling only grows when I walk down the hallway and spot Jenna's apartment door ajar with her set of keys dangling in the lock. Why in the world would Jenna leave the door open with her keys still in it?

Worse, as I get closer, I notice something that makes me sick to my stomach. It's not Jenna's keys dangling in the lock. It's *my* keys. My *missing* set of keys, with the spare key to her apartment pushed into the door.

"Jenna," I call out, my voice quivering in my throat. There's no answer. No noise, other than Crime Junkie's Britt in my ear, shouting, "Don't go in there. Turn around. Don't go in there!"

But instead of backing away as I should do, retrieving my phone from the taxi driver and calling for help, I advance farther into her apartment.

"Jenna?"

Silence.

There's a commotion in my chest as I tiptoe from room to room, searching for any sign of my friend. Nothing. Except for in the kitchen. When I enter the small space, I spot it right away, the hairs on my arms rising. I stare at the bottle of Prosecco sitting out on the kitchen island. Sweat beads drip down the glass like tears. I bring a hand to touch it, and it's still cold. My eyes fly around the room, landing on two champagne flutes by the sink.

Someone was here, and not too long ago. *Two* people if I'm to judge by the glasses. But where did they go in such a hurry with the keys still in the door?

I'm sorry, but this is just too weird.

I let out a deep breath. *Think, Lucinda, think.*

There's still one place in the apartment that I haven't checked.

My stomach is doing somersaults. Suddenly this whole Nancy Drew thing seems like a bad idea. A *really* bad idea.

I grab a knife from Jenna's butcher's block for protection. Then, I hurry down the hallway to her bedroom.

I say a prayer as I wrap my hand around the doorknob, and…

CHAPTER 49

Do you know what it's like to see a lifeless body in person?

Well, thank God, neither do I. I was half expecting to find Jenna dead, but her bedroom is just as empty as the rest of her apartment. If she met foul play, it didn't happen here.

I breathe a sigh of relief, but it's short-lived. Because where the hell is she? And why was her front door open with my key in the lock? Unless someone came here looking for her, got spooked, and ran. Maybe she lost her phone, and everything is fine and dandy.

Yeah, right.

I fire off another text on the off-chance Jenna miraculously sees it and decides to respond:

Seriously, where the fu*k are you? I'm in your apartment. The door was open. Please don't come home until you call me.

A loud beep makes me jump. I glance around the room nervously. My eyes find the closed closet door. My stomach twists as I realize I didn't check the closet. How could I not have checked the closet? That literally should have been the first place I checked. I tightly grip the knife in my hand as I cautiously cross the room.

"On three," I whisper, working up the nerve to open the door. *One, two, three...*

I yank open the closet door and swing my knife around as I step inside. I slash through racks of expensive clothing, kicking shoes and boxes with my feet, but no one is hiding in there.

I step back and survey the mess. Oh boy, Jenna is going to be pissed. I will owe her a shopping trip for this, that's for sure. Though clearly, shopping is the least of our problems right now.

Beep. Beep. Beep.

Where in the world is that beeping coming from? I survey the space again. I check under the bed even though her frame is so low, you'd have to be about four inches thick to squeeze underneath.

As I rise to my feet, I spot Jenna's iPad on her bed.

Aha! Found you, beep.

Jenna's comforter is rumpled, but thankfully she's not rolled up in it. I sit on the edge and press the screen, bringing her iPad to life.

Jenna's Instagram page fills the screen. I examine her most recent picture, which has over five thousand likes and hundreds of comments. According to the time stamp, she posted it this morning.

#newbeau

There's a picture of Jenna looking as gorgeous as always with a hunky chestnut-haired guy. Unsurprisingly, he's incredibly good-looking because Jenna only dates incredibly good-looking guys, even if most of them are complete assholes.

I zoom in on the picture. As #newbeau's face grows, I notice something markedly distinct about him. It turns out brown eyes *can* be distinctive. You know that saying—eyes are the window to the soul? What does it say that one of his brown eyes has a streak of gold running through it?

I drop the iPad as if it's been set on fire. It's *him*—the masked man from the park who tried to kidnap Delilah.

I break out in a sweat as my pulse throbs in my head. I need to find her.

But I don't even know where to start. She could literally be anywhere right now. Well, anywhere but here, obviously. She's clearly not here.

I pick her iPad back up and rush out of the apartment, grabbing my keys from the door on the way out.

THE PERFECT NANNY

My heart is racing as I run down the hallway to the stairwell. As I descend the stairs to the lobby my mind swirls with all the terrible possibilities of where Jenna might be.

But at least one thing has gone my way today—the taxi driver is waiting outside, as promised. I hop into the cab.

"Thank you," I say. "We can go to the police precinct now."

The driver turns around, looking me over curiously. I glimpse my reflection in the rearview mirror, and wow, I am seriously a hot mess. My hair has started to frizz, and the bangs I thought sounded like a good idea when I saw Zendaya rocking them are curled within inches of their life. My mascara is running down my face, which has taken on a very unattractive reddish hue.

But I don't suppose any of that matters.

What matters is finding the man who tried to kidnap my daughter and may now be trying to harm my best friend. *Or is my best friend trying to harm me?*

No. No. No.

Because my face isn't red enough, I send Detective O'Brien a text as my taxi weaves in and out of traffic.

I'm on my way to the police station now. Would you mind meeting me outside and paying for the cab?

It will be the second cab he's paid for today.

He writes back immediately.

I'm outside waiting.

Sure enough, as we pull up to the precinct, I spot Detective O'Brien standing beneath a metal awning, waiting for me. It looks like I'm not the only one who's a hot mess. The detective's shirt is rumpled with armpit stains on both sides. And as I step out of the taxi, I notice how the purple shadows have nearly swallowed his hazel eyes.

"Thank you," I say after the detective settles my very large tab. Apparently, it's quite expensive to leave a taxi meter running for thirty minutes in a New York City cab. But at least I'm here, and now we can get this ridiculous drug test over with and get to work finding Jenna and this mystery man.

Jenna will be fine, I tell myself as I follow Detective O'Brien into the precinct. Everything will be fine.

CHAPTER 50

MANY YEARS AGO

I'd probably have gotten better treatment in prison.

Judy hadn't let me out of my room in two weeks other than to use the bathroom. I hadn't even showered but, really, what did it matter? It's not like I was going to see anyone. And it's not like Judy offered up the opportunity for me to shower. When I needed to use the bathroom, I'd have to ring a bell, and eventually, Judy would come to escort me, waiting outside the bathroom door to make sure I returned straight to my room, where she padlocked me in.

Judy had taken to leaving my meals sitting outside my bedroom door. I also had to ring the bell if I wanted to eat. Other than that bell, I had zero communication with the outside world. For several days, I was able to resist eating, but then the stomach pains became too intense, and all I could think about was food.

I made a concerted effort not to eat. But really, who has that kind of willpower? Not me. Especially not when Judy was pulling out all the culinary stops. She might as well have lit a dozen food-flavored candles in my room. I wouldn't have been surprised to find a fan in the hallway wafting the aromas of her gourmet meals straight under my door.

I couldn't spite myself forever to spite her. I had already altered my dress, and if I maintained my hunger strike, it would have been hanging off my already-tiny frame by the time prom arrived.

So I gave in.

I tried to focus on the bigger picture. *Prom.* I could hardly wait for it. I needed to get the hell out of my house. The days ticked by incredibly slowly. Dougie hadn't returned to visit, but I took comfort that I would see him soon enough.

And then we would leave.

I knew the day was approaching, but the knock caught me completely off guard. I'm not sure if you could even call it a knock. It was more like a banging, a fist pounding against my bedroom door.

Why bother knocking at all? She had the key; besides, I couldn't open the door if I wanted to. I lay in bed staring out the window with my back toward the door. I certainly wasn't going to make things any easier on her. She could fish out her dang key and open the door herself—which she did.

"How are you so incredibly lazy?" Judy asked after letting herself into my room.

"What, Judy?" I didn't turn around.

"Get up." She threw a stack of clothes at my head. "Today's the big day. Back to school, you go."

I sat bolt upright in bed and gathered the clothing in my arms. "Yes, ma'am."

Judy surveyed me curiously. She clearly was not expecting me to be so agreeable. She shook her head, seemingly annoyed by my bonhomie.

"I've taken the liberty of searching your backpack for weapons."

"Judy, I've barely left this room since I got suspended. And we both know I did not bring that knife to school."

Judy clenched her teeth. "Let's go. Now. Breakfast is waiting downstairs. You look like a skeleton."

I knew without asking that a shower was out of the question. I quickly dressed and fixed myself up as best I could. Then I shuffled down the stairs for breakfast.

I looked around for my siblings, but the house was deserted. Judy must have gotten them off to school and daycare before waking me up.

And then, I watched from the kitchen doorway as Judy mashed up a pill and sprinkled its powder into a plate of eggs. I blinked several times. Was I hallucinating? Judy was awful, yes. But would she drug me? That seemed extreme, even for her.

Still, I slipped out of view and listened as Judy set the plates on the table. Then I casually walked through the door. Judy pointed to a chair. "Sit," she ordered.

When she turned back around to pour two glasses of orange juice, I did what any sane, rational person would do.

I switched our plates.—

Judy and I ate breakfast in silence. I tried not to look at her, but each time my eyes involuntarily rose from the plate, I found her staring at me. It was almost as if she was waiting for something to happen.

Something would happen if my suspicions were correct—just not to me.

Judy was halfway through her meal when her face paled. Her fork dangled in midair, suspended above her eggs.

"I don't feel so good," she said, swaying in her chair.

"What was in the eggs, Judy?"

"What are you talking about?" Her words were beginning to slur.

"I saw you. I saw you slip something into the eggs."

Judy's eyes widened. She looked at my plate and then down at hers.

"What did you do?"

I smiled widely, setting my fork down and leaning in toward her. "How does it feel?"

"Oh, God." Judy brought a hand to her mouth. "You're making a terrible mistake."

"Oh, am I?"

"You gave me your medicine."

"What are you talking about? What medicine? I watched you drugging my food."

Judy rose suddenly from the chair, stumbling back and knocking it over. She wobbled across the kitchen, grasping the sink for support. Holding herself upright with one arm, Judy reached for two bottles of pills with the other.

I watched with bemusement as she attempted to throw the bottles across the room to me. They traveled all of two inches in slow motion, landing at her feet.

I walked over and picked the bottles up. I stared wide-eyed as Judy lost her grip on the sink and slid to the ground. She looked at me helplessly, but I didn't go to help her. I finally had Judy where I wanted her—where she could hurt me no more.

I turned the prescription bottles over in my hand. The names were obliterated by black marker. I read the labels—dosage, instructions, warnings.

> *May cause drowsiness. Do not operate a motor vehicle or heavy machinery until you know how this medication will affect you. Do not take with alcohol.*

One of the bottles was a benzodiazepine. I'd seen these before in the bathroom cabinet.

But the other bottle... I'd never heard of it before, so I ran to the computer in my dad's office to Google the name.

An *antipsychotic*?

Why in the world was Judy drugging me with a benzodiazepine and an antipsychotic?

Unless...

CHAPTER 51

Detective O'Brien escorts me into the police station. I'm not under arrest for anything (ahem, I didn't do anything), but I nonetheless feel the side eyes shooting from every direction as if I'm some common criminal he pulled off the streets. My palms drip as we walk through a metal detector past an armed guard. We pass by a few holding cells, adding to my growing anxiety.

I should feel safe here, surrounded by those who serve and protect, but honestly, I'm having second thoughts about agreeing to come here in the first place. Should I have willingly submitted to taking a drug test without talking to a lawyer? It kind of seems like a bad idea, even for an innocent person. Which I am.

Detective O'Brien's words roll over in my head. *They expressed concern that you're taking drugs.* What a preposterous accusation. I've been forgetful lately, but I just had a newborn, for goodness' sake. Baby brain is an actual thing!

Detective O'Brien leads me down a narrow hallway flanked by doors on either side. I swallow the lump in my throat.

"Here it is." He points to a sign on one of the doors—Laboratory—and then knocks before opening it.

A man in blue scrubs with a five o'clock shadow and mussed-up hair greets us at the door. I glance around the room nervously, somewhat relieved to discover a phlebotomy certificate with his name, Steven Allen. Knowing the name of the man who's about to violate my veins is a relief. And that he's allegedly qualified to perform said violation.

"Hey, Dick," Steven says, extending a hand. "I'm all ready for you."

Detective O'Brien shakes his hand, then signals for me to have a seat in the phlebotomy chair. "Just try to relax," he tells me, placing a hand reassuringly on my shoulder. Easy for him to say...

"How long does it take to turn this around?" I ask. "I'm proving to my husband and nanny who wants to sleep with or already has slept with my husband that I don't have a drug problem."

Steven Allen's eyebrows shoot up. "Oh."

"Sorry, I'm not sure why I told you that."

He gives an awkward half smile. "Don't worry, Mrs. Douglass. I'm sure you'll get this all sorted out. We'll have the results within the next few hours."

Steven then pushes a pair of wire-rimmed glasses up the bridge of his nose. Oh God, does he have impaired vision? Can he even *see* my vein? I fight the urge to hyperventilate. I'm going to be sick. I wonder if they could use a vomit sample instead of my blood.

It's not too late. I could still refuse to provide a sample. Call a lawyer.

But I don't. Instead, I slip down into the stiff leather chair.

"Which arm?" he asks.

I shrug. "Left, I guess."

Steven snaps on a pair of latex gloves. I shift in my seat. He ties a rubber band around my left bicep, effectively cutting off the circulation to my fingers. Then he instructs me to make a fist.

I picture Bree's face as I fold my fingers into a knot, squeezing so tightly that my knuckles go white.

"Now, take a deep breath," he says. "You're just going to feel a little prick."

I flinch as the needle slips into my vein, but I don't dare look. I can't stand the sight of blood.

"And done." A few moments later, the needle slides out, and Steven slaps a Band-Aid over my puncture wound.

"That's it?"

"That's it."

Okay, so it wasn't that bad. I haven't taken drugs other than when I smoked pot with Jenna once in college. I shouldn't have anything to worry about. And not trying to rip on President Bill Clinton, but I didn't inhale either. This test will come back negative, and we can all get back to investigating.

So why can't I shake the feeling that things will not play out how they should?

Let's see... Maybe because you suspect your husband and nanny are having an affair and are attempting to get rid of you. And your best friend is dating the man who tried to kidnap your baby in broad daylight in Central Park. Right, there's all that.

As if on cue, my phone vibrates with a text from Bree. I don't know how this woman has gotten inside my head.

I swipe the screen to read her message.

I think we should talk, Lucinda. I'm at the apartment. Will you be headed back from the gallery soon?

I start to type a response and then stop. Maybe this is a good sign. If Bree had spoken to Andrew, she'd have known I left the gallery ages ago.

I turn to Detective O'Brien. "There's something I need to tell you." He trains his eyes on mine. "Can we talk in private?"

Detective O'Brien nods and leads me to an empty interrogation room. We sit across from one another at a metal table, and I open Jenna's iPad.

I'm about to show him my best friend's #newbeau when—

Where is it? I tap on the screen a few times, but to no avail.

Someone deleted the post. There's no #newbeau. No #oldbeau. No #beau.

For a split second, I wonder, *was there ever?* Of course there was.

"What is it?" he asks, interlacing his fingers on the interrogation table.

"I...I..." I can't tell him. The guy already thinks I might be taking drugs. Telling him about a post that doesn't exist won't exactly make me look any better. "I just wanted to let you know that I found my missing set of keys in the door of my friend Jenna's apartment. But she wasn't there. I'm kind of worried about her."

"Okay..." He looks down at the iPad.

"Her iPad was on the bed. I thought maybe it could help you locate her."

"I see. So, now you're adding a missing best friend to my list of things to do?" Detective O'Brien scratches a patch of silver stubble on his cheek. "She's an adult, Mrs. Douglass, so unless there's a pressing reason to search for her, we're not going to be able to get anyone out there looking for a while. In the meantime, I'm heading to the Morgan residence to interview Chad and Marly, and after that, I've got hours' worth of security footage to sift through. I suggest you pick up your baby, head home, and wait."

"Just wait?"

"I'll call you with what I find."

"Um..."

"Here." Detective O'Brien reaches into his pocket and pulls out his wallet. He hands me a crisp twenty-dollar bill.

"I owe you dinner," I say gratefully.

"Just stay safe, okay?"

Advice of the day, it seems. "I'll try."

As I leave the police station, that uneasy feeling I've had all day intensifies. It's as if I'm standing on the precipice of something *really, really* bad happening. I just don't know what.

I shoot a text to Bree.

I am hopping in a cab. Be there shortly.

It's the tail end of rush hour, so I'm surprised at how easily I am able to hail a cab. Except, I manage to flag down a taxi without an operational air conditioner, which might explain why it's so easy. It must be at least eight hundred degrees in here. Worse, the windows in the backseat don't appear to be working either. Worse, worse, I left my drink at the police station. I'm so thirsty I could drink my own sweat.

But I suppose I've bigger things to think about than my thirst.

Namely, how am I going to fire my nanny?

CHAPTER 52

Yes, I've unilaterally decided to fire Bree. And Andrew won't be there to stop me. I'm sure he's still busy at the gallery trying to put aluminum me back together.

As I sit in the cab, I practice what I will say.

Bree, I'm sorry to tell you this, but we will no longer need your services.

Too formal.

You've been great, Bree, but after everything that has happened, I think we should part ways.

Too gentle, considering.

Or maybe—

Here's some advice for your next gig: don't throw yourself at the man of the house if you want to keep your job. And no, I will not give you a reference.

Yeah, I've no idea what I'm going to say. Maybe I'll get lucky, and Bree will just quit.

I pull up the Nannies of the Upper East Side Facebook page while stopped at a light. I scroll through all the nannies looking for a job (there are an obscene number of nannies looking for a job). Bree should be pretty easy to replace.

I don't know what makes me do it, but I find myself typing her first and last name into the search bar on the Facebook page. I wait for her face to pop up, but to my complete bewilderment, there are no hits. There must be some mistake. I recheck the spelling, but no, I typed it in correctly the first time. For good measure, I try spelling her first name like the cheese—Brie. But there's no Brie Miller in this group, either.

I recall our conversation in the bar when I interviewed Bree two weeks ago. I had asked her about the headshot, and I'm confident she said she read on the Nannies of the Upper East Side Facebook page that including a picture helps you stand out. But Bree would not have had access to the Nannies of the Upper East Side Facebook group's private posts if she wasn't a member of the group. Which means—she wouldn't have had access to me there either.

So where the hell did Bree Miller come from?

Thank God I ran into Ms. Randall the other day and had the foresight to ask her to take Delilah until I sort this mess out. The mess that just keeps getting messier.

The cab pulls up at my building, and I step onto the sidewalk, my head spinning. It doesn't make any sense. I know my track record on details has been a little sketchy lately, but the more I think about it, the more confident I am about what Bree told me. Now I'm second-guessing everything, including her reaction to passing Ivybrook when we walked to Central Park. Did she ever actually work there?

Who is this woman masquerading as a nanny in my home?

Oh God, I feel queasy.

I take a deep breath as I pass through the revolving doors to my building. *Great.* Ashton is still staffing the front desk. He must be working a twelve-hour shift.

My doorman is just about the last person I want to talk to, so when Ashton gives me a signal to wait a moment for him to finish speaking with another resident, I pretend not to notice and walk briskly to the elevator.

I rush onto the lift and repeatedly press my penthouse keycard against the panel. Thank goodness I found my keys. If not, I would have been forced to ask my doorman for help. I haven't asked Ashton for anything, so why is he pacing toward me like he's about to push me out of oncoming traffic? He's waving his hands around, mouthing something I can't make out.

Whatever he's trying to tell me seems awfully important to him. I bet he wants to apologize for his behavior with Detective O'Brien this morning, As if I give a flying you know what about that right now. I flinch as his fists pound against the closing elevator door. It's not until I reach the fifth floor that I no longer hear him calling my name.

I try to push Ashton from my mind as I ride the rest of the way to our apartment. I think about Bree. Maybe I'm looking too much into things. She *could* have been a member of the Nannies of the Upper East Side Facebook page and taken down her profile once I hired her. Right? Or maybe she blocked me after hearing about the horrors at Andrew's studio? Only an insane person would want to tangle herself up in that.

I'm probably freaking out for no reason at all. Well, aside from the obvious reasons, but still.

When the elevator doors open, I'm relieved to find the hallway empty and the door to my apartment closed. I stick the key into the lock and let myself in.

The apartment is pitch black and dead quiet. Every single light is off. The sun is already starting to set outside, accentuating the darkness. Odd, considering Bree asked me to meet her here.

I debate slipping back into the hallway. Maybe Ashton *did* have something important to tell me—like there's an electrical maintenance thing or something of that nature. But if that were the case, wouldn't the elevator be nonfunctional and the lights in the hallway out?

No, it can't be that. There's clearly no shedding load or power outage.

I check my text chain with Bree to ensure I read her message correctly. There's no misconstruing it—*I'm at the apartment.* So why does the place look like an abandoned warehouse?

"Bree?" I call out, flicking on the light switch by the front door. As suspected, there's no power outage. But why are all the lights off? And why is it so dang quiet?

Something tells me not to bolt the door behind me. I leave it cracked, just in case.

God, I'm paranoid. Bree is probably just in her room waiting for me to get home. Maybe she was too upset and distracted by packing to hear me calling her name.

I set my keys on the entryway table. Despite the horror movie vibes, I enter deeper into the apartment and call Bree's name again.

Nothing.

I walk into the kitchen next and flick on the lights. My eyes shoot around the room. Something is off, but I can't quite put my finger on it. I open the fridge and grab my Stanley full of tea. I take a long sip and try to calm down. I'm sure there's a logical explanation for all this.

Something catches my eye as I make my way through the kitchen archway into the living room. I hit the light switch, but nothing happens. Seriously? Of all the times for the bulbs to burn out!

I turn on my phone flashlight and shine it on what I saw. Well, that's great; there's a stain on my thousand-dollar carpet. Someone must have spilled their red wine last night. But wasn't I the one standing in this spot? I don't remember spilling any wine.

I bend down to survey the damage, running my fingers over the spot. My heart beats so loudly I can hear it in my ears. It can't be red wine from last night. It's too wet and sticky.

Like blood.

CHAPTER 53

I can't breathe. Why is there blood on the living room carpet?

My eyes shoot around the darkened room as fear runs through my veins. There's another spot a few feet away. And beyond that, another. There's a literal trail of blood across my carpet. What the hell happened here?

"Bree?" My voice cracks in my throat. I take another sip of tea and try to pull myself together. Maybe Bree cut herself in the kitchen and ran to her room to bandage it?

But why would she do that? There's a first aid kit in the kitchen. Unless Bree didn't cut herself at all.

I stumble to my feet and back away from the blood into the kitchen. I should leave the apartment and call for help, but I don't. For the second time today, I find the butcher's block of knives and grab for the sharpest one.

Except... Oh. God. The knife isn't there. Just a long, empty slit where it should be.

Holy shit. Someone is loose in my apartment with a butcher's knife. They may have stabbed my nanny. Or my nanny may have stabbed them. Who cares? Someone was obviously stabbed.

All the bravado drains from my body. I need to get out of here fast, to call for help. I grab the next largest knife with shaking hands, wrapping my fingers tightly around its handle. I position it in front of my body, making my way back toward the front door. I race around a corner and am steps away from the open apartment door when I almost smack knife-first into my best friend.

Jenna stands in the archway of our apartment door, a look of horror painted on her face. "Lucy!" She shields her body with her hands as I stop short with the knife inches away from her stomach.

I nearly burst into tears. "Jenna! You're alive!"

"By the grace of God, Lucy. You almost stabbed me. Would you mind putting down the knife?"

Something tells me I *shouldn't* put down the knife—maybe the fact that there's possibly an intruder in my apartment, a missing butcher's knife from the kitchen, blood on the carpet—but I drop it onto the entryway table next to my house keys.

Jenna steps into the apartment, closing the door behind her. Also, probably not the best idea...

"You can't be too careful these days, can you?" She winks. "You said it yourself—there are a lot of wackadoodles out there."

"Like my nanny..."

"I hate to say I told you so."

"Go ahead, say it." I cross my arms and nod.

"Fine. I warned you about hiring the cheesy beer."

Sheesh, not this again.

"Where have you been, Jenna? I've been trying to reach you all day."

"I was mugged, Lucy. They took my phone and wallet. I've been at the police station trying to sort it all out."

"Oh my gosh, that's terrible. Are you hurt?"

"No, no. I'm fine, physically, anyway. It will be a real bitch to cancel all my cards and get a new license and keys. I sure could use a drink right now."

"A drink?"

Jenna rolls her eyes. "Yes, Lucy, you know the liquid you pour into a glass?" She walks past me toward the kitchen.

Wait, no. "Jenna, stop!" I trail her into the kitchen, grabbing her elbow. "Listen to me...I think there's someone in the apartment. And...and...I'm pretty sure there's blood on the living room carpet."

"Blood?" Jenna raises an eyebrow. "Are you sure it's not red wine? You were sloshing it around quite a bit last night." She pours us two large glasses of red wine as she says this.

Could she be right? Could it just be wine? I remember walking across the room to take Delilah from Bree. Could I have spilled it?

"But it was wet and sticky."

"I guess you've never tried to clean up recently spilled red wine from the carpet before. Wet and sticky." She shrugs.

Well, now I feel like an idiot.

"But...Bree told me to meet her here, and all the lights were off, and there was a missing kitchen knife. Look—" I point toward the block of expensive knives on the countertop.

Jenna walks over, stopping at the sink along the way. She reaches into the basin and pulls out a knife. "Is this the missing knife you're talking about?"

Well, I'll be damned. It *is* the missing knife I was talking about. How is that even possible? Did I not check the sink? Now that I think about it, did I look anywhere other than the knife block before I started freaking out?

"Looks like you need this more than I do," Jenna says as she hands me a glass of wine. I had zero intentions of drinking tonight, but after working myself into such a tizzy, I think she's right.

Except, the uneasy feeling is still there. Because where is Bree?

As if reading my mind, Jenna says, "I'll go check the apartment. Try to relax. Take a few deep breaths. And sips. You'll feel better." She winks and leaves me alone in the kitchen with my wine.

I slosh the liquid around the glass, trying to spark a memory of spilling it last night. I would feel so much better if I could remember spilling it. But the memory doesn't come. No matter what Andrew, Bree, and Jenna think, I was not spill-your-drink-all-over-the-carpet-and-not-remember drunk.

I take a long sip, savoring the taste before swallowing. Wow, this is some good red wine. It's smooth, like velvet on my tongue. I lick my lips, a relaxing, tingly sensation flowing through my body.

I can't even remember what had me freaking out. It almost makes me think I'm losing my mind. Bree is probably in her room, packing to leave. Neither Jenna nor I will shed any tears about that.

I'll just leave Jenna to it and finish my glass of wine. I take another large gulp, lean back in my seat, and try to relax.

CHAPTER 54

MANY YEARS AGO

I left Judy crumpled on the kitchen floor. It was a beautiful day outside. The birds were chirping, and spring was in full bloom. I'd have to walk to school, but that wasn't so bad. I took my time smelling the flowers along the way.

I hopped on the trail across the street from my house that led to the school. It was popular among runners and stay-at-home moms who power walked and wore thick headbands and tennis skirts. Surprisingly, today of all days when the weather was about as picture-perfect as it could get, the trail was deserted.

At least, I thought it was deserted until a familiar voice made me jump.

"You shouldn't have done that."

"What? Dougie? Is that you?"

Dougie popped out from behind a tree. I held a hand up to my chest. "Jesus Christ! You scared the bejeebers out of me!"

Dougie had the loveliest smile I'd ever seen. When he smiled, a dimple formed on his right cheek. I waited for it, but the dimple didn't form. He wasn't smiling.

"I came to your house," he said tightly, staring at me stone-faced. "I thought I would surprise you and bring you to school. I remembered today was the day you got to go back."

My mouth suddenly felt desert dry, as if I'd inhaled a bag of cotton balls. My tongue was a strip of sandpaper. "You came to my house? But when? Where—where were you?"

"Outside your kitchen window." I quickly did the math. Dougie was outside my kitchen window, which was open because it was such a beautiful morning. I examined his face. The corners of his lips twitched as if uncertain if he wanted to scream or cry. Oh, God. He must have seen and heard everything.

"Let me explain. I can explain."

"No, I don't think you can." Dougie folded his arms across his chest.

"Please, you don't understand. At least give me a chance."

"I'm listening." Dougie glanced down at his watch. "You have two minutes."

I tried to explain it to him—all that had happened since my mother's sudden, unexpected death. He let me talk, his expression even. As I finished my harrowing tale, I looked at him expectantly. Surely, he would understand. Surely, he would forgive me. I had no choice. It was her or me.

But Dougie's lips dipped down. "You could have called for help. You just left her there. What if she dies? I'm not going to tell anyone what you did, but I never want to see you again." He turned on his heels and disappeared down the street almost as quickly as he'd appeared.

I stood, frozen in shock. This wasn't happening.

It felt like hundreds of tiny knives were stabbing me in the heart. I turned back and began walking home, unsure what to do. Dougie wouldn't be running away with me. He wouldn't be talking to me ever again. Hot tears burned my eyes.

There was no coming back from this. I had lost everything.

What would be there at home? Was Judy awake, waiting for me? Or was she already at the school, with police in tow? Did she tell them I drugged her and left her on the kitchen floor? She definitely would. And the school would tell the police about the knife. No one would believe a word I said. Dougie certainly didn't.

And what if Dougie was right? What if Judy died? What happened then?

I began jogging, then running full speed. I had to get home before Judy regained consciousness or someone found her. I would flush the remaining pills down the toilet. No one would ever know what I had done. She couldn't prove it without the evidence. It was her word against mine.

I let myself into the house. It was utterly silent. Had she already left? I checked inside the garage, but Judy's car was still there.

"Judy, are you there?"

I ambled toward the kitchen, my heart thumping in my chest. Judy was lying right where I had left her, curled up in a ball on the floor. My shoulders sagged with relief.

I moved toward her slowly. "Judy, I'm back. You can get up now."

Judy didn't stir. She was as still as a statue. Too still.

Like Buddy.

A wave of fear washed over me.

My legs felt like Jell-O as I knelt beside her. I placed a hand on Judy's cheek. It was cold. Come to think of it, her skin also looked kind of blue. I brought my ear to her mouth. I examined the leopard-print blouse fitted tightly to her breasts, waiting for the rise and fall of her breath that never came.

Was she dead?

Oh God, what should I do? She certainly looked dead. But I sure as hell wasn't sticking around to search for a pulse. I needed to get out of there.

I didn't mean for this to happen.

"Stop looking at me!" I grabbed a dish towel and threw it over Judy's face. I retrieved the two pill bottles from the countertop and buried them in my pocket. I ran briskly up the stairs, stumbling and banging my knee. I forced myself up and going despite the stinging pain. I rushed to my closet and collected the bag packed with a few changes of clothes and reminders of my mother.

Then I ran from our house and never looked back.

CHAPTER 55

Wine always makes me tingly. Today is no exception. It feels like I have pins and needles in my fingers and toes. But like I said, it's so good. I get up to pour myself another glass.

As I stand up, though, I notice it's not just my fingers and toes that are tingly. It's my entire body. My legs are gummy, and the room is ensconced in a haze as if there had been a fire. To be fair, there had been a fire, but that was a good two weeks ago.

My eyes flit up to the smoke/carbon monoxide detector Andrew took the batteries out of the other night. My lids start to sag. Oh goodness, is there a gas leak in my apartment? Is that what Ashton wanted to warn me about—possible carbon monoxide? Why oh why didn't I stop to talk to him?

If I can just get to the window, let in some fresh air…

But I can't move my legs. It feels like I'm moving them but not going anywhere. It's like I'm sinking into quicksand. I drop to my knees, but that doesn't get me any closer to the window.

With my last ounce of strength, I scream Jenna's name. Then I rest my head against the cold tile.

"Lucy?" Jenna's voice floods me with relief. I hear her footsteps approaching. But then, a fresh wave of fear takes over. It can't be a gas leak if she's completely coherent. So what is it? What's happening to me?

Jenna's shoes come into view. I struggle to speak. "I don't feel so good, Jenna."

Jenna purses her lips, twisting her face like a funhouse mirror. But she doesn't move any closer. Oh God, why isn't she trying to help me?

My eyes find my phone a few feet away. Jenna follows my gaze. "Oh, Lucy," she says as she walks to the table and takes it in her hands. She runs a finger across the screen, shaking her head at me. "Lucy! That detective texted, and you tested positive for drugs."

"But that's impossible. I don't do drugs."

She paces around me to the kitchen island, where she opens another bottle of wine and takes a long swig, even though a bottle is already open and a perfectly good glass is sitting on the table. "I can't believe my best friend is a drug addict. Best friends are supposed to tell each other everything, Lucy."

"But I do tell you everything. I swear to you, Jenna, I am not taking drugs. You believe me, don't you?"

"Liar!" Jenna's face twists as she swipes her hand across the island, sending wine glasses from the night before flying. They fall to the tile, shattering everywhere. Shards soar through the air, pricking my skin as they cascade to the floor.

Wow, now my best friend *and* husband think I'm a drug addict. What next?

I guess I can understand why she's so upset. But wait, no, I'm not a drug addict. You have to take drugs to be a drug addict. And I did not take any drugs.

"Just look at you," Jenna says as she stands over me. "You're pathetic."

"Jenna, please, I'm sorry I've upset you, but honestly, I'm not lying about anything."

She bends down so that we're almost face to face. "Is that so?"

"Yes, so."

"Okay, then, why don't you tell me a little about you and Chad."

My blood turns to ice. How does Jenna know about me and Chad? And why is she so angry?

This feels eerily foreign. Jenna's never gotten mad at me before. We've had one argument in our entire friendship. But right now, my best friend looks like a bull ready to charge. I don't recognize the twisted expression on her face.

"Look, I'm sorry I didn't tell you. I've always had my shit together, and then I made this horrible mistake. I didn't want you to look at me differently."

"It's a little late for that, Lucinda."

She called me Lucinda. Jenna never calls me Lucinda. Now I know she must be *really* mad.

"Look, Andrew and I were having a rough patch. I screwed up, and I was embarrassed. That's the truth. I'm sorry I didn't tell you."

"You mean the rough patch when he was cheating on you with his paralegal that you *also* didn't tell me about?"

"You knew…" How could she possibly know about that?

"You're not the only one who knows everything, Lucinda."

"Okay, fine, Jenna. But I'm telling you, I didn't take drugs!"

"Oh, but you did."

"Excuse me?"

"You took quite a bit of drugs. So much, in fact, I'm not sure how you're even still talking to me."

Jenna's eyes travel to the empty wine glass on the table.

"I don't understand…"

I'm so confused. From the drugs?

"You *drugged* me?"

It feels like I'm about to pass out from shock and the drugs I unknowingly ingested. But before I lose consciousness, I hear another set of footsteps, and through the haze, my eyes find Bree.

"Jenna?"

Jenna smiles widely. "Hi, Izzy Bear." Then she steps over me and gives Bree…a *hug?* Surely I must be hallucinating. Why would Jenna hug Bree? She hates her. And who the hell is Izzy Bear? Someone better call me an ambulance and quick!

"Bree, help me, please." I try to say that, but my words come out like gibberish. What the hell did Jenna slip into my drink?

"What did she say?" Bree asks, looking at me curiously.

"Beats me."

"How much did you give her?"

"I emptied the bottle."

"You gave her an entire bottle of Xanax! Shouldn't she be dead already?"

"I guess she's built quite a tolerance with all that tea." Jenna laughs.

"Well, it's only a matter of time, unless you'd like me to finish her off now. Where did you put the knife?"

"Back in the block. I found it in the sink. That was a nice touch, sis."

Sis?

There are big black spots all over my vision. And though I'm scared to death, my heart is beating incredibly slowly. I'm so tired I could fall asleep on the tile floor.

No, I can't. If I go to sleep, I will die. Andrew will think I died of a drug overdose; well, I will have died of a drug overdose, but I didn't know I was taking drugs. Oh God, this psychopath will keep living here and raise my baby. I can't let that happen. But then, I can't do much of anything to stop it right now.

Still, I fight to keep my eyes open.

And then I hear it—a key turning in the front door.

"Who is that?" Jenna asks.

"Maybe Andrew?" Bree says.

"Go. Now."

Bree runs from the room. I faintly hear her talking in the hallway with my husband. *Please find me, Andrew.*

"I think we should go pick up Delilah, Andrew," Bree says.

"Lucinda isn't here."

"That's odd. I tracked her phone here. You haven't seen her?"

"Nope, haven't seen her."

"Well, we need to find her."

Need to find her? For what?

D.L. Fisher

The last thing I see is Andrew walk through the frame with #newbeau. My heart breaks on the spot.

Did my husband set me up? Did they all set me up?

I say a prayer for Delilah and let my eyes close.

THE PERFECT NANNY

CHAPTER 56

MANY YEARS LATER

JENNA

I am what you might call Instagram famous. Almost a million faithful followers hang on to my every word. I tell them whatever I think they want to hear. I show them what I think they want to see. And then, I sit back, relax, and watch those numbers grow.

Thanks to my best friend's wise investments and entrepreneurial endeavors, I've done very well for myself. Well, enough to purchase an art gallery on Wooster Place in the heart of Soho. When Lucy's husband Andrew decided to become an artist, I thought it might come in handy one day. Boy, did I hit that nail on the head!

I've been posting online daily since college, except for the two months I spent in a psychiatric ward. The downside of putting yourself out there in the social media world is that anyone can find you. My father found me. One afternoon, he surprised me in my dorm room with my (not so baby anymore) sister, Isabella Grace.

Izzy.

"What are you doing here?" I asked, folding my arms across my chest as I blocked the door with my body.

"Oh Jennifer, we've been so worried about you." My father had aged quite a bit over the past two years, with deep wrinkles lining the sallow skin around his eyes. Surely, the guilt of what he'd done to my mother was eating him alive. "I've missed you."

"You've *missed* me? I know what you did, Dad. Judy told me you killed Mom." That was what she'd whispered in my ears all those years ago, my father murdered my mother.

"Please, Jennifer. Hear me out."

I moved aside so he and my sister could enter the room.

"I didn't kill your mother," he said, plopping down on my bed and interlacing his hands in his lap.

"But Judy said..."

"I know what Judy said. She told you I let your mother die. The truth would have destroyed you."

"What truth?"

My father lowered his eyes. "I'm sorry Jennifer, but the truth is, your mother didn't want to live. She killed herself."

He was lying. He *had* to be lying. Why would my mother kill herself? She was pregnant. She would never have done anything to hurt the baby. Unless...

It was all coming together.

My father filled me in on the events of the past two years and on how worried they'd all been about me. All those years ago, after they found a bottle of antifreeze in my room and they suspected it was me who had killed our dog, my parents didn't know what to do with me. "The doctors said you were delusional, Jennifer. You were always talking to people who weren't there, making up wild stories. It was only getting worse. You needed help, but nothing was helping. And then your mother's pregnancy with Isabella was so similar to yours. She was worried—"

"—that Izzy would turn out like me."

My father nodded, unable to look me in the eyes. Because there was the truth that I'd run away from. My mother killed herself so she wouldn't give birth to another me.

"You wanted a brother or sister so badly..."

"Wanted a brother or sister? I already had four."

"*Four?*" My father looked me over curiously. "Isabella Grace is your only sibling, Jennifer."

I felt sick to my stomach. *Was my father telling the truth? Can you actually make up human beings?*

"After your mom died, Judy tried to help. She really did. But then you tried to kill her."

"I didn't try—" Wait, *try*?

Dad must have read the confusion on my face, because he added, "Judy is fine, Jennifer. She forgives you. She knows you weren't in your right state of mind. We all just want you to be okay. I'm afraid of what might happen if you don't get the help you need."

It was such a lovely, Jerry Springer-like family reunion until two big burly men busted into my room and escorted me out of our dorm. Apparently, my father had convinced the powers that be that I was a danger to myself and others, and that was enough to get me locked away on an involuntary psychiatric hold. Thank God Lucy wasn't there. It would have ruined everything. I left her a note with some nonsense about traveling abroad.

I met James Homestead in the psychiatric ward at Lenox Hill. It's incredible how quickly you can bond with someone over microwave dinners and mental illnesses. James and I became instant confidants—we told each other everything.

Except, according to the doctors at the hospital, I wasn't a very reliable source. My psychiatrist explained that my mind made up stories and conversations which felt so real, I believed them. All I needed to do was take my medications, continue therapy, and the voices would fade.

But did I want that?

Because James had a different theory—he believed everything I told him had actually happened, and someone was trying to cover it up. They were all in on it—the doctors, nurses, my dad, Judy, and Dougie. It was one big fat conspiracy.

Everything James said made so much sense, and he was super cute. The alternative was a wrinkled lab coat with tufts of white puffy hair.

I chose cute.

James taught me how to fake-take my medication. The trick was to wedge it into the side cavity of my mouth where no one was looking. They assumed once I lifted my tongue, I had swallowed it. James did the same with his.

One thing Judy told me rang true all those years later—a man always believes a beautiful woman. I was out of that place in two months. James, on the other hand, was there for much longer.

About a year ago James finally got out, and we set our plan into motion.

It wasn't Lucy that I wanted to hurt at first. She was my best friend. I cared about her, and she cared about me. We told each other everything. Well, obviously, I didn't tell her everything, but that kind of goes without saying. How do you tell your best friend, *I poisoned my dog and tried to kill my father's girlfriend? Oh, and my mom killed herself because she didn't know what to do with me and was afraid my baby sister would share the same dangerous and delusional tendencies.* Right. You don't.

I thought Lucy was the strongest person I knew. When I sent her the pictures of Andrew looking too cozy with his paralegal, I thought for sure she'd leave him and his life would be ruined. But then she stayed, and on top of that, she didn't tell her best friend about it! What kind of sociopath does something like that?

If Lucy wasn't going to leave her husband, then I would make sure Andrew left her. And imagine my surprise when I found out she actually *was* cheating on him. The picture I snapped of her outside of the Wall Street Hotel making out with Chad was priceless. Add that to her list of betrayals.

Maybe she and Andrew deserve one another after all.

I can't take credit for everything, though. James came up with the brilliant idea to get Lucy to hire my sister Izzy as a nanny. If there's one thing I know about Lucy, she always has to be right. Even when she's wrong, she finds a way to be right. So when I told her she should, under no circumstances, hire the headshot girl, Bree Miller, I knew that was exactly who she would hire. And Lucy says Andrew is predictable! For extra insurance, though, I contacted all the other applicants Lucy had shared with me at the coffee shop, plying them with one crazy story or another.

THE PERFECT NANNY

Come on, Lucy, who orders a vodka martini on the rocks with blue cheese olives at ten thirty in the morning at an interview for a nanny position?

It was also James's idea to stage a kidnapping at Central Park. What better way to endear Bree to Lucinda? I mean, how could Lucinda not love Bree—she saved Delilah's freaking life!

Maybe my younger sister should have gone a little easier on the whole, throwing herself at Andrew part, but she blamed him for ruining my life.

I bet you're wondering why? I'll get there in a minute.

I texted Marly while Lucy was in the bathroom the day of the interviews to invite her to dinner. Then, I poured pine nuts into the pesto sauce while I took a call (from James), stuffed the walnuts she'd bought into my bag and snatched Lucy's keys from hers. I knew that would drive her crazy—and make everyone else believe she was crazy. I would do whatever it took to split her and Andrew apart. Was poisoning an innocent person extreme? Perhaps, but I never liked Marly very much to begin with. Besides, if Lucy had responded to the pictures like any normal human being, I wouldn't have had to make this last-ditch effort. Desperate times...

And then there was Lucy's lifetime supply of Mother's Milk tea. For someone so smart, my best friend is awfully gullible. Who gives away a lifetime supply of breastmilk tea? I stocked my closet with hundreds of packets, lacing each with the prescription medications I didn't take, and brought it up as if it were a delivery every time I visited her apartment.

Lucy has ingested such an obscene amount of medication over the past month and in that glass of wine that it's only a short matter of time before she dies.

And now, it's time for Andrew Douglass to pay.

Oh Dougie. If only he'd run away with me like he promised. We would be happy together living in this apartment with our own baby. But no, after that day he confronted me in the woods, I never heard from him again. Not until I saw him hitting on my friend in our sociology class at NYU. I tried to move on; I did. I wanted Lucy to be happy. But Dougie was mine first. It wasn't fair.

And it's all come to a head. In a few minutes, Dougie and Lucy will die in a tragic murder-suicide.

James, Izzy, and I will casually walk out of this building, waving goodbye to Ashton, who couldn't identify a banana in a fruit lineup.

When an appropriate amount of time has passed, I will alert the authorities and report my best friend missing. Then, I'll sit back and wait until their sad story airs on the five o'clock news. Since Lucy made me the godmother, against Andrew's better judgment, I'll have Delilah Bear wrapped up in my arms in no time. James and I will raise her as our own. She won't even remember her parents. Dad and Judy will make wonderful grandparents. And we already have help lined up.

Izzy will make the perfect nanny!

CHAPTER 57

I'm not dead yet.

My eyes are closed, and I'm drifting in and out of consciousness, but I can still make out bits and pieces of the heated conversation around me.

"You don't want to do this," Andrew says. "She's your best friend, Jenna. You can work this out."

So maybe my husband *wasn't* in on this? Is it possible that I have this all wrong?

Jenna laughs, a sickening sound that makes my heart momentarily stop beating. Or maybe it's the drugs. "Have you still not figured out who I am, Dougie?"

"Dougie? Who is Dougie?"

"Don't play dumb with me. I'll slit Lucinda's throat right now."

"Please, don't, Jenna. I'm listening."

"You were supposed to take me to prom. We were going to run away together. And then you just left me."

There's a long pause, and I wonder if I've finally succumbed to death. But then I hear my husband's voice. "That never happened, Jenna. I was never taking you to prom. We were never running away together. I don't think we even had an actual conversation until college. I remember you from high school now, but you didn't talk to anyone. You were always talking to yourself."

"Liar!" A foot to my ribs brings me back.

"Please don't hurt her."

"Don't you dare come near her, Dougie. There are three of us and one of you. I'll kill you both."

"Jenna, please, can we just sit down and talk about this rationally?"

"It's a little late for that, Dougie. You've had all these years to make things right with me. But it's like you can't get far enough away from me. You've lost your chance. It's too bad Lucy cheated on you, and you killed her in a jealous rage. The pain must have been overwhelming for you to kill yourself, too. It's over, Dougie."

"Stop!"

A familiar voice fills the space. "Not in my building, you won't..." *Ashton?* Now I know I must be hallucinating.

"*She* dropped this," he says, pointing an accusing finger at Jenna. "It's a letter. You need to read this, Mr. Douglass."

There're a few moments of silence before Andrew's voice rings in my ears. "You were blackmailing my wife? Did you ransack my studio as well? You're sick, Jenna. Sick!"

And then, a slow wave of relief washes over me as Detective O'Brien's voice fills the space. "We have video footage of these three exiting your building the day your studio was defiled, along with video from the park and this building. Jennifer Murphy, Isabella Grace Murphy, and James Homestead, you are all under arrest for the attempted murder of Lucinda Douglass and the attempted abduction of Delilah Douglass. You have the right to remain silent. Anything you say can and will be used against you in a court of law..."

It's over. It's finally over. I picture Delilah's gummy smile as I lose consciousness one last time.

The next thing I see is a bright light. I'm either dead or nearly dead. What's that they say in the movies, go to the light? My eyelids involuntarily flutter. The light is obscenely bright. I must be getting closer. They flutter again. Wait, why is there a hand attached to the light? That's weird.

I blink. The hand is attached to a body in a white coat. He has a name tag on his jacket. God wouldn't be wearing a name tag, would he?

"Do you see that?" he says. "Her eyes are responding to the light. That's a good sign."

"Is she going to be okay?" Andrew asks. My husband is in the room. Oh, thank God. Jenna didn't kill him after all.

"She's in there," the doctor says. "But there's really no way to know at this point what cognitive function she has. We have an EEG scheduled for this afternoon to assess her brain activity."

"So you're saying my wife may be ... brain dead?"

"Look, Mr. Douglass. We are doing everything we can to help her. But these things take time. She ingested a lethal amount of medication. It's a miracle she's even breathing, to be honest. It may be a while before we fully understand the depth of her injuries."

I feel the warmth of a hand on mine. It's Andrew's. Tears well up in my eyes. "Look," Andrew says. "Lucinda's eyes. She's crying."

"That's probably from prolonged exposure to the flashlight."

"Oh." I can practically taste the disappointment in my husband's voice, which makes me realize how incredibly thirsty I am. My tongue finds my lips. I need water. *Can someone get me a glass of water?*

"Andrew?"

"Did you hear that?" Andrew calls out. "She said my name."

"I heard it, Doctor," a woman's voice says.

"Open your eyes, Lucinda. Open your eyes."

I push against my lids and open my eyes.

By a miracle of all miracles, I awake with my brain and body fully intact. Don't get me wrong, I feel like absolute shit, but at least I haven't done any permanent damage. The psychological trauma will take longer to recover from, but I'm well on my way.

Ironically, the drugs Jenna slipped in my tea did me a favor. If it weren't for the zealousness with which I drank it to keep up my milk supply, I would be dead. After holding me for observation for a week, they finally released me from the hospital.

I'm lying in our bedroom when Andrew brings Delilah in. By the good grace of God, my daughter was minimally affected by the drugs. It's a good thing kids are so resilient. Delilah smiles widely when she sees me, and I know now that Bree, erm, Izzy, was wrong. It was never gas. Why I ever listened to that psychopath is anyone's guess.

Speaking of psychopaths—Jenna, James, and Izzy have all been committed, pending psychiatric evaluations and subsequent trials. I heard they are all taking the insanity defense. They will spend the next twenty to thirty-five years in a psychiatric ward or a maximum-security prison. Either way, they will all be locked away for a significant portion of their lives. They can no longer hurt us now.

I still plan on returning to work, maybe not on October 1st, but definitely when I'm feeling better. Hopefully, it won't be awkward. Chad and Marly visited me once. We buried the hatchet, though we'll never be good friends again—if we ever were, to begin with.

Ashton and Detective O'Brien, on the other hand, will be my first guests once I'm back in the kitchen. Until then, we'll eat all the meals dropped off by neighbors and friends. Now that the baby gifts have finally petered out, we have get-well gifts and dinners up the wazoo.

As for Andrew and me … we spent hours talking and crying and crying and talking while I was in the hospital. What an elaborate scheme Jenna put together. It turns out, with the right angles and impeccable timing, you can make just about any situation look bad. Andrew never was cheating on me after all. He did take his paralegal in training to lunch, and she was a little too handsy for my liking, but Andrew didn't notice. He really is just that clueless. I should have known he would never cheat on me with anyone, let alone our nanny.

As for what I did with Chad, thank goodness, Andrew has forgiven me. I realize I didn't make the best decisions, but I am committed to doing better. And no, our marriage will never be the same moving forward. It will be stronger.

No more secrets. No more lies. No more Jenna pulling strings.

There's a knock on my door. Ms. Randall enters the room, holding a tray of scrambled eggs, bacon, French toast, and orange juice. It turns out Ms. Randall is not only the perfect nanny, but she's also a fantastic cook.

"You need to eat," she says with a smile.

"I'm not very hungry right now, but thank you. I'm sure Andrew would love to eat that. It smells delicious."

Ms. Randall places a hand on my arm and squeezes. "I said eat."

I nod and take a bite.

"One more thing, dear," she says, her hand still hovering above my arm. "For goodness sakes, call me Judy."

The End

ACKNOWLEDGEMENTS

Thank you from the bottom of my heart for all of the love and support you've given since I embarked on this thrilling adventure. What a fun ride it's been! To my family, friends, editor, readers, reviewers…please know that every single review, post, mention and email warms my heart. If this is a dream, I don't *ever* want to wake up.

Keep reading, and I'll keep writing!

Follow @dlfisherthrillers for information on upcoming releases. And keep reading for a sneak peak at My Husband's Son coming to you in 2024.

All the best,
DL Fisher

MY HUSBAND'S SON

PROLOGUE

"How could he?"

"Mrs. Winter?"

"I just... I don't understand."

I bury my head in my hands, then look up at the detective sitting across from me in an interrogation room not quite the size of a Manhattan studio apartment.

"Unfortunately, these things happen."

"These things *happen*? I'm sorry, Detective, but I beg to disagree. These things don't just..." I air quote my fingers around the word "...happen."

But he has a point, I suppose—these things do happen; they just don't happen here. At least, they didn't until Bennett's son TJ moved to town.

"I can't believe what he did." I shake my head, letting our current predicament sink in. "It's sick."

The detective watches as I mentally untangle the web of the past twenty-four hours. It's wrapped around my neck like a noose.

I draw a deep breath as every emotion known to humankind fights for space in my head. "This doesn't feel real," I offer, looking for validation from the man sitting across from me.

Tell me:

It'll be okay.

You couldn't have known.

It's not your fault.
Something. Anything.
Maybe even explain:
How has this fallen on me?
Because right now, I'm struggling to make sense of any of it.
Or, say nothing.
When the silence becomes too much to bear, the gravity of what's happened really sinks in, followed by the tears.
"I can't believe he's gone."
The detective narrows his eyes on me. "You can't believe he's gone?" He repeats my question, folding his hands on the metal table between us.
"Yes, that's what I said." I wipe my face with the back of my hand.
"You should believe it, Mrs. Winter. I mean, you are the one who killed him."
I shift uncomfortably in my chair. The metal legs screech against the concrete floor like nails on a chalkboard.
"I didn't mean for it to happen. I swear. I…"
The detective pushes a box of tissues across the table. I quickly grab one and dab at my eyes.
"Please, Mrs. Winter, just start at the beginning."

CHAPTER 1

THREE MONTHS EARLIER

When Bennett and I married on a yacht in the South of France, I thought I'd won the freaking lottery. The water was crystalline, and the weather, absolute perfection. Surrounded by friends and family, I stared into Bennett's Caribbean blue eyes and wondered how I had gotten Fortune to smile down on me.

It's not every day that you marry the literal man of your dreams.

Today?

"Carrie!!!" My husband's voice roars through the house like a blow horn.

I run up the stairs, taking two at a time, until I find Bennett in our bedroom, displeasure written across his handsome face.

"What's wrong?" I gasp, winded from my sprint into what looks like a war zone. The floor and bed are streaked with red, snippets of deep color splashed across a canvas of natural linen. It's as if I've stumbled onto a crime scene.

"My red power tie, Carrie. Did you pick up my red power tie from the cleaners?"

Bennett motions toward his closet, where thirty red power ties dangle from his tie rack. They're pretty similar to the other thirty littering our bedroom floor.

"I'm sorry, *which* red power tie?" I try to look conciliatory, but I'm helpless to hide my confusion.

Bennett blinks rapidly, the expression on his face softening. "I'm sorry. I didn't mean to yell at you. You do everything for me and...I'm just, I'm so sorry, Carrie. Can you find it in your heart to forgive me?" He bats his impossibly long, thick, dark eyelashes at me, and I'm a goner.

Yup, I'm the luckiest woman on the planet.

And trust me when I say I'm a bit of an expert on the matter. When you find the *right* one hidden in a sea of *wrong* and *very wrong* ones, you dig your nails in and never let go.

"It's okay," I say, meaning it. "I know how nervous you are."

The corners of Bennett's lips curl up, crinkling the skin around his blue eyes.

"Understatement of the century."

I offer a sympathetic smile. I'd be nervous if I were him. I'm nervous, and I'm *not* him. Damn fentanyl. Why did Bennett have to have the biggest mediation of his career today? Why couldn't it have been tomorrow? Next week?

I feel the slightest twinge of resentment.

Has he forgotten?

I brush against Bennett as I enter his walk-in closet. "This one," I say, selecting a tie with tiny blue circles that will make my husband's eyes pop and is a beautiful accompaniment to the navy suit designed especially for him.

As I slip the tie around his neck, Bennett brings his lips to mine. He pulls back just far enough that I can still feel the heat of his breath.

"What did I do to deserve you, Carrie?"

My lips curl into a smirk, and I wink. "I guess you just got lucky, huh?"

"Lucky you didn't give me third-degree burns."

I stifle a giggle. "Who told you to walk into me while I was carrying a tray of hot coffee?"

"Who told you to distract me with that short, tight skirt? All the paralegals at my firm wear pants. And besides, if you hadn't scalded me, we may never have found one another."

I smile widely.

Unlikely.

"I wish I didn't have to leave you. Today of all days." Bennett runs a hand across my face. His fingers are smooth like a baby's bottom, nails perfectly manicured. I exhale a deep breath, resting my cheek against his palm.

He remembers.

Of course, he remembers. Bennett never forgets anything. The man has got the memory of a gosh darn elephant.

"We will have lots to celebrate tonight. The settlement..." I say as I cross my fingers in front of my chest. "One year of wedded bliss."

This time, it's my lips that find his. Even after a year of marriage, I find it hard to keep my hands off my husband. If I were a dog, I would pee on him.

Bennett runs a hand through my hair, gathering it into a loose fist. "Watch it," he warns jokingly. "You know, once you get me started, you'll be responsible for what happens next."

"If you didn't have that meeting today, I'd happily accept responsibility for what happens next." I wink conspiratorially, then pat Bennett on his sculpted chest. My husband is like that cliched bottle of fine wine—he really does get better with age. You'd never guess by looking at him that he's more than ten years my senior.

"I had Linda make reservations at La Mer."

Unless you heard me squeal like a little girl. "My favorite! Please, thank her for me."

"And..." Bennett opens the door to my closet.

I nearly pass out. "How did you know?" Hanging on a velvet hanger is the cutout Givenchy dress I've been eyeing at Neiman Marcus. A little fancy for dinner, but you only celebrate one year of the most amazing marriage ever once.

"I know everything, darling." Bennett winks at me, giving me full-body chills.

Because, come on, no one knows *everything*.

"I guess I should get going." Bennett flashes a sheepish grin.

I reach around his neck, transforming his silk tie into a perfect knot at the base of his throat.

"You look amazing, babe. Knock 'em dead." I grimace at my horrifically inappropriate pun. "Oooh, I didn't mean it like that."

Bennett's cheeks dimple as he flashes a line of perfectly straight, sparkly white teeth. "I can't wait until tonight, my love."

"Good, because neither can I, Mr. Winter."

"Until then, Mrs. Winter."

One last soft kiss, and I watch as my husband disappears from our bedroom.

***

I find all sorts of imaginative ways to keep myself busy around the house while I wait for the clock to strike six and our celebration to begin. I load and unload the dishwasher, mop the floors, and tend to our vegetable garden out back. The bell peppers are an impossible shade of green—juicy and plump. I'll throw them in a salad tomorrow.

I need something to do while Bennett's out working.

I never thought I'd retire before thirty, but Bennett insisted my fingers are too beautiful to type. I'm not going to argue with my husband, who is allowing me to enjoy life without the headaches of commuting into the city for work.

And unlike most days that stretch like an endless ball of yarn, today is flying by with unusual speed.

At four p.m., I hop into the waterfall shower in our master bathroom. There, I spend an excessive amount of time exfoliating my skin and shaving until I look like a hairless cat. I rub on enough moisturizer to permanently rehydrate a ninety-year-old's skin. A little excessive for twenty-eight? Perhaps.

But Bennett Winter didn't get where he is by not caring.

Neither did I.

I'm thumbing through the latest issue of Vogue, waiting for the lotion to dry, when I hear the doorbell chime. A grin spreads across my face. My amorous husband must have sent me flowers or some other romantic gift.

I pull up the Ring app on my phone. A young man is standing at the door with his hands shoved deep in his pockets, staring at his feet.

I squint my eyes, scanning through the images on the screen. Funny, I don't see any flowers. Or balloons. Not even an Edible Arrangement.

I throw on my silk robe and shuffle down the stairs to see what this visitor wants and send him on his merry way. I still need to get dressed, do my hair, makeup...

With the chain latched, I crack the door open. "Can I help—"

All the blood drains from my face as he looks up at me, and my heart sinks into my feet.

No, it can't be.

Suddenly, our anniversary celebration is the last thing on my mind.

Made in the USA
Middletown, DE
06 December 2023